HIGH TIDE

HIGH TIDE

INGA ĀBELE

Translated from
the Latvian by
Kaija Straumanis

OPEN LETTER
LITERARY TRANSLATIONS FROM THE UNIVERSITY OF ROCHESTER

First edition, 2013
All rights reserved

Library of Congress Cataloging-in-Publication Data:

Abele, Inga
  [Paisums. English]
  High tide / by Inga Abele ; Translated from the Latvian by
Kaija Straumanis. — First Edition.
    pages cm
  "Originally published in Latvia as Paisums."
  ISBN-13: 978-1-934824-80-1 (pbk. : alk. paper)
  ISBN-10: 1-934824-80-1 (pbk. : alk. paper)
  I. Title.
  PG9049.1.B45P3513 2013
  891'.9334—dc23
                    2013010621

The publication of this work was supported by a grant from the Latvian Literature Centre,
State Cultural Capital Foundation, and Ministry of Culture of the Republic of Latvia.

KULTURA.LV

Printed on acid-free paper in the United States of America.

Text set in Garamond, a group of old-style serif typefaces named after the
punch-cutter Claude Garamont.

Design by N. J. Furl

Open Letter is the University of Rochester's nonprofit, literary translation press:
Lattimore Hall 411, Box 270082, Rochester, NY 14627

www.openletterbooks.org

HIGH TIDE

IN THE BEGINNING

IN THE BEGINNING

GOD didn't create words.

In the beginning there was a dream.

And at the end there was again nothing but a dream.

God appeared to a woman in a dream that was like death.

God found the woman within this dream and said to her:

"If you agree to live your life in reverse, you'll have the power to give life back to your lover, who died young. Just don't get your hopes up—your meeting at that crossroads will last about twenty minutes, no more. Then he'll continue on toward old age, but you, back to childhood."

The woman agreed immediately.

God said:

"How strange. Do you really value your own life and experiences so little that you're willing to undo all of it without a second thought?"

The woman said nothing.

She remembered this dream when she awoke.

TURNS OUT—WE'VE LIVED

SHE doesn't need any more advice—models, examples. Maybe she's just on a whole new level, but right now she doesn't need it. She doesn't read books, newspapers, or magazines, doesn't use the internet or watch TV, doesn't go—God forbid—to the theater. It's like being wrapped in a blanket up to your chin: you see and hear everything, but can't move a muscle. Everything is right there around you, within arms' reach. She wanders the house and now and then picks up something, grabs onto something, touches on something. A sentence from a newspaper, a phrase from a Mexican soap opera, an idea from Proust. They're all always going to be right.

On her walks, Ieva goes around the forest in circles. Then on her birthday she asks herself a question—why do I walk in circles, like a dog chained to a post? Because of my fears? Only because of my harsh, bitter fears? I can walk in a straight line, she tells herself—and whenever I want. But when she does finally walk straight she only *feels* like she's actually getting anywhere. Her surroundings change, but the content doesn't. Big cities are all essentially the same, and every country has farmers wearing plaid, made-in-China shirts. Any new place that she ends up she eventually has a close group of friends a lot like the last. The group will always have a mentor, a lover, someone

she'll betray, someone who'll betray her, an enemy, and friends she
can talk to and with whom she can find spiritual healing, rather than
wasting money on therapy.

Once in a while she breaks from the campaigns, the marathons,
the expeditions, and returns to the doghouse and sits next to her
chain. Sits absolutely still, like a Bedouin gazing into the distance,
and then writes. Script writing is usually complicated, but all of her
scripts are about the same thing. All very clichéd, and when she tries
to make excuses to the director he tells her: I need you precisely for
the clichés. Because the ending needs to be something predictable.

Her scripts are about how nothing happens because nothing can
ever happen. Not a single molecule is lost in the eternal cycle between
the earth and the heavens. Only a pure soul can hope to break free
from the carousel of life and death, into the cosmos through the tunnel of light and at a speed that makes everything down to the smallest
particle feel simultaneously heavy and weightless. Everything shrinks
until it disappears, until it's erased from the memory of the world
along with time. But to live your life until your soul is pure—don't
laugh, it's not that easy—you have to become a Buddha, a Christ,
or a Mohammed. You have to become light itself, a pure soul. Then
you can be on your way. But it's a long way and you'll be scrubbed,
doused, and wrung clean until then. Those few mistakes that will
haunt you, jolt you awake at night, and force you to keep going on,
these mistakes that you carry with you your entire life—in the end
they'll destroy you. But keep thinking about them, keep thinking. It's
gratifying to keep picking away at them. It will heal you.

Eventually she doesn't even write the scripts herself anymore, just
touches up those written by others and sends them in. She takes the
finished product and objectively embellishes them. She's done work
like that before—adding details to bulletin posters in her school days,
a pioneer in the last generation of an aggressive Soviet empire. Her
homeroom teacher called it "giving life" to something. "Take it to

Ieva," the teacher often said, "she'll give it some life." And Ieva would take her black marker and give the dull pencil sketches some life, be it Lenin or the Easter Bunny. A wavering shadow in the distance, a gleam in Lenin's eye, and the tense muscles in his jaw, something she'd seen in her father's face when he shaved in the morning. And Lenin would come to life. The Easter Bunny would, too.

Everything is proof of it—this forced gift of existence—even the tired face of a small-town bus driver in the early morning; it speaks of longing, the endless patience you have when scrutinizing good fortune that has unexpectedly dropped into your lap. And what does life offer in return . . . the quiet hum inside the bus where you can warm up, a change from the frozen and bleak winter landscape . . . What does it offer in return? A kiss goodbye from your wife before you head out, and the mildly bitter taste of coffee with cream? The early morning fog and a dead moose on the side of a road? Like an Indian who gets glass beads in exchange for gold, you trade the suffering of existence in return for the smell of baking bread. The feel of a dog's wet nose against your hand. The look in your children's eyes. A bird feeder. May it all bring you joy, says this opposing, unwanted, huge opportunity—Life. Truth everywhere, like rows and rows of weeds that need only a bit of rain to grow: a handful of TV shows, a handful of philosophical essays, a handful of tight-lipped snobs, a handful of bartering vendors.

Her mother's mother, Gran, used to say: You'll never know where you'll lose something or where you'll find it, and, if you knew where you'd fall, you'd put a pillow down first. In many ways Gran hadn't outgrown childhood. She had never experienced passion, never been disillusioned, but had remained an innocent; that was her destiny. Her cheerful daily greetings were proof she had never discovered herself, her own anger, or her deeply hidden doubts. Doing so would mean being sent into freedom, out of the Garden of Eden. She had stayed in Eden, playing in rows of sun-ripened, wild strawberries. And among the bustle were all life's sentences: her parents' deaths, her husband and children, the people she loved. But she never said "love" because she didn't know the word, hadn't evolved to words. Gran had been her parents' pride and joy, a helper at the dairy farm with her white apron and silky ash-blonde hair, someone who had never grown to know hatred. More precisely, she was oblivious to any daggers of hatred aimed at her. Instead they went through her like she was nothing, because she didn't believe in bad people—just people. Her only sins were her pride and self-reliance. She always had tickets for sugar and bread, but also always had more for extra things. A kind word and a helping hand, the sense to put others before herself . . . She believed it was her choice and responsibility. She didn't need anything from the Lord God, just some nice Lutheran Christmas songs and spiritual peace. She hadn't unlocked that little door in her heart that led to spite. She stayed in her bud, her entire life spent in it and as a child. God and humanity attack these kinds of people more than anyone else because there's something obnoxious about them. But neither God, nor humanity can use their endless recipes for disaster on these people because these people lack any trace of hate—and God can take a vacation since there's no one to peddle vices to. Having fulfilled her duty to everyone she loved, Gran quickly retreated to her inner child, back into that bud. A small, polite girl who always walked on the sunny side of the street. And that's how she ended her journey. She was stuck in her helpless innocence, and then all the world's charges were piled on top of her. Stay helpless as a baby, an animal, a prisoner, a fool, an alcoholic, a one-legged bum in a tunnel—and the world will quickly chafe you until you bleed, and you'll understand why you've always needed God. You put Heaven on a pedestal while you still have the strength. And when you grow weak you see the devil. Not the one with horns and a tail, but the devil in the hurried compassion of the fast-paced world, the one that will kill you with kindness.

Longing for paradise is nothing different from longing for a strong pair of hands. Forget all the understanding, the kindred souls and greatness of spirit—the most important thing is an Eden of two strong hands when you can't go on anymore, when your mind stops working, when you're just a naked, trembling mass of bare and rotting nerves, a substance without a clear point of view. When you're just a scrap of flesh.

After this experience, after Gran's passing, Ieva lost all illusions she had of herself. No one person can do it all. And though Ieva was capable of a lot, she couldn't maintain the clarity of that stream of goodness. She could fight like a tiger, but it wasn't her thing. There was a story about Ieva—Eve—in the Bible, who ate the forbidden apple and gave it to others, recklessly spreading the poisonous contraband and barreling into death and sin, the dualism between good and evil, the battle between God and Satan. There she was, at the very crossroads of it all, with her black marker in hand. She gave life to everything that crossed her path—sin, holiness, and life itself. She'd never be able to protect anyone, only challenge them. And to what? To life, or death. To find the seven differences between these two pictures.

It's harder for people who are reserved. Reserved people are quiet for years and years, and then they jump off a bridge. But those who constantly hound their friends by whining about their pain and paranoia, they're the ones who keep themselves alive. Knock, and the door will be opened unto you. Maybe not quite opened, but something will definitely change—if that makes you happy. Maybe new wallpaper. Moving to a new apartment. A new perfume. A new perspective. And a new picture. If an irrational hope sparks in your veins now and again, it could even be the moment when you're on the train reading a book translated into Latvian, and in a brief flash you realize that you understand the author, the main character, and the life of the translator. For a second, all three of these personas unite in you, not in a linear sense, but in a predestined, glowing arc. You get inside and can suddenly see through to the bottom of a frozen lake, to the stillness of the undercurrent between motionless water lilies. Then you turn the page and it all disappears. You're back in your own body, you have to buy milk for the kid, and a heart to cook up for the dog—a giant, red, cow heart—and bring it all home, you have to be a hunter because all around you are nothing but frozen, wintery fields that destroy everything warm and alive.

At times it seems best to not go anywhere, to not read anything, to not say anything. Because this world is like the colored bits of glass in a kaleidoscope. Turn the barrel—see something beautiful. Turn it again—see something entirely different, but still beautiful. Ieva knows that the symmetric shapes in a kaleidoscope are created by a system of mirrors; it's the mirrors' fault, they can only create things that are symmetric . . . too symmetric. So symmetric it's scary. Honestly, not even truth is that symmetric—only death is. But mirrors can't work any other way.

She's not a reserved person, she isn't. She walks through the woods and talks to trees, dogs that cross her path, and will even talk to strangers now and then. But she steers clear of giving and receiving advice. She'd like to make it through the woods without a chaperone. She doesn't need an encyclopedia of plants or a map. At least not now. But she does need the woods. A full-blown forest with trees, moss, and that intoxicating scent of the sky—the cold air and the icy dampness of tree roots under a blanket of ferns in the fall. It's the best in November. Or in the heavy, stuffy July swelter, when everything is dry to the bone and like the forest itself is storing up fire, it's as withered as an old miser hunched over his pile of riches and as dangerous to itself as a propane tank by an open flame. The forest is in her schema and in the schema of others like her, her chemical make-up contains this secret element—the woods. But then she goes to the desert and observes its inhabitants, observes its elders, who understand that they can't go anywhere. You can't take shelter from anything in the desert because there isn't anywhere you can hide. All you can do is stand still in the narrow shadow of your hut and gaze into the distance with chewing tobacco stuck under your mustache, or without the tobacco. Just sit and observe, without any progress. No forest, no progress. The elders sit and look into the distance and watch the imperceptible, forever shifting traces of wind and water on the sands.

But those who have a fire inside them, they put the fire out as best they can—Ieva included. She separates herself so the fire no longer reaches her thoughts. All her running around is nothing more than putting out fires. And sometimes she takes the dog along with her because it's no good going out by herself. Some of the scenery opens up in her chest like a crashing wave of joy. Other times it's like slow foam at her feet. Other times still are like a shot to the veins—like a burning that makes her heart beat rapidly and sweat break out on her forehead. Something always opens up to her when she goes walking. Oh, this small illusion of movement. She doesn't need anything else.

People just need to be understood, she thinks to herself. The world needs to be understood. People are like shoes—you can't fit every one onto the same shoetree. The leather of every shoe has unique curves, seams, wears. And it takes time to see this.

She's already been on her share of carousels—there's nothing wrong with that. After a typically calm breakfast, she throws herself into the passage of time, lets herself be rattled apart so she overflows with awareness and all the trivialities that keep her alive. She pours the tiny, crushed pieces at the foot of her impasse, wails, cries, and then everything is quiet for a while, wonderfully quiet, still and frozen and beautiful. The world works like a well-oiled machine with parameters, barometers, altimeters and chronometers. You like long and short distances, beginnings and ends, and are particularly fond of the middle ground. Going to work, home and car loans, children and parents, even unmarried godmothers. If it weren't for the cold and the constant rotation, who knows if you'd be able to value that small mechanism—the stirrup, hammer, or anvil, whatever that little bone is called—the balancing mechanism in your ear that keeps you upright. Your vestibular apparatus.

The red substance of everyone's blood is the same—slow-flowing and completely saturated with time and diverse archives. It's always a hot substance; however, which creates more? Time or blood? And if it's both, why live beyond that? After there's no one left on earth to tuck you in, to accept you with implicit love, to take you exactly as you are. To take joy in watching what you do, in whose eyes you would simply be good . . . When there's no one left like that, who will you be able to be yourself in front of? Because you always find a bond with those who tuck you in, or throw you a rope to pull you ashore, or who profess something to you in the world of absolute chaos in which we have to live, where the sun alone moves along the same path and where daylight creeps over the windowsill like ivy. Other than that, everything has changed. And you're not being told anything revelatory, but rather—and aren't the values of the modern world strange?—the same old things you need to survive. Even Ieva has been told something like this. Two—no, three—things for survival. The first two are: never sit on stone before you hear thunder, and don't stand in drafts. Obviously, these have to do with the same damn bundle of nerves. They get damaged by cold and drafts—you'll start pissing blood if you don't watch out. You'll shrivel up like a gnarled branch if you're not careful.

But the third thing was explained to her in a roundabout way—through a story. Her Gran, the person who gave her this advice, had worked before World War II as a servant for a rich family in Riga. She'd only worked for them a month to save up enough for a place to live in this new city.

"Sweetheart," she had told Ieva, "I knew full well I'd only work for them a short time, so I put up with everything with dignity and had enough strength and energy for each new day. When I left them after a month they cried and didn't want me to go because they had never had a servant as good as me."

This story meant that everything would eventually pass, even life. Maybe whatever it was would last more than a month, but it would pass. Each view, each landscape, even you. It's a solution, at least until the moment you're more sick of life than of death, when all you see on the horizon are black, burnt-out clearings, when you hate life so completely that your body is overcome by agonizing tremors just thinking about it. Thank you, Gran.

Because, honestly, Ieva doesn't call herself a girl anymore, and sometimes even says that beautiful word—middle-aged. Yes, right now she'd like to consider herself middle-aged. She's already experienced middle age physically—the thought came to her on the morning of her thirty-third birthday. On that morning she felt she was standing at the very top of a mountain. And this mighty, craggy mountain ridge extended in both directions, its outline melting into the distant golden sunrise. The ridge was tall and black, but oddly enough there was plenty of oxygen and her blood wasn't coursing out of control. Instead there was a damp, refreshing easterly wind, up there the stars were twinkling, meshing in the blueness like white knots. Things were very good. Right now things are very good, she's not thinking about the road here or about the climb down; everything is here and now, everything is halfway. And the only thing that hurts is the awareness that she has climbed up from the direction of the sea, but has to descend into the desert. The knowledge stings a bit, like a once-broken collarbone that aches every time it rains. But you get used to it.

Then the day comes: her life is halfway over and she's walking through the woods on a fall morning. The golden asp leaves rustle around her, the earth exhales coolly, and the sky is as blue as her boyfriend's eyes. And her life is half-over and, now and then, something will happen as time goes on. For example, there have been a lot of births, a few deaths, there will be something that will ache in her over her entire life, something she will never be able to fix, something she will have to dismiss—and so on and so forth. She walks through the woods and feels that she'll soon reach that critical point when the cup will be full, and when the handle breaks it won't go unnoticed. The cool glass of the milk bottles from her childhood and the triangular tetrapacks with the word MOLOKO on them—she can't forget those either. Or the piles of the newly-freed country's money in suitcases, her first real paycheck—an entire roll of colored paper—frozen kidneys and peed pants, her first time with a boy she would never see again, her first time in an airplane, her first time abroad and seeing strange things. The person you slowly but completely left because he was fading, even though he begged you to stay. Your heart's betrayals, your wild, spiteful spirit and brief moments of respite, your contracts with your conscience, your father and mother, and your travels near and far, when you fell in love with cities, the sky, or entire regions of uninhabited land.

Love doesn't always have to be about people, no, not necessarily. You can fall in love with a city, its many smells, how quiet it is under the snow. Small and large streets and the dusk in the glowing windows that awakens a desire in you, when you stand in the streets with your eyes glazed over simply from wanting to experience every imaginable life, everything behind those windows. You want to tear them from the walls and place them in your chest simply because you know and understand it all. Simply because you love these blinds, curtains, shades, the fraying bits of carpet behind the flowerpots against the walls and windows. A quick or fancy dinner, cats on windowsills, and boiling pots in kitchens. And how calm he is when he comes home from work. And how she tilts her head for him to kiss her cheek. Here is your victory, your life in these basic, little things that everyone will gulp down until the end of time like they're dehydrated and, when they're drunk from it, roam along the courtyard walls, craving only that eternal shift between night and day. The shade and a nap on a striped couch while he makes you tea. A moment within yourself in the cozy warmth, when the hands of the clock don't stab at your dry, tired eyelids like steel knives. You'll crave the solitude of an old woman, her cat, her parties, and bed full of crumbs from the grand-children, especially in November, and inside is bright and cozy while outside it's dusky and cool, and a little freezing. Outside where you stand with your only heart and life in your chest, knowing it all—but how?—and loving, loving, loving it.

But there is only this moment in the present, this excessive, ruth-less sense of awareness, and the acrid scent of the earth.

Why do I walk around with an orchestra playing in my head?

And she starts to crack like a pine tree. Her bark peels—layer by layer, falling off in flames. The forest breathes and grows, stands mod-estly, doesn't try to prove anything, just exists. She knows the forest is perfect, but the forest itself doesn't know that. Existence asks too much of a person, too much of this complicated structure, this ball of nerves with a heart, brain, and eyes—how can it forget? It's an end-less struggle, a whirlwind of activity, tendencies, thoughts, instincts, responsibilities—and if not those, then at least the slightest inkling of them now and then. Lifting your hand to change channels on the TV, taking the grilled cheese out of the toaster oven or just running the red light at a packed intersection. Or like when you get back home after being abroad for a long time and, as you look out onto the silky reeds under the sliding shadows of clouds, you ask yourself—who's the one seeing all this?

Or when you're in a new place and get word that your mother has died. I don't want to hear it, your tired, scarred, cynical heart cries. Your heart doesn't want any more pain. But something inside you trembles, shivers—a tiny, significant dream right before you wake up, or the screech of an animal as loud as an overworked motor—and you get the piercing realization that your next breath could never come.

But it does, and you're simultaneously thrilled and inexplicably disappointed. Because the question of the heart remains. If someone was once close to you, very close, and is now dead, and you imagine their heart, which you've never seen, but can pretty well imagine—and why shouldn't you—as a once functional, but now stiff, immobile shell at the bottom of a grave. And you try to imagine what the heart is doing down in that grave. Has it cultivated a soul, that sought-after pearl, or not? Most likely not. There isn't a pearl down there, no archeologist has ever found a pearl in place of a heart. It's unheard of. Maybe you yourself are the pearl, the fruit and creation of this strange life, but the sudden stillness of the heart, the coup of that flesh, which you possibly loved more than your own, can drive you insane in its stillness and assimilation to the earth. And the decomposition of the heart, its imperceptible transformation into earth and worms, soil, roots—it hurts you, and you're ready to dig it up out of the dirt, bring it into the daylight, this useless thing that has no spark, no movement, no echo. It's an obsession.

But her thoughts have peeled away; at least that's done with. She takes a hesitant step away from the lee side of a pine tree and moves forward. Sand mixed with black soil, so loose that she sinks down into it up to her ankles. A firebreak freshly tilled in the anticipation of forest fires. There won't be any more fires. Her thoughts have peeled down to the moist, living pith. Down to her being, to the present, free of the past, the future, genetics, ancestry and contemplation, from high school certificates and notices from detention centers. It suddenly seems to her that this spiritual peace is thievery. Like an unending and painful embodiment of others' lives—it was such a deep hole, but now it's just a thick layer: the woods, the road, and the sky. That has to be proof of suffering, she wants to shout, but falls quiet. And if that ends up being the only chance to keep going? Stoop down and grab a handful of your shadow along with the sand—nothing but the woods, the road, and the sky. And you. A thickening of matter, an accidental obstacle to the sun's rays, a being without genes, without ancestors, without a past, or a future. An observer, someone who has seen one or two of the most beautiful moments of her life in nature. There aren't many of these moments, but there are some, and she can't stop thinking about them. She thinks she'll even remember them in her final hour, like fog snaking through the city on a swelter-ing summer morning. The movements of fog animals in the empty city streets, when the mist slips its tendrils into the ancient river val-ley. Movement without movement. Or when the first snow falls on the lake in the forest. A black, clear mirror that glitters endlessly, a disappearing curtain of white, an army of snow, billions of flakes that cease to exist as soon as they touch the clean, black void.

Yes, but was there ever ugly scenery in the woods? Wasn't the darkening sky every fall evening when, if you were able to persuade yourself to stop for a few seconds in a clearing to see a pair of ravens fly off with a low "craw-craw," to see the white jet trails of a plane in the gleam of the setting sun turn redder and redder, and the fine lace of the north-facing treetops grow mysteriously blacker and black-er against the rich yellow sky . . . wasn't that beauty? Just like the concentrated color of an expanding sunset before the night thickens, before the earth sinks into itself—there's no sign of the ideas the wind carelessly sowed where the forest stands in the crisp, wintery stillness, immersed to its roots and tips in a meditation only it can know. A beauty for itself, yet simultaneously meant for her to see. Meant for her, a single body so small in this large clearing. And the glimpse of life that finds her in that moment is rapid and just as insignificant as a train whistling as it leaves an empty station. An essentially unneces-sary gesture, a superfluous signal without an addressee; because there isn't anybody here, just the surge of tracks from horizon to horizon and the inky wall of frozen spruce trees, along which the train carries its cry and the warm electric glow of its windows.

She once read, though who knows where: You'll fall from grace more than once, but it's okay. It boggled her mind and she thought it over for a long time. It seemed to her that someone was playing a sick joke. What she saw as a sin was nothing more than a lesson to someone else? She couldn't believe it, but at the same time felt the tiniest hope that this sentence could take responsibility for its words. And what was sin, what kind of word was it? As someone once told her, like the greatest Dostoevsky novel in its both satanic and holy natures, sin was not what people called upon when chasing murderers and thieves to the gallows, oh no, that was another, much more brutal matter, undeserving of that fine whisper of a word "sin". Sin, he'd said—look into your heart, look at the momentary shivers of hate, desire, pride, envy, gossip, and jealousy that are born in it—that's sin, locked up in your heart's emotions, the same heart that also has forgiveness and the eternal balance of peace hidden in it; look at the agitated surface of your blood and you'll have something to confess to—it doesn't matter to whom, a priest, the sea or the Holy Mount Kazbek; measure how level your heart is and you'll find that it's not the other person you hate, but rather what he provokes in you, your dishonest desires and weaknesses. That's what you hate, not him, he's not at fault; he's like a child, how could he be at fault? But these ripples of resistance coming from your heart are yours, they have your eye color and your facial expressions, not yet put into words or to use. Your heart hides sin in its thoughts. Then suddenly this—you'll fall from grace more than once, but it's okay. Get up and move on. Don't make the same mistake twice. If only she could graft this thought onto her body, like cultivating a double-blossom flower in hopes for a thriving species.

You have to be the most careful when driving in the car, yes, of course. That is, if you can even look up. Oh, secret . . . locked chest of time . . . serious and melancholy expression . . . impossible closeness.

A bowl that cannot be filled even when there is too much, a cup that cannot be emptied—human! If you consider how many gears need to fall into place for even a shadow of intimacy, a figment of intimacy, an imitation of intimacy to be possible . . . But if it's true intimacy, the immensely aching, desperate attempt to overcome time and bodies and to make out the darkest chasms within each other? Then to be able to look each other in the eye after all of it—isn't that a miracle? And when you're in the car you see the right side of his face. The right side is supposedly from God. So it's the best one. The first one to be lost in war. But it's also the most beautiful, without a doubt. And the road itself is beautiful, as is the destiny of the landscape rushing by to flash and reflect in your face and eyes, to change.

That's why you're careful when he offers to take you to Paris— well, maybe not Paris, but maybe to Helsinki, Tukums, Kaliningrad or Lake Baikal. The road shines in his eyes and it's always beautiful. No one is more beautiful than a person on the road. He's carefree and pulls you along with him. The road, the beauty, an aching. But hold on to even the tiniest piece of your critical mind. We grow more irrational with every year and, it's very possible, may someday even understand Russia—no, nonsense, we don't have to understand Russia, just blaze through it wild and barefooted, doling out their penance. But try to maintain even the tiniest bit of your critical mind, so things don't totally backfire, so the dark Russian land doesn't swallow you up. Or at least maintain your belief in yourself. Leave yourself the freedom to wake up the following workday and walk to the lake and back. You won't really go anywhere; you'll slump into the trolley or your favorite Rolls-Royce and head off to work. But leave that afterglow of freedom in your mind, that possibility to just go down to the lake—and you won't have to go anywhere. You'll be at peace.

What's the reason for her restlessness and desire? It's simple to the point of cliché. She's once again overcome by this wave and doesn't know if the wave is crashing over her, or if she's the wave itself. Respectively, what's putting her through her paces: destiny or free will? The reason is ridiculously simple, the same reason why she doesn't like or read those so-called "books on relationships." They're garbage and dangerous. As soon as the words "she" and "he" appear on the page she slams the book shut and throws it into the corner with a crash because it'll probably be the same old story about that maternal instinct that makes women get involved with jackasses. It could just be Ieva's own miserable experience making her rebel. Because love has once again come down on her, but not a relationship, God no, there's no sign yet of that swampland called "a relationship." She's been overcome by a clean and pure love, and she'd like to reduce this fire to embers as soon as possible, so everything would once again be ruled by calm and the quiet crackle of coals deep in the ashes. This peaceful state is her favorite: cinders on the outside and a quiet move-ment in the depths, the hidden smoldering of the coals. She likes it, but it's not possible to burn anything out faster than it's meant to, life is fire, love is fire, days are sprouts of light on the stem of an evening primrose, light is fire, and time is fire and warmth. And then comes the high tide, then comes the ninth wave and, if you're the only one who can't hold her breath long enough to dive to the next low tide, then grab hold of him and soar over it all.

The reason is so cliché and simple that she's angry with herself and cries, but she doesn't want pity. No destiny but her own, no advice, no help. She wants her own experience. Why try to avoid it—so she won't make mistakes? She needs mistakes, needs them! Fear of mistakes has been stitched into the spacesuits of astronauts and launched off to Mars for years and years. The need to make her own great mistakes surfaced as she trudged through her detached years. She wants the forest and silence, and to see how it'll all end. And how they'll start, if they'll start at all. What she does know is that after the beginning comes the end, and after the end comes the beginning. But whether or not something will outlast her—that she doesn't know. The most valuable thing she owns is an old Chinese Book of Changes. It hasn't lied to her a single time. She only turns to this book in rare cases, when it's no longer possible for her to go on like she usually does. And she's not looking for keys to the past or future in this book, no. She's noticed that the most significant thing lacking in a person's life, and a frightening habit at that, is the ability to be aware of the present situation. She often asks the Book of Changes one question—where am I? And the book has never lied to her, it tells her the place like a well-drawn topographic map: Breakdown.

Observation.

Justice.

Or something else. Defeat turns into assault, structure into debris. And the characters, they're the same ones you see in your dreams. Now that she's in love again, she asks the book and the book answers: Swan. It's the truth. But unfortunately, she's not a swan when she's in love. She's a cat. And the swan never reaches shore. She laughs at herself—look! She's in love. But does she need it again, she's so tired and knows all the horrors of it from start to end, like she knows her multiplication tables, so why, and for what? Again with this sighing feeling of existence, this diploma of life. This stream that pulls her forward and makes the pit of her stomach flutter.

She catches cold so she has time to weigh her options. So she can sit motionless by her kitchen window for hours and watch the land-lady, the pigeons, the veins in her hands, the creases at the corners of her mouth in her reflection in the window, her thoughts and feelings, all before she jumps to her feet, calls him, runs and throws her arms around him. Because . . . is there value in anything without love? Woman has always been and always will be the strength in what's weak and the great in what's small, but of her own volition—don't forget that.

Outside, coincidentally, is the harsh Baltic seaside climate. When she was little she believed it was the only world that existed. There, by the sea, three months of sun and nine months of darkness seemed as natural as being in her own skin. The change of the seasons, the velvety tips of budding flowers, drawing sap from birch, or the patter of green, wet leaves against the roof of the house in fall—she was so close to it all, though her head was no higher than the ferns and her fingertips could just reach Gran's knobby knees. Granddad Roberts sometimes brought his wrinkled face down to hers, coming into view like a piece of brown driftwood the wind had slowly unrolled from a skein of waves. He'd sing:

> "Over the fields sweeps
> a low spring wind,
> a violin cries sadly along.
> The violinist plays,
> he once was young,
> the heart in his chest was once full of love . . ."

And then he'd play the same melody on his silver harmonica.
Back then Ieva had asked:
"Granddad, does that mean your heart isn't full of love anymore?"
"Always," he laughed, "my heart is always full of love."
Roberts smoked by the stove and told Ieva that the glowing rolls of paper he always held between his fingers were also lit by the flame in his heart. Pipes are for those who like breathing in fire, he'd laugh. Then Gran would scold him, call Roberts a smokestack and to stop feeding the child nonsense. But there was no real reason to scold, Ieva had eyes enough to see that Granddad lit them by picking out an ember from the grate.
Ieva hadn't yet learned to read when Roberts told her all about the nature of clouds. How clouds, this everlasting gloom from fall to spring, were a second sea above the real sea. That up there where birds live, above people's heads, was another lead-grey surface, which

the wind constantly swirled about and chased into waves. It was lit by the sun and the sky above it was just as clear and blue as in the summer. Now, many years later, she's been to the desert and has already felt that the door is open—she could escape from the swamp to the equator by myriad paths. She just doesn't want to. She wants to feel like a child again—to be in the depths of the clouds. To be at ease in the depths around her heart.

The screenplay she's just started is sitting on the table, but right now, as far as she's concerned, it could be on the surface of the moon.

And what is she looking for? Can she ask anything more of life than the privilege to trust a single living person, and him alone?

And what can she ask of everyone, of the one and only God, of outer space, the Universe, but the desire and basic hope to never betray or hurt another?

On a shelf she finds letters she wrote to her brother as a teenager. And sends her brother a text message—an entire forest of exclamation marks. He responds with a single question mark.

Turns out—we've lived, she answers.

There's proof, you can touch it. A little black notebook filled with words. If you have one free week, an unpaid vacation, or are part of a stay-at-home clinical trial during which you can afford to spend time in a dusty closet, digging through ink-stained, aging pieces of paper, or to look through photographs of the deceased that still retain some kind of discernable contours—you can touch it, this feeling.

Turns out—we've lived.

GATHERING

MOTHER

MOTHER tries to remember where she's seen it before.

Faces peering at her from a glaring brightness.

Big eyes. Lips that are saying something, smiling, cooing, scolding. Faces that pull her from the comforting darkness and into the light.

An avenue.

For a moment she sees her father; he points out the leaves overhead. She is a child in her stroller, a child absorbing every single detail. She sees the leaves and becomes them, submerges herself in them and their silky movement.

The faces in this narrow room are like the leaves. They form a canopy high overhead, full of rustling movement and a teasing wind. The faces look at her as she lies there like a dried-up worm, wedged between the body pillow and the wall. A pair of hands throw open the curtains—a window fills with light.

"Good morning! Time to get up," a light voice says.

The face leans in very close—it's a woman's face.

Mother opens an eye. The other is crusted over with pus. She looks at the faces and her toothless mouth whispers a few syllables in greeting. Mother is afraid of the daytime, afraid of the daily routine. She'll be rolled over, picked up, moved, washed—it hurts and it makes her uneasy. Mother wants to tell them she doesn't understand why she needs to get up anymore. She's tired, but they won't leave her alone.

"And the worst is she somehow gets in there with her left hand. She grabs and tears at the diaper and then smears shit all over the place. She's out of her mind. I've got to change the bedding twice a day—all of it."

Mother closes the one eye and pretends this talk isn't about her. For several years now her good eye has been covered by a film, a rapidly swirling fog with tiny black spots.

"You have to figure something out. You can probably do something like tie a shirt over her chest," says a second voice that's lower, infused with darkness.

Mother likes that voice better.

"She doesn't get in from the top, but from the bottom along her thigh. The entire bed is flooded by morning. She pees so, so much. And if there's shit I can't even come in here without gagging. You wouldn't believe the smell," the first voice complains, white and clear as a ray of light.

You can't hide from that voice, so Mother just shuts her eye tighter.

"Maybe like something for a baby. A onesie that buttons up the sides."

"Won't work. Since the last treatment she's completely lost it. Look at how small she is—but she's heavy, as heavy as a rock. She's dead weight, ten times heavier than me. I make her stand up so her legs won't totally atrophy. A few minutes a day. When I come home from work I have her sit up. You can't believe how hard it is. I've sprained my back—it hurts. No, no, no. No onesies, no pants. She can't even lift her legs. It would just mean extra clothes for me to wash. No, no, no. I had an idea yesterday—I'll secure the diaper with electrical tape. Or a wide strip of duct tape. What do you think?"

"You can't do that, Mom. Her skin'll get infected."

"You think so? Well, then I don't know."

Mother pretends she is dead. Pretends this stupid conversation isn't about her. People only talk like that about children who misbehave. She's not a bad child, never has been. No, no, no.

The light voice disappears and the door closes.

Something warm slips under her neck, she feels warmth. Mother feels a soft, youthful breath on her cheek and opens her good eye.

"Drink some coffee, Gran," says the dark voice, "while you can. I'm visiting. So you can have your coffee before washing up."

A white cup enters into view. It moves closer. The hand firmly grips the back of her neck and lifts her head. Mother's toothless mouth and pale, slug-like lips suction to the rim of the cup. Something white, warm, and sweet fills her mouth. It flows over her tongue, which has dried out overnight and rattles inside her head. The drink is heavenly. Mother wants more and watches the cup eagerly as it's moved away from her lips.

"See, it's good. More?"

Mother gives a sharp nod with her pointy chin—almost like she fears the cup will stay out of reach. But it comes back. This time the slug-like lips don't let go of the white cup. Mother gulps down two mouthfuls and sinks back into the pillow. She tries to smile and make out the face. But she can't. The effort clouds her vision even more.

Mother speaks:

"Sweetheart."

"Yes, Gran? What do you want?"

Mother wants to tell her, but there are no words.

A yard divided up by the bright sun and a shadow cast by the roof. Gravel and tufts of grass. In this yard, she is a cat crouching close to the ground on the edge of the shadow.

The cat jumps into a flock of birds sunning themselves in the hot sand.

The birds scatter and the scene crumbles away.

She doesn't call up these scenes; they just come and go. There's the damp smell of moss, a cool spring wind on her face, the breaking of the last layer of ice underfoot and boots splashing into mud.

She sees a clearing and catches the scent of resin.

She sees railroad ties, up close—pitchy wood ties, iron tracks covered in red rust and tiny yellow flowers—so lifelike.

She sees a newborn child, slick with fluids, and they place it in her arms.

She can see everything except the chance to experience it all over again. She thinks a lot about this.

But right now Mother doesn't want scenes; Mother wants what is right next to her. That warm, innocent, dark voice.

Mother speaks:

"Sweetheart."

"What is it, Gran? More coffee?"

Mother slowly sticks out her chin.

"What then?"

Oh, if she only could say.

Mother wants heat.

The kind that can't be bought with money.

Mother wants someone to lie down next to her. Right next to her, pressing side to side.

Like her own mother used to sleep next to her.

Like her grandmother used to on winter nights.

Like her husband used to once she had overcome her cold, distant teenage years—once she had been grown up enough to sleep with a man. The return of the nights when their separate warmths would join to become one.

Like when her own children used to climb into bed next to her.

And wasn't this one here—the one with the dark voice—wasn't she her granddaughter?

A country home in the July swelter. The window is open and not a single blade of grass moves in the stifling heat. She is exhausted from this heat and reclines on the large sofa in the kitchen. They call it the "lyre"; it's covered with a faded, striped cotton blanket that smells faintly of dust. She calls to her granddaughter:

"Sweetheart! Come lie down!"

Like a tiny flame, her granddaughter nestles against her broad back; the flame turns this way and that until it is overcome by sleep. Flies buzz around the brown wood of the curtain rod. Life is so incredibly vast.

Mother wants to say to her granddaughter—sweetheart, come lie down!

Mother wants to say—to hell with bathing, to hell with all the pissing and shitting, the eating—what does it all mean? Coldness, coldness is seeping into her from all sides. Lie down next to me, sweetheart, so I can feel your warmth. Take my frozen body into your arms. Let's look out that far, faraway window for an hour. Two.

Live a moment of my life and you'll feel like a year has passed.

Let's look at our hands against the light, you can read so much in them.

Sweetheart, do you have a little time for me?

Just one night—in the heat of your embrace.

Sweetheart—Mother tries to say it, but only a sigh comes out. So many words in one sentence just to convey one thought. Mother just can't string them together anymore.

Please don't deny me warmth, she wants to say. It's the worst thing one person can deny another.

Sweetheart, Mother wants to say, your face is a beautiful canopy of leaves. Full, soft, alive. That's a good thing, Mother wants to say. It's important for a woman to be attractive.

"Gran," her granddaughter speaks suddenly, close, close by. "Gran, do you remember back when you said that a person is beautiful only once they understand themselves? Gran, right now you're very beautiful. Yes you are, don't shake your head, you are! You are."

The light voice returns above them:

"I went to the Red Cross earlier and got one of those cheap toilet chairs. See, that white thing. They rent them out, but I paid for only a month, since it's not worth paying for a half a year. The man said so—if they're dying, it's not worth it. They're dying."

As these words are spoken a wet towel is scrubbed back and forth over Mother's face. Mother pulls away, squeezes her eyes shut—both the good one and the one that's crusted over—but it's impossible to escape the towel. It's wet and rough.

"Mom, don't say that around her."

"Her hearing is bad. And what does it matter anyway? That's life. The day we brought her home from the hospital, another patient in her ward died. She was this tiny old woman, swore at everyone, complained, was never satisfied. That day they'd supposedly pumped a ton of fluids into her—you know, eight of those huge bags. Well, and she died anyway. She didn't suffer long, maybe ten minutes. Her daughter had just arrived and was standing by the bed. The doctors rushed in and wanted to resuscitate her, they even brought the gurney, but there wasn't anything to resuscitate anymore. They opened the window—for the soul to leave—and then cleared her away, bed and all. And that was it. That morning I'd even told the women working the ward—look how she's holding her hands, crossed over her chest, she's going to go soon! And she did."

Two strong hands wedge under Mother's shoulder blades and sit her up.

"Oh," Mother cries, "it hurts!"

"Nothing hurts, you lump. I rented the toilet chair for nothing. She doesn't understand anything anymore. I sat her on that chair and kept her there for an hour. Nothing. No pissing, no shitting. She doesn't get it. Just sits and dozes. For nothing! She's lazy, just takes care of everything in the diaper. And at night she scratches at the walls, fidgets. One night around three I heard this loud thump. I wondered what it could be, so I come look and find she's fallen out of bed. Flat on her face. Once I'd finally gotten her back up I couldn't fall asleep until morning. I went to work completely out of it. Now I put the toilet chair against the bed so she won't fall out. At least it's good for something. It's heavy, see, made of metal. It's like having iron bars."

Toothless Mother smiles from behind the bars. She smiles at nothing in particular, something melted, sweet, and white beyond that faraway window. But the here and now just won't let her be. Her palms press down onto the bars and force her to push herself up. Her body is crumpled, it doesn't want to move. Her muscles are knotted at the thighs, her legs don't want to stand. It's hard for her, she doesn't understand why she has to stand if her body doesn't want to. But she's propped up with her hands on the bars and is stretched like a piece of leather across a frame as the bottom of her nightdress is rolled up in the morning light. They wash her back. She puts up with it. There's a throbbing and pulsing in her temples. She feels her blood slosh through her bony body and pool at her feet, she is a glass of corked wine balanced precariously high over the emptiness and the white of daylight.

"Good thing Pāvils gave me these yellow rubber gloves. They're really good, see? Before my hands would smell so badly I couldn't

go to work—piss and shit get under your nails and the smell sticks
to your skin no matter how hard you scrub your hands. It's more
hygienic with the gloves. They work! I put a hat on before coming
in here, too. Your hair soaks up smells in a second. I can't talk to
anyone at work about any of it. I never dreamed it would be like this.
She's been strong as a horse her whole life—she worked as hard as a
horse and was as proud as a horse. Wouldn't let anyone or anything
get to her. And look at her now! How long will it be like this? Could
be years. The doctors said her heart was like a horse's. Strong. Her
mind's gone, she doesn't think or feel anything, but she's still got an
appetite."

Mother hears these doubts about her mental capacity and smirks,
then smacks her gums, which are again as dried out as the desert. But
right away she winces as a rough towel digs into the skin behind her
knees.

"Mom, what you're doing is admirable—you're great. You amaze
me. You'll feel good about it afterwards, right?"

"Will I feel good about it? I don't even know how to respond to
your little cheer."

"Cheer? Mom!"

"I don't know. I don't know about anything anymore. I try not to
think at all."

They put a new diaper on Mother and sit her back onto the bed
with a pile of pillows behind her back. A napkin is tucked in under
her chin. A spoon of something red is brought to her mouth. She
opens it like a mechanical beak and swallows.

"Have some fruit, Mother!"

"You should cut it up—she doesn't have any teeth."

Mother nods and swallows the piece of fruit whole.

"She can mash it up with her gums."

"Maybe it would be better to put her in a home. You yell at her.

And one time when I called you were in tears. Sometimes you drink and cry."

"I don't just yell at her, m'dear, I hit her too—with a towel. She's totally shameless. And yes, I yell. She shits all over the bed and pisses all the time. But she still has an appetite. I stand next to her and watch my life fall apart—or what's left of it. An hour with her sometimes feels like a year. I'll drink her medicine, it happens a lot. It's human nature! Don't shake your head, that's life. You don't believe me and that's fine, because you don't know anything about life yet. Think what you want, but I'm not putting her in a home. She's my mother."

"Nurse supervision, good food. She's been proud her entire life, remember, Mom? It might be better for both of you if you didn't yell and hit her with towels. If you didn't cry and drink her medicine."

"Why bother having kids if they just end up putting you in a home?"

"But let's at least think about it."

"You're all trying to push this nursing home thing—stop piling on your advice!"

Mother nods and opens her mouth to have her say, but gets a mouthful of chocolate spread instead. That was unnecessary. Mother hates the chocolate. She shudders and shakes her head. But her gums mash up the spread, and it melts and drips heavily into her stomach.

Mother speaks:

"The white one."

"Mom, she wants the cottage cheese."

"I heard, I heard. I've got it all under control, I'll get through it, you hear me? This is my mother. Alright, let's give it a rest. She's scheduled for an X-ray Tuesday. Can you come help me? To get her in the wheelchair and down to the clinic."

Silence.

Mother smiles.

"I can't do it by myself. She's ridiculously heavy. Every muscle in my body is already strained. It hurts here, on the left side. From my ribs to my thigh—it's like I'm being cut with a knife."

"Are you crying?"

"No. It's some kind of fluid that just drains from my eyes on its own. It's just that everything hurts. I never thought it would be like *this*. I've never experienced anything like it before, you know? She doesn't want anything but pity. But I can't give it to her because of all the shit and the pain. I don't see anything beyond that anymore, and I'm so scared. There's nothing to do about it. Let God pity her— that's his job. I just wash the sheets, get upset, and cry. Eat faster, Mother, I have to go to work!"

"What does she do by herself all day?"

"Sleeps. What else?"

Mother smiles. What does she do by herself all day? Time's a real son of a bitch, she thinks.

Time always pretends it's something else. Sometimes it pretends to be a person. Time pretends to be people's wrinkles, scars, saggy bits. Sometimes it's faraway, unreachable roads. Time pretends to be a road that leads to the sea—over hills, past hidden places, past mysterious destinies that are never understood, over roofs, chimneys, castles and huts, fields of cow-wheat and forget-me-nots, and under the silvery smooth beech trees of manor houses. Sometimes it pretends it's the sea itself. And the sky. Sometimes it pretends to be gravestones, children, the elderly. It pretends to be your veins, your teeth, your dentures, or eyes. In Mother's eyes, these days time usually pretends to be the wall opposite her bed. The window is time. Day and night. Light and dark. Time is yellowed photographs— black and white, figures disintegrating under her failing vision (what time hides from Mother is that these figures are her own faces throughout the years, her children and her husband). Time is a clock that has stopped.

Sometimes Mother's fingers are time—she holds them up against the light and studies them for hours like a child.

"I wanted to ask you something."

"What, Mom?"

"I hope it won't be like that, but if I . . . If I end up like her, shoot me! Or get rid of me some other way. I'll write a letter of permission ahead of time. I'll keep it in my purse with my ID."

"Mom! Don't talk like that around her!"

"See, you're thinking of her again. I'm not blind or deaf—that kind of talk is fine around me."

"Stop it. At least stop making it all about you for a little while."

"I've done nothing else my entire life *but* put myself second—I wonder why she never bothered to do the same!"

There are no more words. They fall silent and hug, then stand next to Mother's bed. A shadow falls over her face. Mother sticks out her chin—this is how it should be.

Warmth! She also craves that heat. She's grown almost completely cold. Tomorrow night's high tide will extinguish her.

A napkin wipes the remains of chocolate from the corners of Mother's mouth. The voices above her keep talking.

Mother finally remembers—she remembers. There were female voices back then, too!

Like a garment cut from nothingness with magic scissors, like a paper crane made of light—she draws closer to the memory—the warm nose of a foal nuzzles her, its breath hot—she has to get a bridle on it!

Mother leans toward the memory, avoiding the invasive spoon, her toothless mouth now and then gulping the cottage cheese. Her bony fingers tear at the blanket corner in her lap, and she remembers . . .

. . . The voices are coming from the kitchen. She is still in part a child, but also in part a woman, on that border when time ties the first rosy knots at the tips of a girl's chest. She's at her mother's house in the country. There's a celebration tomorrow. The spring weather is hot, and the cherries, hackberries, and lilacs are blooming. The kitchen door is open and almost every woman from the seaside town is in there baking, cooking, slicing meat, and grinding onions.

The thick, juicy grass lies flat in the garden like a green, hairy beast, and the leafy branches of the apple trees spill in through open windows. The screams of animals being slaughtered for food has stopped and their rolled-up hides lay haphazardly next to the barn, because the tanner is drunk on beer and sound asleep next to the doghouse. The boys are tickling his mustache with a reed, and he smiles in his sleep. Everything smells of sweat and music. Striped cats purr and wind around the porch pillars.

Steam rises above the pots on the stove, rattling the tin covers like bells. Laughing children dart around the grownups with the neighborhood dogs, stealing slices of smoked bacon meant for tomorrow's bacon rolls. The women scold them and wipe their own sweaty foreheads and flushed necks with white handkerchiefs. They pass around a bottle of lingonberry brew, which you can only have a little bit of at a time, because it's quite strong, quite sacred, quite devilish!

Uncle Jānis blows a horn on the roof of the shed—the song is "The Sea Needs a Fine-Spun Net"—he doesn't know that in a few days the sea will take him in place of the net, and then the women will be cooking for his funeral instead.

Uncle Jānis plays his horn, then comes inside, sits at the end of the table, chats with the women and manages to get a few sips of brew. The women swat him with their handkerchiefs and blush when he pinches one of them in the thigh. His voice is pure, unfiltered fire, strong like the lingonberry brew. The children eye the trumpet on the corner of the table, poke at its yellow, brassy shine, breathe in its metallic scent.

Mother goes outside. It's hard for her to hold herself straight against this bold thundering of life that tears through the air and slams against her little body like the waves crashing against the breakwater. For the first time in her life, she simultaneously feels deep pain and joy. The sweltering happiness in the kitchen and the passionless existence of the blue skies over the sea, with the fragrant clusters of white flowers in the twilight—

—it's hard for her to be outside for long, her heart is being torn to bits by the cold and lonely wind. She wants to go inside, closer to the fire. Rather, she wants it all together, to pour these two worlds into one cup and drink it. To see: is it really like oil and water, can they never mix? To bring the cold inside, or to bring the heat outside.

Soon enough both worlds melt into one, because something happens that night, something secretive. She is recruited—

—because on her way inside she almost runs into a woman. There, in the front hall, is their neighbor, Maija. Maija's right hand holds a bundle of onions and is pressed to her chest, but her left hand is balled up by her mouth—her white teeth biting into her thumb. She is listening from the other side of the kitchen door to what Jānis is saying to the other women. The adults have said more than once that Maija is crazy about Jānis.

Maija looks at her with dark eyes. At the motionless, angular silhouette of a teenager in the doorway against the blue-green horizon over the sea. It's bad to eavesdrop, they both know that. But the woman at the kitchen door burns like a fire, even though her frame is small and her hair is soft and long. Voices can be heard from the kitchen—

"Child," Maija says and puts a finger up to her lips. Her eyes gleam like a cat's.

"No, no!" the child cries out, burned by this fervor.

Then the door opens and someone comes out. Maija lets her into the kitchen ahead of her, into the thicket of steam and life. They cut onions, laugh, cry and never again mention what happened. All she does is now and again steal a glance at Maija. Maija is a woman. She, too, is now a woman. A bowl of fire. A tiny, bright flame, until the Star comes—The One That Brings the Rain—

Mother speaks:
"Sweetheart."
Silence.

She opens her one good eye. She is welcomed by the white square of the window and the black fog the Dark One pulls over her vision.

All that's left in the empty room is the dream called her life. Voices can be heard from the kitchen.

DAUGHTER

IN the darkness of midnight, Lūcija turns on the lamp and looks to see if her mother is still breathing. She's so shriveled. Lūcija is now her mother's mother.

The mother is her daughter's little child.

Her mother's mouth is opened slightly, her eyes closed.

All the witnesses to this horror gleam at her from the dresser top—diapers, sippy-cups, mugs, wet wipes. Creams for rashes and sores. Things for a child. A newborn child. Only this birth is happening backwards—from the light into the darkness.

And then the child becomes strangely still.

Daughter looks at mother. She'd give up everything for her to keep on living. But over the course of their time together all they mostly did was argue.

Daughter looks at mother. Places a hand on her. Her head is still warm, her arm still warm. The last bit of heat.

Leaving is so difficult and drawn-out.

And how this excruciating period of time finally brought them together.

ALL OF THEM

GRAN'S soul is fighting its hardest to get out, fluttering in her head. Her mouth gasps for air. Her relatives take turns wetting her lips with water.

When her light is about to give out, Pāvils jumps to his feet, wails and grabs his grandmother by the shoulders.

He cries:

"Don't fall asleep! Wake up!"

Gran comes to and asks:

"What did you do that for? All of them were coming to greet me."

Gran dies the next day, when all her relatives have stepped out for just a moment.

But how beautiful she looks.

GRANDDAUGHTER

IEVA crouches in the middle of the field and watches two giant tree stumps burn among the pile of branches. The wind has picked up and sparks fly through the air. Gran's things are among the kindling.

Not diaries, letters, or notes—just things. Things from her final months.

The black plastic trash bags melt, split open like blistering skin, and drip into the fire. The flames lick at the dingy shoes, the warped sleeves, lace pillowcases. A mug shatters with a bang, the plastic bottles melt into puddles.

Ieva watches on as if made of stone. The fire melts her down and pours her into a different mold.

There will be nothing left when the fire burns out. Only memories.

ANDREJS'S RELIGION

ANDREJS'S RELIGION

OUTSIDE it's rainy and incredibly windy.

The woman moves into the kitchen and begins to season the meat. Andrejs sits down at the corner of the table.

"What are you looking at?" she asks.

You can't really know anything these days. This is only the second time they've met, and he's kind of quiet. But his eyes are like razors—sharp, cutting. She could easily use them to slice the roast.

"What I'm looking at? Just looking."

"Everyone looks for different reasons."

"I'm not everyone. I'm Andrejs."

"Pass me the fillet knife."

"Which one's that?"

"With the threaded cord."

Andrejs hands her the knife, she cuts the roast. It's raining outside. You can't really know anything. These days.

But she's a woman, a real woman. Seasoning a roast in front of him with garlic and herbs. She wants to cook it tomorrow in his honor.

He can't look away.

A woman is a real home. Food. Children. Holidays. And shelter. Happiness.

"What are you looking at?" she asks again. She should stay quiet, the idiot. She'll ruin the entire night with her questions.

"You're cutting and cutting," he answers.

"I'm done," she says and wipes her hands on her apron, then takes it off and hangs it up. "Now what?"

They go to watch TV, but Andrejs wants her to just take off her panties already.

Outside is rainy and cold. And all the while Andrejs feels the woman next to him. He feels as if he's the only one in the world who understands what a woman is. She doesn't even get it herself. Look at her head dropping onto his shoulder. She's dozed off.

At that moment, Andrejs is visited by Ieva. By memories of her. Violently, as usual.

An awful fate.

But still—it was his fate, too.

He's a little unsettled by the Black Balzam he drank for warmth and courage—just 100g of Balzam.

He glares at the TV, then at the woman asleep next to him. The movie of her life projects itself under her eyelids. It's fascinating and sad to watch that kind of movie.

In his consciousness, his life separates itself into two lives. Though technically into one—at the Zari house with Ieva, plus his time in prison. He doesn't call the prison he's now locked up in "life." It's a strange waking state where he thinks about life, remembers it, but doesn't actually live it. The whole time there's this distance, this space between him and existence. Right now he has a woman, the woman has average breasts, an apartment, and a roast, and obviously some feelings for him. But all he can do again and again is chase his own memories. Somewhere hides the thought that it would be possible to organize them all onto a shelf.

A stupid thought. Because these memories don't do anything but unleash insanity and the feeling of being ripped open. The desire to drink, get drunk, get away from yourself. Memories go around in his head like on a carousel and drive him even deeper into the cage that is his body. They strengthen and cement one-of-a-kind people like Andrejs: thirty-nine years old, divorced, one daughter, fifteen years in prison for murder, released early for good behavior, saving him five years' time, during which he just worked in the same town the prison was in. Hasn't even gone more than a kilometer from the barbed wire fence. Alright, so he's crossed a few sand lots, closer to the highway. His carpentry shop is right here, everything is right here—a shack heated by a wood stove and with an outhouse behind the sheds. A dirt-colored building, dirt-colored porch, dirt-colored scenery behind moldy blinds. All the brambles and raspberry bushes and clematis— nature's colors. Clothes, the neighbor's dog, the never-ending spring or fall, who knows. A dusty steppe between the highway and a ditch.

But what's that flame, like a wandering ship between the blinds every day and night? It's his prison. The powerful searchlights, the thick stone walls, the tangled network of barbed wire—it all glows white, even in the fog, even in blizzards beyond the distant field. Andrejs's prison. His prison.

The black swan.

He looks to the window. This is the woman's apartment on the other side of the river, he doesn't see the prison when he looks out— just the town and a church.

Not good.

He is overcome by awe, he has goosebumps.

What is he without prison? He hasn't been away from it in so long that it seems like he never left.

He's comforted by the thought that he doesn't have to go far. He could leave right now if he wanted to. Push the woman's head off his shoulder, put on his jacket and go. Cross the bridge, cross the river. He'd stop in the middle for a smoke. It would be nice, a nice breeze over the middle of the river—cool, wide. Free.

Andrejs's doctors don't let him smoke. His hand hurts; his right shoulder, knees, and heart all hurt. The doctors told him to quit smoking. To cut back. He went to three doctors in a single day, so as not to waste his time—otherwise all you do is go from one clinic to the next. And that's where you'll stay.

He didn't cut back, but quit the very same day. Then the doctors said worse things could happen if you quit cold turkey. Your body has grown used to smoking. Your body will be stressed and deprived. Fine, let his body stress out a bit. He never liked smoking anyway. It's just that those were the years, those detached years, where if he hadn't smoked he would have completely fallen apart. And that isn't just some kind of saying or, what did they call it—a metaphor?—no. He would have fallen apart. Literally. Because during those years, not having a cigarette was like not having a watch. A cigarette an hour. If he was awake, of course. But the closer he got to being released, the less tired he was. Tick tock, tick tock.

He had once asked Ieva in disgust: Why do you smoke? She said it was to calm her nerves. Back then he had thought she was sick. Then he got sick himself. Was for fifteen years.

And Ieva. What about her? She'll always be Ieva.

But the woman next to him is asleep. She's tired. Smells of spices. She's an accountant at the prison, probably. He hasn't asked her. She could be over fifty years old, but she looks good. Maybe she works at the prison. Everyone in the area does. So he can say he's spent a lifetime together with this woman in the same prison. Him in the cell and her in accounting.

Let her sleep. They'd first met last holiday season at his neighbor's house. Andrejs had helped him dig a cellar and had been invited to the big New Year's dinner. He'd thought it over for a long time, then ended up going so he wouldn't be some completely uncivilized jerk. And she was there—a relative or friend of the hosts. Andrejs noticed her immediately, maybe because her eyes were dark, heavy, like from a secret. But no, there was no outer indication of sorrow—she smiled and joked, and the men at the end of the table where she sat drank twice as much liquor as those at the other end. It was her doing, getting them all riled up. Oh, Demeter, fruitful earth!, he had thought.

At midnight Andrejs had pressed a ladle with melted tin into her hand and said, "Pour my New Year's fortune." Who the hell knows why he had her do it. Maybe he was drunk. Then again maybe not, he doesn't like to drink. But she had laughed and taken the ladle, tipped the melted tin into water—poured a sort of bitter fortune. You couldn't make anything of the result; the tin whistled as it hit the water, then there was the flash of her plump hands, a splash, and her laughing eyes, but the piece of metal she fished out left an unpleasant impression on him. Smooth arcs of tin, like a naked person with a bowed head as if in mourning. He'd grown sad. Incredibly so. He'd taken his naked fortune, put on his leather jacket, and gone home. She had said she felt responsible.

But at the market today—they'd been so happy to see each other again. Genuinely happy. Andrejs was out looking for a new yardstick since his old one broke the day before yesterday, and the tape measurer was sometimes impossible to keep steady. But instead he bought a pork hock and left with this Demeter, who was now sleeping soundly against his shoulder. Tomorrow is his name day. He hadn't imagined he'd be spending his name day in a strange place. Life's funny like that.

Although, he could just leave. It was always an option. You could leave wherever you were as long as you were alive. Buy cigarettes and a book of matches at the gas station, stop and smoke one halfway across the bridge before throwing the rest of the pack into the river so they can't tempt him. Then take a right and head toward the small Russian church. Then across the train tracks, where little red and green lights glitter welcomingly in the shallow ravine. And past the tracks he was already almost home. Five kilometers—and his shed. Probably as cold as ice by now. The heat gets sucked out of the shed in no time; it's no surprise since the walls are so full of cracks that the wallpaper flaps in the wind.

But it's nice to get a fire going.

Open the flue.

Pile wood into the stove. Pack enough newspapers in the middle. Then light it.

Close the stove door and regret throwing the pack of cigarettes into the river. It's nice to have a smoke while lighting the stove. Surrounded by the dark, cool room, where the roaring flames reflect yellow onto the walls and he can see the white puffs of his breath. Regain warmth slowly, along with the floor, the ceiling, the bed and table, along with the bricks and wood. It was all somehow very nature-like.

Andrejs remembers how Ieva used to do that sometimes at the Zari house. It was too bad he didn't smoke back then. It would've been pretty great with the both of them. One over the course of the entire evening. With Ieva. But they never had anything together.

But this woman here—she's a typical woman. He told her how he'd quit smoking and right away she started going on about how good that was, and how she'd have to keep an eye on him so he didn't pick it up again. That thing all women have, that kind of habit of ownership, they're supposedly the weaker sex, but they're all just calculating bitches. They net you with their promises, tie you up, hold you to your word like they're yanking on the reigns, school you, keep an eye on you, babysit you. Just wait until she wakes up, then he'll tell her what's what, tell her not to get her hopes up, not to expect anything. She'll learn only the things she's entitled to learn. And give everything else a rest. Prison is his past. And that's all he'll say.

But why is this accounting thing bothering him? Ah, right, because of the photograph. She showed him a photo album—well parts of it, a few photos right at the beginning. And he'd accidentally seen the next page—kids in the prison visitation room, in the corner with the iron swing set. He recognized it right away, even though he'd only seen it a few times since he'd been released. When you're in the prison you don't see how pretty it looks from the outside. It's white. With fences and searchlights. And that strange alarm tone that goes off once an hour. And a swing set in the visitation area. His prison.

He recognized the yard by its masonry. The kids play on the swing set by the prison while their mother sits in accounting—he decided that's how it went. Two kids. Two's always better—it's always more fun. Now she's alone, he can tell by her slippers and toothbrush. Who knows if her husband died or left her. Actually, he doesn't care. She can tell him as much as she wants to. What's done is done.

But the handwriting under the photos is familiar. The number two in the year is like a swan with a curled neck. Maybe she was one of the people in accounting who accepted payments for visitations back then? Back when Ieva still came to see him? Who knows why he's being nagged by memories of that slanted "2"; he probably saw it on some receipt when Ieva came to visit.

Sweet little accountant. She's pretty in the pictures, and still looks good now. He told her this. So she wouldn't be offended that he wasn't really into the whole pictures thing. What's done is done. What's the point of photographs—your eyes never change. You're not going to love a woman made of paper. But the one resting her head on his shoulder, that's something else entirely—warm, full-figured, lightly snoring. Very quietly. Andrejs knows she's asleep. Because in prison you learn to tell by the sound of someone's breathing whether or not they're asleep. The rhythm is completely different. Especially the exhale.

And what says they'll even get around to talking? He could just ask her straight out about the accounting. But what if he suddenly wants to go home? Or tomorrow morning, even—bail while she's still sleeping? You can't force your heart to feel something. Visiting is great, but being home is even better. And if being home is better, then conversation is definitely not mandatory. Burden yourself with excess information. She already managed to talk about a few things while she was seasoning the meat. Show him the photo album. And ask questions. He won't say anything. What for? For more heartache? It's pointless and disloyal.

So she's sleeping. Let her. It's a nice moment. A couch under him. A woman beside him. The strips of light cast from the wall lamps long and muted. To the right a window, and beyond it darkness and cold. A TV in front of him with the volume turned down. Warmth all around him—not the abrasive, dry heat of a stove, but the soothing blanket of centralized heating.

It's his, Andrejs's moment. A moment of existence. He's gotten so good at capturing these moments over the past years. He sniffs them out like a bloodhound, extracts them like a pearl diver and brings them to the surface of his consciousness, breaks and grinds them down like a nutcracker. He's almost happy, dammit—happy!

He doesn't need much anymore. The waves that used to crash over him have thinned out. Soon the sky will be visible through them. He's almost convinced that its dark corners no longer hide any threatening shadows that could bring him suffering. It's his fate—to spend his entire life as a toy in the rolling waves of life. To do something and only realize it after the fact. Life brings nothing but pain to people who live like that. He's had enough. It's nice here, in the shallows. And his memories are within reach if he ever wants to feel something.

He was also happy back when Ieva still came to see him. But it was a tormented happiness. Kind of like what he feels now, when he replays the scenes of his life over and over, even though he should relax and enjoy the warmth, this moment of existence. Why let yourself sink in the past when you can't change or undo it? To feel that troubled happiness? Life is life, it has everything; the contents in that pot are so thick that, in the moment something happens, you can't tell if you're still happy or not. But only the good things remain in your memory.

Back when Ieva still came to see him, he would start waiting for her three months in advance. Once you'd shown you were hardworking and could behave, you'd get an extended visit. One visit per season. He'd carefully fill out the request form, put down Ieva's passport information, and write "wife" in block letters on the line above "relationship." Back then he had a wife.

They usually brought Ieva in first. The prison's hotel room was a long, narrow bedroom with a window at the end of it looking out onto the inner prison wall. Two beds against opposite walls. Two bare, ugly nightstands. No frills.

She was always sitting on the bed when the guards brought Andrejs in. He liked to think that she sat because her trembling knees would give away her excitement. But maybe she sat so she'd resemble a painting. Because she knew full well—in this empire of ugliness she looked so unnaturally beautiful. Who the hell knows. He was never able to fully understand Ieva.

He already had the feeling back then that she was slowly pulling away from him, that she was already associating with people who stayed out of trouble. And it was only the prison with the clanking of its hundreds of doors, the jangling of keys, narrow hallways, the spots of light on the guards' uniforms, Andrejs's shaved head and large eyes in his gaunt, dark face that fused them together—the way only prison can do.

When she stopped coming, he spent the next four years entertaining the thought of killing her once he got out. But that lasted only four years, not longer. No emotion lasts longer than four years without support from God. It was around that time he found *that* book by the stove in the prison boiler room, read it and calmed down. For life. The only thing he asked of God was to never see Ieva again. Now he's always on edge whenever he goes to Riga to visit their daughter. Ieva is probably around somewhere. Why shouldn't she be?

Just as alive as back then.

His hands would still be behind his back, even though it had been more than thirty seconds since the guard had removed the handcuffs and left the room. Andrejs grinned like an idiot every time—maybe Ieva didn't notice, at least he liked to think so. Grinned like an idiot and rubbed his wrists.

Then—and then he'd rush to the bed and pull her into his lap like a cat, warmth all around and their scents mixed together. They'd sit for a long time, pressed into each other, filling each other's contours, almost motionless. Breathing each other in.

And then they'd start to talk.

Finally Ieva would break free and they'd start to make dinner. Outside would be growing dark.

Like in that one song—just the two of them, alone in this world— what was that song? It doesn't matter. There are so many songs like that and all the singers in the world sing about it.

But the feeling was so rare. It was like the world had just been created. And they were the first two people in it.

Two people protected by a barbed wire fence, dogs, and guns.

It had been so beautiful. As if Andrejs even understands anything about words, anything about the word "beauty," for example, because no one ever really taught him the meaning of words. Everything he knows he knows from observation. Jesus!—who was going to teach words to a farm boy like him? "Get lost!" or "Take 'im, he's in the way!"—behold, his lesson. Ieva added the word "beauty" to his vocabulary later, but she spoke differently; she was his Gospel. She would even read aloud to him at the Zari house. Books. At night! Before going to bed—like for a kid.

But that's just how she was: she'd spend the day thinking and talking to herself, and at night she'd look for answers in books and even read aloud to him. And why not? It's tough when you live out in the country, surrounded by black woods. Where the darkness quickly thickens in the snowless winters, and you can hear the constant rush of the ocean from the north. You could go crazy. But they had their little room and their large bed, and the yellow-painted light bulb hanging bare above them. And Ieva reading out loud to Andrejs. He'd warn her ahead of time that he'd fall asleep. That kind of reading reminded him of his mother's lectures. Ieva was his Gospel, his mother—the Law. The only time his mother could hold him when he was little was at bedtime; the rest of the time she could neither control him, nor find him. Skis, a shotgun, a hunk of bacon, and his dog—that's all he needed.

True, when Ieva read Knut Hamsun to him, he didn't fall asleep so quickly. The woods, a dog, a girl. The dog shot dead in honor of the proud girl. Andrejs understood all of it, there was nothing to discuss.

There was also—who was it again—Trygve Gulbranssen, *Beyond Sing the Woods*. Another Norwegian writer. The woods, darkness, horses, and the proud Christina. And everything carried this sense of a larger, more respectable life. It was natural.

How beautiful, Ieva had said.

Beauty!

To her, the greatest beauty could be found in the thing Andrejs hated the most—some kind of statement or phrase. She'd read those phrases over and over again and almost tremble with joy.

Ridiculous.

Why spend so much time digging around words? Outside there was real life, the woods, a tractor, livestock, and most of all—a husband. Andrejs gave up so much for them to have a life together: his skis, his shotgun, and even the woods. Because they had to make ends meet, save money. But she just re-read sentences. What's the big deal, he'd often ask, it's a nice sentence, so move on! But it's not something real. It was better to steer clear of fantasies, awful things that they were.

Like that novel *The Idiot*, which Ieva found particularly beautiful. Jesus Christ! The definition of boredom.

When she opened that book, he'd fall asleep without the tiniest hint of regret. Dostoevsky could mess with your mind, and let him, but you were responsible for paying attention and drawing that line when the time came. Andrejs remembers what the book looked like: a Soviet era publication with a bluish-grey canvas cover, with a really stupid-looking cherry red picture at one corner of a man and woman with tiny waists caught up in dance. Ieva was pregnant then. He remembers what she looked like just as well as he remembers the book. The soft skin of her round stomach, the silky, soft triangle at its base and her breasts, hard and protruding like the horns of a stag, and with large, dark tips. None of that tiny waist crap. At that time all Ieva would eat was sprats with rye bread. The effects of the pregnancy were like that—she'd make him run into town for sprats if there weren't any in the fridge, even if it was the middle of the night. Downed them with rye bread like a madwoman. Lost a lot of weight. The doctors warned her, but nothing helped. She was stubborn.

They made love each night, and sometimes afterwards Ieva would read aloud.

It all happened in that one year—falling in love, a child, turning eighteen, a wedding, the collapse of the Soviet Union—boom! An entire lifetime over the course of twelve months. Ieva cried. The whole year. It's no surprise Monta grew up so sensitive. If anything she's neurotic, because Ieva spent the entire year crying. Pregnant women shouldn't act like that, he's convinced. Even if the empire collapses.

Monta was born while he was away. He'd driven out to the border to clear a forest in Nīkrace. He tore all the way back across Latvia to get back home to the Zari house once he heard the news. He wanted to bring his daughter home himself, in the tractor. Ieva wouldn't let him, said she wanted to get home by taxi. Again with some kind of fantasy she'd gotten from a book.

When Andrejs met Ieva on the front steps of the hospital holding the baby, it seemed like several years had gone by instead of several days. Ieva looked disheveled and bright-eyed—unfamiliar. She had probably expected a flower from him, but he didn't have one. She shouldn't expect something from him that he wasn't going to give.

He looked at his daughter—cute. He called for a taxi. So be it.

But he fell asleep in the cab. No surprise since he hadn't slept much the last few nights. A cast-iron stove had smoked away in the loggers' barracks, and all night there was nothing but charcoal and the howling of the village dogs. Now and then he'd light a cigarette and listen to the snoring of the other workers. The heavy night pressed the smoke down and constricted his chest. But maybe it had been from the excitement that he now had a daughter.

The taxi driver woke him when they were already back at the house:

"Wake up, Dad! You should've carried your newborn in yourself!"

The yard was empty. Ieva had already run inside with the baby to hide her tears.

He'd slept through it.

Ieva, of course, was silent for the next few days. His daughter obviously meant nothing to him if he could just fall asleep like that. Did he do it on purpose? Wasn't he happy? He was happy; he just couldn't show it on the outside like everyone else.

In his opinion, Ieva's sadness was a huge cover for how spoiled she was. Both of her parents had worked and her mother had migraines, so they couldn't keep both Ieva and her little brother. They had sent Ieva off to the countryside to live with her grandmother, but that's where all hell had broken loose. She hadn't had real life conditions there, the way he saw it. It was like living in a conservatory. Books. Laziness. The sea. Her Gran did everything for her. And the little princess just lay on the couch, reading—and from the age of four!

Andrejs hated know-it-alls. Smart people. Writers. Who needs them? Fine, everyone can come up with one great thought in their lifetime, a single, strong thought that's their own. You can't run on empty, so to speak. Something goes on up there, all the time.

Alright—two great thoughts in a lifetime, like Andrejs had.

Yes, he can count two great thoughts of his. The first is the one he'd love to remind Ieva of, in case she'd forgotten. That, despite everything that's happened, plus prison, he never turned into some pig.

They say your own people will get it. He won't explain anything more to anyone else. Those who don't get it can just drop it. Who needs explanations. He won't say anything more. It's such a massive thought and so completely applies to him that chills run through his body when he repeats it to himself and fully realizes it.

The second thought is about life. He'll tell Ieva about it someday. And she and all her smart people will pale at the idea. Because they're all liars. Shelves stuffed full with books. Fakes! Because a person can come up with one, two great thoughts in his lifetime, but then there are people who knock out a book a year. It's obvious to Andrejs that they just make money in the name of boredom. That's how that world works—the less sense you have, the more others will take advantage of you.

Three thoughts, what lies. Three is impossible.

He's told Ieva that. She drove him nuts with her talking, pissed him off. He had felt so unprotected, so forced into solitude and darkness, that he had screamed it right into her face—I hate know-it-alls!

She'd screamed back—but I crave knowledge!

A yeller. She'd been consistently raised like that, to be proper and positive. Undisciplined and lazy.

Oh, Ieva. His Ieva. What's wrong with him!

At times he's actually pretty scared. Things will just fall into place and this wave builds up inside him. Then he becomes afraid of himself. Something hidden deep within him shifts; something he's never known and will never know about. At moments like that, both life and death seem trivial, and an intense pain rips through his heart. No, not pure pain, but some kind of twisting, a rope of aching, longing, rage, hope, and dread; it runs so deep that it constricts his entire chest.

He can't breathe and he's afraid of himself. At moments like that he's happy his heart has destined him for loneliness. God forbid someone else has to have this wave crash over them as well. Only Andrejs can bear that weight. He holds this wave like Atlas holds the world on his shoulders.

The woman resting on his shoulder moves. His collarbone must be digging into her cheek.

Andrejs quickly reaches his free hand behind his back to grab a cushion, and tosses it in the corner of the couch. Then he puts his arms around the woman and draws her down with him. There's a tickle in his chest, and even though this movement lasts maybe a second, he feels like he's caught a giant fish and is sinking into the depths of the ocean.

The woman mumbles and doesn't want to lie down, and struggles a bit, the idiot, she probably thinks he's going to start groping her, but he doesn't intend to. Alright fine, maybe he thought about it a little, but he's only human, he can see she's tired from work, and also from preparing the roast, so let her just sleep. Her cheek presses against his shoulder, a string of drool hangs from the corner of her mouth onto his shirt like a silvery thread.

"Sleep!" he strokes her hair. And sniffs it. Strange. Her scent isn't really something that would make him want her right now. He sensed that from the start. But he can't exactly push her away, either. Like there's a secret flowing through her. That's a good thing. He likes a woman with a secret.

She makes a noise like a content cat when he strokes her hair, then drifts off again. Makes sense—it's nice with the two of them together. Close, cozy.

And it's nice here in the warmth, nice for Andrejs to think about Ieva without interruption. These thoughts always drag him away from wherever he is, carry him through the air and to a strange and enormous house, where it takes a long time to inspect and check all the cellars, intersecting hallways, antechambers, rooms, mansards, stairwells, pantries, attics, guest rooms and hidden passageways, and then clean and catalog them until next time. Tonight he's just getting started. Until he's made it through it all. Let this Demeter sleep. There's nothing left to miss out on. That's how time works.

Ieva's visits were beautiful in their slow pace. There was no rush. "We'll be back tomorrow at ten!" the guards would remind them as they left. And then time would suddenly start back up for Andrejs, whose life orbited a bewitched circle, where the same actions took place every morning, every night, and every year, forever winding up back at the beginning; a life where the mirrors are frozen and always reflect the same image. He had been shunned from time both physically—in prison—and spiritually—within himself.

But then one morning Ieva would show up and time would start again.

Even the guards noticed it because they said they'd be back in the morning to separate them. Andrejs suddenly became worthy of keeping track of time—this body the court had sentenced to age hidden from sight. Something overflowed and pushed out, the floodgates burst open—a powerful torrent rushed forward from 10 AM through 10 AM the next day, and it took his breath away to see how elastic and shifting time was, how material and flowing it was.

On those days he hated the clock. On those days the clock once more had meaning, and it mocked him as much as it could, like someone born to be a prison guard—someone with tormenting in their blood, someone who makes sure you'll never forget them.

He and Ieva would sit and exchange unhurried words, they could see the prison wall from the window and watch inmates wander around the yard like livestock, like a dazed flock in bluish parkas or white shirts, depending on what season it was. Sunspots moved across the floor. They talked about neighbors, Ieva's job, his friends and prison life, their parents, money, and Monta. Andrejs would look at photographs of his daughter, if Ieva had been able to conceal them well enough in her clothes, and say he'd put them in a plastic binder. He had an entire collection of photographs like these hidden under the false bottom of his nightstand.

Andrejs would study how time had changed his daughter's face. When she was born she had looked exactly like him, like she'd been shaped in a mold, a tiny copy of him, an imprint in dark metal. Then her face started to change, jump from his features to Ieva's expressions and back again. Of course, a lot depended on the angle of the photo and the lighting, but in the end Monta became Monta. It was impossible not to notice it.

He'd timidly beg Ieva to bring Monta with her. And Ieva would firmly answer that her daughter would never set foot in a prison or ever breathe this prison air.

"And if I die?" he asked.

Ieva shrugged.

And that's how she was, a straight-up bitch. It was because of her Andrejs was in prison, because of her and that ass Aksels, but see, she made herself to be this noble, white dove who visited him like a dream once a season. But she was absent at the same time. Naiveté—or rather, what was it called again?—immaturity. Exactly.

An immature infant. And a bitch. She comes to prison, but doesn't breathe the air. That idiocy comes from books, of course. I am what I am, and where I am is where I am. But see—it's easier to deny reality, to linger in the dream, to pretend, to observe.

Stupid.

Independence and betrayal. The entire breed of book readers are traitors. Because they use words however they see fit, and they're as sly as foxes. They'll forever twist the world into something they like better. Everyone else sees black, but they say it's just the opposite of white. Obviously you can say it like that, too, but it will always be connected to a selfish purpose so tangled it's sickening.

That was when the fight started. The time when he gave her his shirt as she left because it was pouring outside. May showers—loud and spattering, or in a gleeful disarray.

And she never came again. Just sent back the shirt with a note—*Everything's over for real now. Ieva.*

There wasn't actually a fight. He'd just told her what he was thinking. And suddenly it was over. So their time together had been based on nothing but lies—on lies and silence. But that had been clear for some time.

That time she had showed up kind of disoriented. Like she was in the room, but not.

And then suddenly—she asked if she could talk to him about Aksels.

The trump card. He even swayed a little, he hadn't been expecting it. They never mentioned things like that. Because, first and foremost, they both had their own version of what had happened.

And second, the walls had ears. All the walls in the Soviet Union had ears; they couldn't be so naïve to think that a prison that had never been reconstructed would be clean of wire taps.

But she asks—can they talk about Aksels?

And then she just went off with almost no segue—she reminded him of a person up to their knees in seawater and with the tide coming in fast. He could tell right away that she had been holding it back. She'd probably spent those four hours in the train talking to herself.

About how, see, he shouldn't have shot Aksels. That it had been a kind of neurosis, and now how were they supposed to fix it? That she hadn't done right by Aksels, but instead turned him into some kind of animal.

Jesus Christ! Andrejs had just looked at her and smiled. If she had been anyone else but his Ieva, he would have yelled back at the top of his lungs. Obviously it had all been a load of bullshit. That scrawny, sickly drug addict, and that whole history and theory they had been drifting on for years like on melting ice. Eternal love. I want to die in your arms. My life and death are yours, and your life and death are mine.

"Ieva," Andrejs had asked, "tell me the truth—don't you know that you were both completely insane?"

"And what about you?" she asked.

"I happened to be there. If I had a second chance, I'd do it again."

First of all, so you wouldn't. Second, because I hated him. He got on my nerves.

Ieva had jumped to her feet, her face pale, spots at her temples.

"You just don't get it! So if we really were insane, then you're sitting in prison because of two complete jackasses? Think about that! You're wasting your life because of two idiots?"

That was uncalled for, he thought. Then he answered—"Yes!" And what else could he say, when she had him cornered like a rat?

Yes!

Like Croesus, squandering lives.

Total bullshit.

He has to think about it every day.

They both went to the kitchen. Fried some eggs and bacon, carried the pan to the room and ate. Then they went to the second floor TV room, sat next to each other in the soft, red chairs behind the potted palm. At night they made love, and it was good for her. Insanely good for her—Andrejs felt it. Maybe she was seeing someone out there, on the outside, but he didn't care. For him the sex always seemed secondary. It was like being lazy. The important part was for her to be next to him, for her to feel good, and then he was also able to sink into that whirlpool. That was the last thing. And he'd wash away his anxiety, stress, the sediments of time, wash it all away. Lightning struck and traveled down through the lightning rod, down to Ieva's world. Then it was a new morning, sparkling and clean. A new page could be turned. A pure, white page, still clean of any marks. That's what the sex was like for Andrejs, but for her? Who knows.

She didn't say anything.

That night, toward morning, the light of an unusually bright full moon flooded the room. He tried hard to convince himself that he was asleep, but in reality was laying wide awake with a deathly weight on his chest, hugging the precious body next to him—and then she woke suddenly with a scream.

He wasn't able to calm her down, even though he was able to pull her into his lap, stroke her hair and her ribcage and knobby knees. She sat there, curled into a ball, and whispered that she'd sensed an evil in the room!

The devil had been in the room. Andrejs rubbed her back and tried to calm her, said the devil didn't exist, it was something people had made up, but she cried and told him her dream: she and Aksels had been standing high up on a hill, everything was green and happy, and there was a rainbow behind them. But when they had taken each other by the hand, gashes appeared on their palms and blood streamed onto the ground.

Jesus, at that moment Andrejs would have been ready to shoot Aksels ten times over, riddle his dead body with more and more holes, so he would go to hell once and for all. That little shit, that son of a bitch! He was in Ieva's dreams, even though he was long dead. He stomped around Ieva's dreams!

Andrejs wasn't able to fight him, no one can fight in dreams, because you don't break into dreams, you're invited in. Andrejs could only hate him—hate him more than he had ever hated anyone else in the world.

And he said this to Ieva—said that at this exact moment she was with a murderer.

Told her not to call it what it wasn't.

And that she was a bitch if she let Aksels wander freely in her dreams, while she was sleeping with Andrejs. And that this institution, in case she didn't know, was built for people just like Andrejs, because out of a hundred people who feel hatred, only one will actually pick up the shotgun, and that person is him, and he doesn't regret any of it.

Ieva had looked at him with such fear, the bluish whites of her eyes glazed over in the moonlight. He could tell by her breathing that what he had said was slowly sinking in.

"You shot him only because you'd learned how to kill in Afghanistan?"

But of course! The shotgun had been right there, loaded, and what's more—Ieva had handed the gun to him herself. But of course, love! When would he have had another opportunity to get rid of the little bastard who'd ruined his entire life?

But he didn't say *that*—because *that* thought was as wispy as a rose-colored, papery autumn sky—that he had possibly caught himself in his own lies. Now he was saying one thing, but at other times, like when he was sitting in the dust of the prison yard, watching the wind tug at the leaves of the elm trees, and Ieva was so far away at the other end of the world past the barbed wire fences and one hundred twenty-four kilometers of forest, rivers and bogs, or when they made love, he was able to break free of himself, from the biting harness, he felt her contented breathing, and at those moments Andrejs could do the unthinkable—let all the happiness of the world flow into Ieva, because she herself was valuable, because she was worth it. And if she loved that son of a bitch Aksels, then at those moments—even though it was unthinkable—he was able to let himself imagine that she was even allowed to love Aksels. Even Aksels! And at those moments some kind of serpent, vibrant as a Latgalian wool mitten, would hiss into Andrejs's ear that this was the kind of true love written about in the Bible. A love that didn't hate, wasn't jealous, didn't destroy, wasn't submissive, just carried you toward the sun—carried, carried, carried you, forever carried you.

But that wasn't something Ieva needed to know.

He only added that he was the only one who could call her a bitch and, forgive him, but if he hears someone else call her a bitch, he'll slit their throat.

"You've made me your personal swamp," she said calmly after a pause.

Maybe it was then that she had already made up her mind.

Then they probably both finally fell asleep.

In the morning it was overcast, and the air was full of the bewitching scent of spring buds, but Ieva was unnaturally pale and silent. Even that usually beautiful final hour they had, during which they normally dressed, cleaned up, and wallowed in thoughts of parting, memories and glances—now it was hard as stone. And the guards had forgotten about them.

Once they'd dressed they sat stiffly on the beds facing each other, looking like they had met for the first time in their lives. The time came for them to go their separate ways, but the guards didn't come. The black tentacle of the clock slowly slid to four minutes past ten, then to ten minutes past ten.

The room grew darker and darker, until finally the black-blue cloud outside broke open with a mighty crack, struck the earth with a blinding thorn, and unleashed a grey downpour. Rain beat against the windows with such force that it rattled the windowsill like a tin drum. Andrejs sprang to his feet and started pacing back and forth across the room, then suddenly took off his jacket and unbuttoned his shirt. It was a violet-colored shirt with dark stripes, possibly the nicest piece of clothing he had ever owned. And he put it around Ieva's shoulders.

"Take my shirt," he said, "you'll get soaked."

"That'd be just perfect—to forget about us in prison," she said, letting out a fake laugh and glancing at the clock.

Five more minutes passed. Andrejs thought he was losing his mind.

"Just think, my shirt'll be free in a few minutes," he said, just to say something. Just to fill the eerie silence.

The sound of the rain droned on forever, then was suddenly extinguished like a candle that had been knocked over—the guards came in and Ieva and Andrejs both jumped up.

Andrejs obediently put his hands behind his back; there was the click of the cuffs, the jangle of keys, Andrejs at the door, her profile outlined by the flash of lightning, and then she was by him, close, close, a kiss, more like a bite in its desperation, warmth, her scent, the guard prying her fingers from Andrejs's shoulders: "Your time's up, ma'am!" Andrejs goes, turns a few corners down the hall, he knows which doors have glass windows, Ieva waves, hurries behind them, the fluttering of shirtsleeves and the hem of her white dress, she waves, her face, then another corner, then emptiness, the zone, and the storm.

The prison yard and silence, then it's over.

Your time's up.

And yes, after that at the next visitation time he waited for her in vain. All he got was her note: "Everything's over for real now. Ieva." And the shirt.

The hastily folded material still held her smell and the softness of her breasts. She had been here! She left a duffel bag with the shirt and the note. Stood in line some fifty meters away, shit, nothing between them but walls and guards—but he'd sensed nothing! His senses were deadened, she'd been here, but he hadn't grown anxious, hadn't moved, hadn't felt anything—like an old camel, like a rundown Arabian horse whose nose can no longer sniff out water.

He hadn't even dreamt of her.

Oh misery, godforsaken!

He hadn't been prepared for the worst—for Ieva to leave him half-way, alone in prison. In the end it was betrayal; they were both up to their necks in the same shit. And then this!

She knew him too goddamn well, that was a fact. He'd carry his sentence until the end. But how could love so quickly turn into searing hate?

"Everything's over for real now. Ieva."

And the shirt.

But in living with Ieva, you had to be prepared for something like that. Naturally.

He wasn't ready. He'd spent four years of his remaining sentence planning revenge.

Prison had become his home. And what's to keep him from coming back home if he's got a good reason? He had decided to erase Ieva from the face of the earth.

And then there was that unforgettable fall day—icy moisture dusted the skies, mud splashed up over his shoes and the frost bit through to the bone—the day Andrejs had wound up at the furnace.

Bound stacks of paper were brought to feed the zone's boiler-room furnace. Leftover magazine issues, failed books, educational materials. And on that day, a blue, cloth-bound book of Ancient Greek myths for high school courses was lying among the frozen clumps of sawdust. Almost without reason, but mainly driven by curiosity and laziness, Andrejs smoked a cigarette and read a page in the book, then found himself unable to put it down.

There! He dug his unshaved chin into the collar of his down jacket. If only Ieva would come see him again, he'd read this book to her—there was no clearer way to say it. What Andrejs's people referred to as love was complete bullshit. Talking nonsense by candlelight.

The Ancient Greeks knew that the gods were immortal, and told immortal tales. Once he's placed in time, a mortal isn't able to think of an immortal tale, much less tell one. A person's existence winds around birth and death like a ribbon around two magic wands. He was curious to see how they'd solve the issue of immortality—if a story has a beginning, but no middle or end, what kind of skeleton is the meat of the story holding on to? If a god isn't moved by his own death to act, then what does that god think about? It turns out—the gods think of nothing but power. The principle of power classifies existence under immortality.

Andrejs took the book. He tucked it under his shirt instead of throwing it into the furnace. And at night, he read about Odysseus by flashlight:

"After many days traveling they came to a place where thick osier bushes and tall poplars hid the entrance to the underworld; the travelers pulled the ship ashore and stayed to guard it. Odysseus went on alone. When he came to the entrance of Hades, he proceeded as Circe had instructed him: he first poured the libations of milk, honey, wine and water, then, to draw out the ghost of Teiresias, killed a black ram and spilled its blood into the pit he had dug in front of the entrance. A swarm of ghosts appeared at the pit to drink of the warm blood, but Odysseus kept them at bay, so that he may first hear the ghost of the graying Theban augural Teiresias, which was slowly approaching the pit."

Andrejs thought of Aksels. If Andrejs had a blood-filled pit at the entrance to the underworld like that, then Aksels would definitely be lurking by with a ravenous stare.

"Then Odysseus' mother neared the pit; she had died of grief in her son's absence."

Andrejs thought of his own mother. When Ieva stopped coming to see him, his mother slowly took her place. But that was completely different. His mother brought him a bag filled with bacon, eggs, onions, black tea, and cigarettes, made him dinner and then fell asleep exhausted from the work. In the evening she'd wrap up her hair, kiss her son once on both cheeks, and cry when they parted the next day.

Her visits to her son in prison were like visiting a ready-made recreation center.

She'd quickly tell him a few important pieces of news—what was new, who had died—and then was quiet.

"Then Odysseus' mother neared the pit; she had died of grief in her son's absence."

Andrejs thought of his mother's large, overworked hand as it hung over the side of the bed, where she slept like a log facedown on the pillow.

"Then Odysseus' mother neared the pit; she had died of grief in her son's absence. She told Odysseus that his home in Ithaca was still amass with relentless suitors for Penelope, who faithfully awaited the return of her husband, but that his son, Telemachus, was too young and weak to drive the suitors away. Old Laërtes, who grieved the fate of his son Odysseus, had left the city and was living in the countryside among slaves."

Andrejs thought of his father. His father didn't care about Andrejs's fate. Maybe a quiet ache smoldered somewhere deep down in him. The rest had been eaten away by a lifetime of hard work. He knew how to take good care of his tractor—but never of himself. His father hadn't let himself want anything for a long time. Not his son, not his future, not even his past.

His father's two great thoughts:

—you have to live the life you've been given;

—a person lives and works, and then one day he's clocked from behind with a shovel and pushed into a grave.

"Old Laërtes, who grieved the fate of his son Odysseus, had left the city and was living in the countryside among slaves. In winter he sleeps on the ground by a hearth, and in warmer months sleeps in an orchard on a bed of soft leaves."

And yet. Andrejs's mother had said his father had been getting soft in the head with age. He was supposedly dried up and fragile as a bird, and cried a lot. He's on his way out, that's why he's grown as brittle as shortbread, laughing through his tears.

He doesn't want to experience that, wouldn't be able to watch it. This abusive, hard, and spiteful man who didn't have a heart—a crier?

Anything but that.

Once, his mother came with a secret. Unlike the other times, she was kept awake by an unusual restlessness. She sat on the bed, chewed the hard candies she'd brought for him, swung her leg back and forth, and watched him as he smoked by the window. Outside it was a hot summer afternoon.

Andrejs looked back at her and finally asked her straight out: "What?"

His mother blushed, wiped a handkerchief across her forehead, then spoke rapidly:

"Ieva came to visit."

Andrejs sat backwards on a chair and drilled his stare into his mother's lowered eyes. She glanced up at her son and grew frightened, understanding that she had to quickly finish saying what she'd started:

"She's a big deal now, been to all kinds of schools, has a car. She went up to Dad, and he flung his arms around her neck and cried, told her she would always be welcome in our home. But I . . . I couldn't just stand there . . . Eh, and how could I, I had to say it, told her she'd damned and betrayed my son, left him to rot, and for her to keep far, far away from my house, or I wouldn't be held responsible for my actions!"

His mother grew red in the face as she spoke, and gestured wildly as if trying to push the image of Ieva away from her:

"But about your girl, I told her she could hide her wherever she wanted—when Andrejs gets out of prison he'll see his daughter, no doubt about it!"

Andrejs turned back to the window. Mom, you're lying, I know you too well—he could have said it. You know you love Ieva, he could have told her. But he said nothing. Outside a cat walked along the carefully raked strip of sand.

Having unloaded the weight on her heart, his mother fell asleep quickly.

Outside it was a hot summer afternoon.

He had found his religion in the Ancient Greek myths. He read about Scylla and Charybdis, about the Cyclops Polyphemus and the nymph Calypso, about the suffering of Prometheus, and the courts of Hades. Andrejs, who spent his days and nights with murderers and thieves: he read and understood.

A son who, instructed by his mother, took a sickle and castrated his own father, whose blood mixed with sea foam to give birth to the goddess of love. A father who, terrified of the power of his own sons, swallowed them whole. The Graces, muses, and Moirae—almost every prisoner had his own; distance, isolation, and desire raised them above the gods. Zeus was Andrejs's favorite. Thirsting for knowledge and afraid of losing power, this guy had swallowed his first wife, which was what his mother had wanted. "Zeus swallowed wise Metis, in doing so both eliminating an heir and gaining Metis's wisdom."

He understood that kind of love, not the whining adoration coming at you constantly as songs on TV and the radio. He'd like to swallow both Ieva and Monta, they'd be in his stomach—Ieva's wisdom and their daughter's beauty, everything together in one place, home. He didn't know how to love, only wildly desire, and it was among the Ancient Greek heroes that he found where he belonged. Here, in prison, there was no shortage of jealous women just like Hera, who murdered her rival's children and took sleep away from her so she would have to wander the world like a ghost; until Zeus took pity on her and gave her the power to remove her eyes so she could finally rest. There were those like Danaus, who made his daughters kill their husbands. Or those like Tantalus who, in an act of unbelievable arrogance, sacrificed his son and offered his flesh to the gods. And those like Demeter who, distraught by a great loss, blindly ate everything the goddess of fate put before them, even the flesh of others, and not to mention such delicacies as sorrow, desperation, and alcoholism. Here you could find Ares with all his evil forces, whose sons were Terror and Fear, and who found joy in bloodshed.

Andrejs liked the retelling of these stories because they were about a time before anyone had been crucified for the sins of others, and before anyone had been saved.

Prison was the place where priests fished for souls day in and day out like pearl divers—forever looking to take confession. This frightful, shaved, robust, dark-eyed mob, *a priori* guilty, was the perfect material onto which they could cross-stitch those pearls.

He went to mass and listened, but never for a moment felt in his heart the main thing the priests asked them to feel—the desire to fall at the feet of Christ and call him their Lord and Shepherd, to transfer the responsibility for what they'd done onto their Lord and Shepherd and to beg for forgiveness. Andrejs could fall at the feet of Christ like he'd fallen to the floor next to the dead body of a stranger in a darkened cell. There was no question that Christ had definitely been a regular guy. He could wash Christ's feet and trim his toenails, like he'd done on more than one occasion for an aging cellmate who had been exhausted to the point of lethargy. But he was unable to feel the most important thing—the desire to shift his guilt onto the shoulders of some Lord. Andrej's guilt was his business, it was a part of him. Here he stood with his entire life and was completely aware of it. Though it was hazy, he could sense his freedom and responsibility within it.

King Oedipus, having unwittingly killed his father and married his mother, was unable to afford a single indulgence. The curses came true, but there were never any indulgences. No one had ever been crucified for Oedipus. He had to accept blindness as his fate all on his own. He had to accept himself for what he was and stab out his eyes, and wander the road with his walking stick, mourning his fate and that of his children.

In turn the Ancient Greeks were stingy with lessons. There were only two in the entire book—a lot like those real thoughts a person could think of in a lifetime. Both lessons were briefly laid out in a section about Medea and Jason in Corinth.

"But the happiness, honor, and praise they had hoped for never came to their Greece. Her own words came true: 'Bloodshed begets bloodshed.'"

Medea had murdered her brother for Jason.

The goddess of love, Aphrodite, who gave so much joy and happiness to people, was also often merciless. "Passion that is more powerful than conscience brings the worst kind of evil to mortals."

Medea had murdered children for Jason.

Andrejs remembers the moment he read those words, down to the smallest detail. His four cellmates snored away in their dark cell, which was hot from the stove and thick with bodily odors. He was lying on a bottom bunk facing the window; outside, a November storm carried a large, white lamp back and forth, so it looked like someone had hung a full moon up by a string and was waving it over the prison wall. The corners of the cell rustled with cockroaches and a draft, and Andrejs's blanket glowed from the flashlight he held under it. Having finished reading about Medea, he turned a stony gaze upward to the metal bedsprings above him.

The woman was lying there with her eyes open.

Andrejs's arm had fallen asleep. But to the point where he couldn't take it anymore. He woke up—or rather, snapped back from his trance-like state of thinking—and tried to pull his arm out from under the woman's back, and when he glanced at her he saw that she was lying with her eyes open. When had she woken up?

Afraid that she'd say something and interrupt the story, he instructed:

"Sleep some more!"

The woman obediently closed her eyes.

That night with Medea he'd been healed, because he'd finally seen himself from the sidelines. A tall, immobile, idiotic sack under a thin prison blanket.

That night they let him go. Enlisted him in the reserves. He knew that he would never kill anybody again. Not even Ieva.

Something had ended, the passion suddenly broken. Turns out his fate had been hanging at the end of such a fine strand of hair. Now it had matured, fallen out and slipped away. The shedding of an unnecessary skin.

How strange—when love was flowing through him he didn't need anything, not even his only shirt. He had done terrible things, but they could all be justified. His, Andrejs's, love.

Now that it had burnt out, he could start anything, though nothing would give him his fill. And he couldn't imagine what more he could need that would fill the massive space surrounding him.

Andrejs didn't even try to understand what happened in his brain when he read the story about Medea. Maybe the two things just fell into place—Medea and the release of his own passions—and both of them had nothing else in common but the horrible events over the course of a single night.

Maybe Aphrodite had never meant to be there in the first place? On that night, had the goddess of love ripped the deeply-lodged, festering arrow from Andrejs's heart, and then disappeared without a trace? Without the core of the arrow his body crumpled like an empty shell.

He remained half way without Ieva, without reason, without a future. He knew that from there on out things would be calm and he would soon be released. He was a broken clock, a defective mechanism—why fight it? They don't keep people like that in prison.

In truth, he should have stabbed out his eyes that very night.

"Want some champagne?"

The question spoken into the homey darkness scared the hell out of Andrejs because the woman shot it out as suddenly as a flare gun.

She had been lying there with her eyes open again.

He asked:

"Now?"

"Why not?"

They pulled themselves to their feet, turned on the kitchen light and rubbed their bleary eyes. He watched the movements of her plump elbows. The kitchen was small, and the woman filled the space right away. Andrejs liked this—just watching. He was ready to go sit in one of the corners when the woman said:

"Hand me those glasses!"

"Where?"

"On the shelf by your head."

He turned toward the wall and came face to face with his own drawing. He stared at it for a long time, as if seeing a ghost, and then asked the woman:

"What's that?"

"Glasses."

"I see the glasses. But behind them?"

"That? Oh, that. A card."

Andrejs very carefully took two fragile champagne flutes in his calloused hands and handed them to the woman. Then he took the card leaning against the wall behind the glasses and sat on a stool next to the small table. He studied the yellowed paper as intensely as a war refugee who's been pulled from the water and given a passport, and who can't believe this thing could save his life.

The card was drawn with lead pencil on regular notebook paper and then glued to cardboard. Its edges were decorated with barbed wire, which connected at the top in a knot around a red rose. The lettering *For Ludmila—Ruslans* was separated by a date, in which the number two looked like a swan with a proudly curving neck. The drawing also had the North Star and the aurora borealis. Small lettering at the bottom read: *She dreamt that in the Caucasus steppe . . .*

So she wasn't an accountant! So that's where he'd seen that handwriting and date before! How could he forget?

Andrejs asked:

"Ludmila?"

"Yes."

She sat on the opposite stool at the table and twirled a strand of hair around her finger. Like she was flustered, clueless. When she lifted her eyes to meet his, they were bright with tears.

"That's the last card my husband sent me."

She wanted to tell him more, but he silenced her with an impatient gesture. He still couldn't decide if he should go home right away, or later. If he started to talk now, it would mean he wouldn't go home until later.

But he started to talk. He hadn't become a heartless monster yet. "You don't need to tell me. I drew this."

The expressions on the woman's face changed as quick as the wind, chasing after one another like the shadows of falling leaves— while she sat very stiff and straight, her eyes searching his face to figure out what his words could mean.

"Ruslans and I met at the Central Prison Hospital. He was already admitted when I was brought in. We were together for a week, or less, I don't remember. In any case no more than a week. I was there when he died."

The woman let out a weak scream, and the tears finally overflowed. She wiped the wetness across her cheeks with the back of her hand. Andrejs handed her a towel, which she immediately bundled up into a kind of squirrel's nest and hid her face in it. He waited patiently for her to look up again.

"You could say I was the prison artist. I framed photographs by sewing plastic wires around the edges, drew on materials using safety pins and colored thread, etched wood, sketched. Ruslans found out and showed me your handwriting. Asked me to draw a card and write the words like you did. He really liked your handwriting. I recognized it right away, but thought that you worked at the prison as an accountant."

The woman nodded feebly. She rummaged in a drawer without looking away from him and placed a candle on the table. She burned her fingers with the first match.

"Tell me how he died," she said, her voice somber.

"He died at night. I was writing a letter to my wife, he was lying down. I thought he'd fallen sleep. Then he suddenly started coughing, ran to the door and banged on it like crazy. All at once, about a bucket of blood spewed from his mouth. And then he fell over. I lifted him a bit and held him, but he had already started with the death shakes. The guards came and took him away."

There was a moment of silence.

"Don't worry, it happened quickly. He didn't suffer. It was over the second he ran to the door. Later the nurses said one of his pulmonary veins had burst."

More silence.

"But he managed to send the card out. When's your birthday? Sometime in May, right?"

"May second."

"And what's this about the Caucasus, if it's not a secret?"

"He was a really good person," she finally said.

"I know. So what about the Caucasus?"

The woman thought for a bit.

> "She dreamt that in the Caucasus steppe—
> He lay still, a bullet in his breast . . .
> And yet, I am Ruslan's now,
> And will be faithful to my vow."

Andrejs propped the card against the windowpane so its edges were surrounded by the reflection of the candlelight.

The woman said:

"We liked poetry, like Pushkin's 'Ruslan and Ludmila.' I'd read it to him when our kids were still little. Before he got mixed up in that damn gang and robbed that gas station . . . He was so surprised that there was a poem like that—about us, he said—just imagine! About us!"

The woman stood and opened the refrigerator. She pushed the champagne toward Andrejs, having suddenly grown very calm. He opened the bottle just as calmly and poured the chilled liquid into the glasses. In the reflection of the flame, the bubbles dancing in the sparkling wine seemed like lonely planets.

Andrejs lifted his glass:
"Well then—to us! To all of us."
The woman nodded, and they both drank. Bliss—ice-cold bliss.
The woman spoke:
"And yours got better?"
"What?"
"Tuberculosis?"
Andrejs rubbed his cheek. The champagne made him feel very alive.
"There was actually nothing wrong with me. Time was running out. The last thing people had on their minds back then was prisons. There was famine in the prisons, actual famine, unemployment, and insanity. In order to survive I ground sugar into powder and inhaled it. A lot of people did it. And man, the lung spots it would produce on the X-rays! Say what you want, but the food in the hospital was much better. But after a while I started to think I really was sick. Every night the taste of blood in my mouth, at first in my dreams and later for real. You spit and see blood. Every night. Nothing during the day. During the day—powdered sugar."

They'd emptied their glasses. The woman reached across and poured another.

"But the night Ruslans died . . . It was like—what's so terrifying about it, people die! I was in for murder. That's how it went."

He said it before he realized what he was saying, and looked at the woman. She looked straight back at him. There was no fear in her eyes, no surprise, no questions, just an unwavering stare.

"But that night he died, it happened so fast. Didn't even take five minutes. He was alive, and then all of a sudden I was holding him in my arms and everything was covered in his blood. The guards came and took him away. And then it was quiet again. I went back to my bed and found the half-written letter to my wife. I couldn't finish it, the pen moved around the paper on its own, my thoughts had left me. Just five minutes—and it was like the letter was finished by someone else. Understand?"

He downed the champagne and gritted his teeth. Words, words. The devil had once again urged him to wear his heart on his sleeve. There was no point. He should have left when he had the chance.

"Another drink, artist!"

The woman poured the rest of the champagne. A good woman. A woman was supposed to be like that—warm as a bread oven. He wanted to tell her everything, but it wasn't possible. There are certain thoughts you should keep to yourself.

"If I can, I'll recite a poem for you."

This kind of courage made him break into a sweat. Ieva had always encouraged him to write poetry, but he'd never been good at it. Ieva, on the other hand, was—you could even say that she put everything that happened down on paper. Like photography, but what you could do with photography was still entirely different from what-ever prompted words. Write what you felt the moment you opened your eyes this morning, she'd urge him. He sat down with a piece of paper and sighed and complained until he was done. He thought it needed to turn out good if he gave into Ieva's pushing. But it wasn't good, he knew so. Ieva thought so, too; she was quiet for some time after she'd read it. "I woke up early, the alarm clock rattled like a chainsaw . . ." It went something like that, and it wasn't like it didn't make sense. What Andrejs saw was nothing like the morning or an alarm clock on the paper, but rather his own useless, Sisyphean battle with language, with words. And this nerve-wracking battle left that particular morning in its wake, that morning—one of many, but so unrepeatable. He hadn't known how. But now?

"—black woods surround you, wipe your forehead
black swamps surround you, stay here and live
the teeth of the white dog cannot reach to bite you
black fields hold their hissing hands out to you
take shelter behind the pine forest, gather dropwort
black swamps surround you, wipe your forehead
your retreat to the ninth breath was not in vain
keep your sorrow behind you, your joy in your arms
there will be a sharp fog when you open your eyes
the teeth of the white dog cannot reach to bite you
the breath and the palm, they will guide you
black woods surround you, don't cry, but sing . . ."

He had been left alone in the dark expanse and tore the lines from deep within his chest like flaming bullets, like his life depended on it. They died and were born from the death of the last, joined like the links in a chain of logic that only he understood, and they held fast. In it wavered his childhood, moments from the murder, serving his guilt and time, glimmers of Ieva and Monta, of his mother and father, and the black woods—places that, when he saw them, always caused a sharp ache in his heart because you could also love a place to the point where seeing it made your chest feel it was on fire.

Then the poem was over and he snapped out of it, thrown back into the shallows, into a strange kitchen where he'd said too much and, even worse, bared his soul through words.

Because of that third glass! Hadn't life taught him all good things come in twos? Two cigarettes. Two glasses. Have a third and the rest of the numbers are redundant.

Andrejs rushed out of the kitchen and started pulling on his coat in the dark hallway. The woman followed quietly behind him like a cat and turned on a tiny, yellow wall lamp. She stroked his shoulders, neck, unshaved cheek, everywhere she could touch his skin.

She whispered:

"Such a beautiful poem. Did you come up with it in prison?"

"No, just now. And what about you?"

"Me—what?"

"He's dead, but you've moved on?"

"Yes, slowly. What else can you do?"

"Prisoners. We're prisoners in this life. Us. Everyone."

He yanked on the door.

"Unlock it!"

The woman obediently found the key in a basket and put it in the lock. When Andrejs was already on the threshold, she suddenly and quietly asked:

"What about the roast?"

Andrejs hugged her to him. Strange lips like an undiscovered steppe.

Screw the steppes, Ludmila, let's forget the steppes and our words, you were Ruslans's Ludmila, but you'll be my Demeter, the fertile earth herself! Someone discovered us long ago, gave us words hundreds and thousands of years ago. How I ache, how I search for this Giver of Words, I want to shake his hand and thank him for his creation—I sense that we won't be the ones to give words, that time will grind us down and scatter our dust thrice over a broken field, the goddess Demeter and me, your mortal beloved—but I'd still like to look into the face of the Giver of Words, he is all-knowing! Look into the eyes of the Giver of Words, and finally find peace.

And then came the abyss, she embraced him, absorbed him, took him in and swallowed him like Calypso swallowed Odysseus, while he inwardly longed for the coldness of night, the bridge over the river and his moment of existence, his long-standing sentence of loneliness.

Too tired to object, he quietly prayed to the Lord, and the Lord came over him and he finally grew calm, having sunk his thorn into His hot center.

When he woke up the next morning, he was alone in the room. The smell of the roast and the woman's singing floated from the kitchen.

It was a harsh morning, misty and cold. They ate. The food was delicious, rich, like her.

He asked:

"Don't you have to go to work?"

"But today's Saturday," she answered.

As if he didn't know.

"These days some people have to work Saturdays, too."

"Oh, that. I work in accounting at the prison."

Andrejs was speechless:

"So you do!"

"When he died in the hospital in Riga, the kids and I left the city. Took a train on a whim, the farther away the better. Got off at the last station, rented an apartment, asked around for work. Turns out this town has a prison and the prison was looking for an accountant. Might as well, I thought! If it's a prison, it's a prison. No reason trying to run from your destiny. Nothing wrong with work, either. It's a good job, stable."

"Yeah it is," Andrejs laughed.

"A person's got to eat. We're prisoners in this life, you said it yourself last night."

They watched some TV. There was a commercial for some movie playing at Cinema Riga.

"Would be good to see a movie," she suddenly said.

"Go to Riga?"

"Why not? I haven't been to the movies in ages! Or to Riga."

He was horrified by the idea, but she was already getting dressed and humming. So be it, he thought, feeling very unexpectedly generous.

The woman had dressed up nicely for the event—she'd done her hair and put on makeup, put on a light dress under a short jacket, silk stockings and heels. Like a girl, he thought. It didn't suit her. But what can you do if a trip like this to Riga happened only once in a while?

The train was full, but they were able to find seats facing each other by a window. Andrejs was embarrassed to look at the woman, her legs seemed too naked for the winter weather, so pornographically, screamingly lewd. This nakedness radiated toward Andrejs and completely unsettled him because something in it was meant only for him, aggressive like a good poem. Oh, Demeter, he thought, staring stubbornly at the reflection of his own dark face in the window, not looking at her once, even though she now and then touched his leg with her shiny, stocking-clad ankle. He even ignored her questions until she grew annoyed and glared straight ahead, the smile gone from her face as she was rocked by the rhythm of the train. Then he could safely scowl at her hair in the reflection in the window.

There was no snow, and after three and a half hours they stepped out onto the black asphalt of the Riga Passenger Station platform. The wind was biting, and the train's passengers burrowed deeper into their coats and quickly disappeared into the belly of the station.

"The movie theater's back this way," Andrejs said. "Let's go along the tracks, and then we'll head down into the city."

"Why that way?" the woman was surprised.

"No point in wasting money for the tram."

The woman hesitated. He still couldn't bring himself to look at her, just leered at her sidelong like a wolf. She was close to tears, trying to keep her jacket closed with one hand and beginning to think something wasn't quite right.

"Let's go! It's not far."

They started to walk along the side of the tracks. Andrejs in front, hands jammed into his pockets and shoulders hunched forward. The woman behind him, with her exposed, white legs and heels, jumping over the ties and rusted iron of the switches. The wind blew open the slit in her dress and her legs were covered in goose bumps. Her nervous footing caught in the gaps between the ties.

The woman finally spoke up:

"So this is taking a trip to Riga, to the movies, huh? You could've come up with a better idea!"

Andrejs answered curtly:

"This is the fastest way."

"We could've taken the tram like normal people!"

"What a princess! Keep moving!"

The massive train track field was at least half a kilometer wide at this point; electric trains went back and forth, signaling their approach from the bend with a whistle, then coming into sight themselves. A fence ran along the tracks, as did paths worn down by bums and bushes containing piles of garbage—below it all were the wavering city lights and din of traffic.

The train to Moscow slowed down and passed them on its way to the station. Andrejs froze in his tracks. He and the woman looked in the direction the train was going. The last car slowly rolled by.

"What are you looking at?" the woman asked.

He didn't answer.

Dogs.

Guards who shove you against each other, throw you, toss you like lifeless sacks . . . But first—dogs, the wild barking of dogs, sinister, horrible . . . Dogs—the devil incarnate . . . Cerberuses . . . Then the soldiers, their boots . . .

On the ground!

On your knees . . .

Hands behind your head! . . . Move, right, left, we'll shoot without warning! . . . Days and nights of waiting in the half-dark without food, water . . . Then suddenly a light, shouting, barking, the wind in your face like rye bread, so fresh, so alive and rich . . . You eat it half-blind, chew it, swallow it—fresh air . . . Until you're herded into a new cell, where they de-lice you, re-clothe you, shave your head, and save you from yourself. On the ground! . . .

On your knees . . .

Prisoner transport cars.

And, having lost all other characteristics of being human, you'll latch onto your kind, will remain nailed to your kind.

"What are you looking at?"

"Prisoner transport," he finally said reluctantly. "You see that last car there on the train to Moscow? The last one's a prisoner transport car. It gets hooked on at some point—in Daugavpils or maybe Krustpils. When all the passengers get out, a locomotive will come, unhook it and push it onto the side tracks. Maybe overnight. Maybe for a few hours. Maybe they'll take it right away to Central Prison. Who knows—maybe only the day after tomorrow—to Jelgava or Liepāja."

This Russian woman had the knowledge of transport cars in her blood; knowledge about where prisoners spent the night before they got put in the stocks, before the sentenced whippings, before being branded with the symbol of shame and exiled to Siberia, when every condemned soul is to be pitied, when you feel compelled to give them a warm sandwich, to drop an apple into their laps, to force your way through the crowd so you, too, can press a coin into their hands.

But she'd lived with that two thirds of her life, and she'd had enough. She didn't want to deal with it tonight, and launched a rebellion. She whined:

"Let's go. I'm cold. C'mon, let's go, good God are you going to stand here for hours? We'll miss it!"

She walked forward a few steps, then stopped.

"That's where all your memories are, all your friends, right? Transport cars and shackles, and dogs, and railroads—right? Well go, run, beg them, maybe they'll let you into that car, huh? That's where your entire life is, snitch!"

"Shut up!"

"But it's over now," the woman said from somewhere behind him, and started to cry.

"What's over?"

She grew scared and got quiet.

"Don't cling to any fantasies or hopes! Don't! You'll get exactly as much as you need. And leave the rest of it alone! I've put prison behind me. And I won't tell you anything more!"

The woman stood on the tracks in the fall drizzle in her see-through stockings and stupid shoes, and trembled. The wind tore at her jacket, hair, and tugged at her thoughts, she looked so pathetic in her fancy get-up and red lipstick . . . and so close.

"Sweetheart," she said, "but it's over now."

He spun around angrily and wanted to head back to the station. Ditch this drama and leave, like he'd done so many times before. But he suddenly felt that he couldn't. It surprised him. He'd told her everything on his mind, but these words suddenly meant nothing, and disappeared like they'd been dropped down a well. Sweetheart, she'd answered, and was still standing there.

And he couldn't go anywhere.

Strange. What's left to not experience, he thought sadly.

He turned back around and started to climb down the steep embankment. She stumbled after him, crying out quietly when her foot slipped in the mud, and balanced meekly on one foot like a child when he brought the stray shoe to her and put it back on. Taking each other tightly by the hand, they dove downward, into the bright city.

FATHER

SEVERAL ducks and a goose idly putter along and nibble stalks of grass by the canal downtown. The weather is hot and humid as a greenhouse. A storm shifts tensely high overhead, but it can't pull itself together.

Monta and Andrejs, having left the apartment, sit outside at the café. Andrejs rubs his thumb over his train ticket—he always buys it ahead of time for the trip home.

Old men play checkers on a bench under the lindens by the café terrace. Squealing children run around the adjacent playground, where the blue and red plastic tunnels, steps, and towers radiate a poisonous heat into the absentminded dust of the city. Punks and National Bolshevisks lounge in the grass in their striped woolen sweaters. But for now, father and daughter have the café to themselves.

Monta tries to inconspicuously wipe the sweat from her upper lip. Andrejs watches the ducks, watches his daughter, does up and undoes the top button of his shirt. As if waking from a trance, they now and then hastily pick up their drinks. The tonic swims with the reflection of the trees overhead and the broken shadows from the straws. Andrejs's straw is yellow, Monta's blue. Andrejs has a strong, almost violent mouth set in a darkly tanned face. Monta's lips are sensual and soft, with traces of red lipstick.

Monta opens her mouth several times without a sound, then resolutely returns her father's stare with her icy blue eyes. When they're together there isn't much use for words.

Some mothers sitting on the long bench by the playground talk about something and then burst into laughter—the sound is sudden and free, like champagne bubbling from a bottle. Monta starts, then bites her straw. Andrejs hears the tiny, delighted squeal of a little boy and turns to wave to him. Monta sees the shadows of leaves chase each other across the aged skin of her father's neck. She looks up at the sky; it's sticky, it's suddenly and completely closed off, blackened by something stifling and dark like soot. But the sky won't open up for a while still, though the foliage might. Moisture gathers on the lindens from the humidity.

Her father faces her again, reaches across the table and touches the back of her hand, where the heat has drawn up a few bluish veins. Now the yellow-painted fingernail of her index finger traces vertical stripes in the condensation on her glass.

A small, mangy poodle runs into the flock of birds. He seems oblivious to the ducks, but aggressively herds the lone goose. The poodle's owner, an elderly woman with a pale face and arms crossed behind her back, turns toward the canal and looks at the bright green embankment on the opposite side. Her ankles are swollen beneath light-colored stockings, knotty like a tree stump at the roots.

Right now this woman is alive. The grass along the canal is unbelievably green. It's as if the thick air is seconds away from unrolling a rainbow over it all. Everything will smell like cool, wet dirt, and air.

That's all in the past, Monta had said—with that accidentally, but firmly dismissing Andrejs's usual landslide of memories. She keeps drawing her fingertips down the side of her glass. Monta feels guilty. She wants to bring her father out of the cave he finds so comforting.

Wants his attention for the physical, flesh and blood Monta sitting across from her father on a woven metal chair. He can't reach that Monta anymore because he's still scattered somewhere in the past as Ieva Eglīte's misplaced object.

She'd be grateful if he'd listen to her selflessly. And he'd listen to her selflessly if he had any room in his heart. But he doesn't, Monta senses that. That's what we are, she thinks. A lost love tames the soul and drains it dry.

Why the fuck did you kill Aksels, Dad?

But she'll never ask him. The question has to do with an entirely different life of his. It would startle him. Maybe he'd feel pain like a snail being suddenly scraped out of its shell with a spoon?

He'll never talk about it. And it's his pride and his downfall.

They hug each other reservedly, then draw away and really look at each other. Then Andrejs leaves on the train, suspended by endless silver tracks that never intersect, never intersect.

And a few station stops later, his head drops to his chest as he falls asleep.

CONVERSATIONS UNDER SHIFTING SKIES

UNDER SHIFTING SKIES

"**HAVE** you ever been outside of yourself?"

"Outside myself? Sounds like an illness to me."

"What kind?"

"Schizophrenia. Like one minute you're one person, but someone else the next."

"That's not what I mean. It's not an illness. It's . . . Alright. Imagine you're you. You're with yourself at all times. You're inside yourself, somewhere. I mean . . . Well . . . I don't know where people normally *go* when they're inside themselves."

"Probably not to their feet."

"But maybe there are people who do go into their feet."

"Could be."

"Of course. Nothing but the feet. A person could be in their big toe, too."

"Or somewhere bigger—the knees, the hips, the ribs."

"Higher."

"The heart, then."

"Sometimes the heart . . . Yeah. But for the most part I think people are within themselves around the eyes."

"Not the ears?"

"It's pretty much the same thing. On the border between the eyes and ears. At the temples. You've been there, somewhere, within yourself the whole time. The whole time you'd call your life. For a while I used to be in my fingertips. When I was a baby, before I could walk."

"Yeah. That was a long time ago."

"But we were talking about how I'm outside myself."

"So talk."

"I used to be very much inside myself. Inseparable. I was one with my actions."

"Remember that time you slit your wrists?"

"I do. It was pretty bad."

"Pretty bad? That's putting it mildly—it was horrifying. It was pouring that night and the water blacked out the windows, the street-lights, and the roads. Mom brought you to the hospital . . . It was a nightmare."

"I was completely inside myself then. But now it's even worse."

"What's worse than a car full of blood?"

"There are things. Trust me."

"Like?"

"Like . . . I'm not sure how to explain it."

"Try putting it simply."

"There's nothing simple about it."

"Then try details."

"Details . . . So you know what it's like right before it rains?"

"Like now?"

"Like now. And hear that bird cry? We're in the city but we can still hear it. A rainbird. The trees are rustling, the treetops shifting. You don't want to touch anything because it's all sort of muggy. Painful."

"Right, so anyway! Now you're talking about the weather and some bird, but you wanted to talk about you."

"But it's all the same. It's about that feeling, some kind of out-of-body feeling."

"Experience—the right word is experience."

"I don't care which one's right."

"Then you risk saying what you don't mean."

"I often wonder if it's even possible for others to understand."

"Explain."

"See, it's as if I'm always somewhere outside myself. Watching myself from the sidelines. Take love, for example. Watch how love takes over your body. It kisses, hugs, makes others happy, makes them sad. Your body changes shape, you'll have a kid, then more kids, or maybe none at all. You'll have a home somewhere, warm nights under a melting sky. Arguments, fear, gentleness. But none of it happens to you—it happens to a body you call yourself. The body you're watching from the sidelines."

"You're sick."

"Maybe, yeah."

"Your forehead's hot."

"It's always hot."

"So what are you saying—that even now, while we're talking, you're . . . So that's why you're looking at me so sadly? I noticed that strange look in your eyes a long time ago."

"And you're not worried?"

"I thought it was like the calm before the storm. I'm not sure if I should be worried or not. Maybe I should be."

"How do I look? Describe it!"

"Like . . . Like you're trying to absorb everything around you . . . Through your eyes. Yeah, like you're trying to come back, into one piece. It's in your eyes. Like you need to anchor yourself to something. That's what you look like—like despair."

"And there you have it."

"Maybe you need to see a doctor."

"What for?"

"Because you feel split in two, even around me."

"Split in two! My god, don't be ridiculous!"

"What? You're the one who said you were split in two."

"I never said that, Pāvils! You weren't listening."

"Sorry, but–"

"I'm not split in two! I'm outside of myself, alright? Outside myself. It's not so bad when I'm talking with someone. When I'm talking with someone it's always . . . detached."

"What do you mean?"

"When two or more people are talking, they contemplate, speak, discuss. They're someplace slightly outside themselves. Like in a shroud of thoughts. People tend to use phrases like 'Remember when . . . !' or 'Next summer I'd like to go to . . .' They converse. They're detached, see? They're back in that memory, or they're in next summer. You can see it in their eyes, or how they twirl their hair around their finger as they daydream. They're traveling. They're outside themselves and there's nothing strange about it."

"I'll be honest—it gets harder and harder to talk to you as the years go on. You make people uncomfortable. For example—no, don't get offended—but I even feel uncomfortable talking to you. The look in your eyes is so tense. So heavy. You're wrong, you know. When you and I talk, I tell myself life isn't like that. Life is about life, not useless and continual concentration. It's bad to be so serious! Why do you want so badly to get back into your eyes when talking to me?"

"Because I can't anymore."

"Can't what?"

"Get back inside myself. When we're done talking, Laura will toddle over with a ball and say 'Daddy, let's play!'"

"And I'll go."

"And you'll go and you'll be you—Pāvils. Pāvils who's kicking a ball, who's Laura's father, who loves Vita, who's writing his doctorate."

"And you?"

"I'll wait somewhere far outside myself, until everything calms down."

"You're afraid of responsibility."

"Oh fantastic! What else—any more genius insight?"

"Well what do you want me to say?"

"Did I ask you to say anything in the first place?"

"If we're having a conversation I have to say something."

"Oh please. The problem is you don't believe me."

"It's not a matter of believing or not. It just comes off sounding stupid. And even offensive."

"Offensive how? Are you offended? If you are I'm sorry, I've never wanted to offend you."

"But you did. And in a really strange way, too. Everyone is inside themselves, in their bodies, but you, you're outside yourself. Like you're a princess, something special. It's terrible. And so weird—like *Pulp Fiction* or something."

"I didn't mean for it to sound like that. But you're right to say it, thanks."

"So now I'm capable of saying something right after all!"

"Don't patronize me."

"I'm not! Did I say something wrong? The way I see it, you have to live free and easy, in a single breath. And if you're having thoughts like these there's a glitch in your system. Something's gone wrong. I don't get you."

"Fine, you don't get me. I can't force you to understand if you don't have the capacity to in the first place."

"So, what will you do?"

"Well finally! The king of questions! *What will you do?* Amazing! Think about these words. What. Will. You. Do. They're like the salt of the earth, but at the same time so simple."

"Hey, don't overanalyze everything—be it breathing or language. It's not productive, it's an obstacle. It was a serious question, pragmatic and realistic—what will you do? Are you going to pine away like this forever?"

"But hold up, these words! Listen—*what will you do?* In that specific order, with that hierarchy, and not the other way around. Not *what do you will?* The will always comes first and the doing always follows. If you look at it the right way, you could pave paths to a better world."

"Great. And what kind of world do you want to discover? One without pain?"

"When Monta was little, her favorite story was about the Golden City. In the Golden City, wolves and sheep are friends. The Golden City doesn't need night to understand what day is. It doesn't need death to value life. It's a world without contrast. You know, Monta almost had me convinced. 'You're sad,' she told me. And I knew then that she'd be perfectly willing to trade knowledge for ignorance if only she could be in a world without pain."

"Without joy and hate? Without sorrow and passion, without desire?"

"That would be a boring place, bored-to-death boring . . . and useless. I said this to her. She argued with me that death is something grown-ups invented so they wouldn't be bored. Grown-ups are sad, grown-ups do all kinds of stupid things just so they can understand something."

"A dead boring world is a paradise."

"Paradise?"

"Or a hell."

"Something solitary is dead boring?"

"Something solitary is death itself."

"And so listen, my little deity, who just a minute ago wanted to create a world sans the shadows of evil—listen! The mind of man is small and his dreams are within reason. They're only the safe, good, and painless ones. It's not worth wasting any energy."

"Evil takes care of itself."

"Wasting energy for evil is even dumber."

"Then what's left? Watching how life lives my body?"

"Yeah, better to chase after events like a bloodhound. This endless clash of black and white is colorful."

"Why did you say that being outside yourself was worse than slitting your wrists?"

"Back then, when I was with Aksels, love justified everything we did. Even the most horrible and incomprehensible things."

"You needed justification? Who were you trying to justify yourself to?"

"Not like that. That's not what I meant. The sense, y'know? The sense."

"Sense. Strange word."

"Well yeah. Now I do everything with consideration, I try to be precise and guided by experience, but all that sensibility goes to waste. It's a calculation! Correctly calculated empty accomplishments and losses. It's all trivial. Once it was high tide. Now it's low tide. I've been washed away from myself."

"I've started a path, but I don't know if it's for my benefit or not. But I can't stop or turn back. It'll be a test, hey!—it'll be an interesting experiment—will I be able to take my idea and create a path? You can write your final dissertation on it! I'm in two. It's the only thing that fascinates me and keeps me alive! Me and my body."

"Maybe it is the onset of some kind of psychological disease. Maybe we can still do something about it."

"You could, but only if the goals of both of *me* line up."

"What's your body's goal?"

"Love, laugh, stay sane, be as strong as a mighty oak for myself and for others."

"And what's your goal?"

"To not be here."

"Maybe you're confused. Maybe your goal is to observe."

"Observe?"

"Observe. If you're destined to be outside yourself anyway. Maybe your joy comes from observing your physical body and the physical bodies of others, to observe life, fate, how they come together and part, and come together again. Observe and believe you understand something when something becomes clear; that it might be the answer to at least one question."

"Thanks, brother. You've got some highly flattering opinions of me."

"You look that arrogant, by the way. You would be the one to come up with something like that."

"When the essence of things reveals itself, you stop doing them automatically. That's what I meant. But maybe something else, though, I don't know. No one is themselves in conversation. It's what does exist that talks through us. A million mouths, a million eyes."

"Don't get mad, but seems to me you can't love."

"That's it?"

"Only love."

"That's almost too simple."

"But it's true. Everything else is trivial and made-up."

"Why?"

"Love isn't in your control. It comes to you. There's no other way. You're whole again. You don't question anything."

"But I *do* have questions! Okay, so it turns out I *don't* have love. And I can't answer any other way in the face of a logical confession. And here we are."

"And so you want me to pity you?"

"No. No need to pity, to be sad for me, to express your opinion, nothing. I'm glad that you met me for lunch today, that you sat here, drank black tea. Thank you for carefully picking the bones from your trout and putting them on the fish bone plate. Thank you for convincing me to order this delicious cod. Fish contains phosphorus, which promotes thinking. Thank you for not talking. Thank you for saying a few things that I can spend a lifetime thinking about if I wanted to. Want is at the center of everything. Simple, straightforward want. So everything happens because we want it to. It's the world we live in. It's so important! You know . . . Sometimes I need this more than anything, for you to be sitting there, across from me, drinking tea. It's like your eyes are a chair I can sit and rest in for a while. Thank you."

"Such lavish thank yous. And thanks for that!"

"You going to call Laura over?"

"Yeah. Laura, honey!"

"Laura!"

"Laura, sweetie, we have to go, say bye-bye to Auntie Ieva!"

"Bye-bye!"

"Bye, Laura, you lively little girl! Laura is beautiful."

"Yep."

"When Monta was little, she used to always say that too—yep."

"Little kids are whole. I already said it, but take care of yourself. Go see a good psychologist."

"That would just be more schooling, not the truth. It's not a solution."

"Truth doesn't exist. But somewhere there's a solution. And you'll find it. You've earned it. Don't look so creepy. Life is good. You're good. Everything's good."

"Thanks, brother."

"Bye!"

"Bye!"

"Pāvils!"

"Yeah."

"Be honest—do you think I avoid taking responsibility for my life? But that someday I'll learn how? Someday I'll get back into myself? But you know I can't rush it, it has to happen on its own."

"Yeah."

"Is that what you think?"

"Yes."

"You make everything sound so unrefined. Everything that's secretive and beautiful, everything that makes sense."

"You can do so much with words. Lie a lot. Embellish. Make mistakes. It's a giant avalanche that crashes over you if you so much as move a word. It starts to roll and picks up other words along the way, and there you have it! You can't even lie with words—but that's giving it too much meaning. Pointlessly passing the time instead of doing something."

"For example, going to elections. To vote."

"Right, for example."

"Rake the yard. Take off nail polish. You're naïve."

"Call me what you want. But I have my convictions."

"And that's why I respect you. Thank you for that."

"Are you back inside yourself when you say that? Where's the thank you coming from?"

109

"The universe."

"Liar, liar, pants on fire . . . Laura!"

"She's getting antsy."

"Go. And God bless!"

"What an old-fashioned farewell! But I'll gladly accept it."

"Do you think God is in one piece?"

"Everyone knows that God is a trinity. At least the Christian God. I don't know. They're stupid word games. See, at times form is enough. To live together. People live together, so there has to be some sense in it. Raising children or writing dissertations, novels, cookbooks, screenplays, even making pancakes! Earning money. Spending it. Expressing an opinion. Fighting for something. Something like that, right?"

"Exactly. Alright, I'm going."

"Go."

"Hang on! How come you thanked me for being quiet for a while during lunch? Were you observing me?"

"No. I wasn't doing anything special. We were sitting. Talking. Time was passing. That's almost the only thing that still brings me joy. The fact that time goes on. Cars drive down the street. It's about to rain. Ducks are nibbling the grass. Nothing makes sense, but the water keeps flowing. Beautiful."

"Beautiful."

"Tell me, Pāvils—are you in one piece?"

"I don't think about it. And I won't. This illness could be contagious."

"Sorry."

"Don't worry about me, I don't have that much free time. I can't afford to."

"What?"

"The same as before. Don't look at me in such a scary way."

"You can tell Laura not to do that. But not me."

"Don't smoke!"

"Hm. Take care. Write your dissertation."

"Thanks. You take care, too."

"Pāvils!"

"Yeah?"

"I love you."

"I know."

"You know?"

"Yes. You love me, the earth, the light, slugs, these tiny green leaves here, you love the past and present, children, strange, old and mean women, horrible fates, wavering stares, new buildings, the sea, clouds, God, and goddesses. Total chaos. It's impossible to love you because you love too much. You love, and at the same time don't know how to, you don't know what love is. You're afraid of life and death, and you desire both of them. You celebrate sadness without really knowing what sadness is. You advertise joy without feeling it. You advertise an empty life without knowing what life without nothing is. Lower your barriers, sis. A dog only becomes a dog when you fence it in."

"I don't have barriers. Aksels was a barrier. And he was taken away from me."

"Maybe you'll get him back."

"He's dead, remember, Jesus!"

"Is there life after death and/or love?"

"There are people who are meant to have only one great love in their lifetime. How do you save yourself for the next one?"

"Do you know who your one great love is?"

"I don't."

"Do you know what tomorrow will be like?"

"I don't know anything."

"Then stop it. And don't look at me like that."

AN OPEN ENDING

SURVEYING the crowd in the Berlin Art Academy café, she was unable to hold back and asked loudly:

"So that's the end?"

The sea of voices drowned out the sound, but a few people sitting closer to her heard. Elias, from Cyprus, leaned his head of black curls toward her:

"What did you say?"

"So that's the end."

"Yes, that's the end."

He smiled over his glasses, his brilliant smile. The Berlin seminar was almost over. Tomorrow—her suitcase and the flight home.

Ieva looked around her: Roberta, Neil, Gojel, and Eduardo were at one table. She, Peter, Elias, Barbara, and Marijka were at another. That day the preview of Sybille Bergeman's photography exhibit had taken place in the exhibition hall, and the café overflowed with attendees. They drank coffee, chatted, smoked. Sybille herself was supposed to show up!—the excited faces of those present read. They'd be able to ask her questions. So close they could touch her. Get her autograph and a smile. The way Sybille would use her lens to capture a smile, a caress, the disappearing shadows and lights in the fluctuating daylight. Now they could get these in excess in person and, when parting, even kiss her hand.

The crowd a single, hundred-fingered hand.

Peter was discussing something with Gojels and the young architect in the red shirt—what was his name again? Marcelle? Mario?—from Berlin. Next to Peter, the otherwise businesslike architect looked like a baby. Noticing Ieva's fixed, introverted stare, Peter turned toward her and waved a glass of white wine under her nose. She broke free from her thoughts and back into the bustling world around her.

"Isn't 2 P.M. too early for wine?"

Peter smiled meaningfully.

"I know what too late means, but not what too early means."

Ieva laughed:

"But I don't know what too late means."

Peter stared at her for a moment and in his typical careless manner flipped his dark hair over his shoulder. Then he said:

"Yes, it could be that it's too early for you to know what too late means."

The small, dark theater slowly filled with students. How many movies were there left to see—two?

"Peter, please!"

Elias's smile! Gojels's, Mario's, and Barbara's profiles. They were all so nice.

Except Peter. When he presented at yesterday's readings Ieva had felt a childish and long-forgotten desire to be protective. He had immediately upset the audience. But those were the rules of the game.

Peter had to be edgy by definition. Strange how the truly edgy are rarely crass or confrontational—this type subconsciously calls out for love, sometimes rather violently. Peter was fragile and ironic, there was plenty of love in him, he wanted freedom. "In these bittersweet pages you'll find the fall of a regime and the past two decades of Eastern Europe"—that's what *Rolling Stone* had written about his play. "Simply a polymath vagabond for the needs of New Europe," Lawrence Norfolk had flippantly added. How could they all place the European label on Peter! Like a bunch of kids who are just worried whether or not they'll be able to hear their mothers calling for them.

In contrast to Germany, people in Hungary had never believed in Communism, so to them the regime was straight-up fact, Peter had pitched during his presentation. Exactly—pitched. With a broad stance, his frail shoulders thrown back, always flipping his dark hair. With an easy smile on his face. Sometimes you want to slap such unshakably ironic people, just to see if they can feel anything.

Shows in six of Germany's biggest theaters. His first piece translated into fifteen languages. Multimedia performances with his participation in over twenty countries. A monthly column in the *Frankfurter Allgemeine Zeitung*. He knew how to play his cards right. The kid had scored a ten on his first shot. And he even looked the part. What's more—he looked like a loner who couldn't be really surprised by anything in the world anymore. Often full of a slight disdain. That's what happens to public entertainers. Just like professional party planners hate partygoers.

But Ieva knew that Peter's disdain was purely symbolic. He was used to looking at the world cynically, he shrunk from anything forced on him. Such imposed, positive emotions are usually just for connecting a writer to his audience. Like Paulo Coelho, who went out in front of hundreds of readers at book fairs—and both sides came together in a convulsive overflow of love. Just yesterday Ieva had overheard some students at the café laughing about Coelho—about his habit of drinking freshly squeezed carrot juice with freshly made warm cream. About housewives who, upon meeting him, jump at the chance to tell him about their troubles with their husbands while the author would listen and offer love-filled advice in a fatherly manner.

But Peter's stare was a warning.

Be careful—his eyes seemed to say as they moved over the audience. But not for my sake. I grew up with the dangers of Hungary. So I warn you—be careful for your sake. The audience sat silently and tried to decode this mysterious message called Peter.

In closing Peter read a fragment from his play in English, but the audience sat in icy silence. Then he asked a translator to read the same fragment in German, saying, "Usually I'm used to seeing more smiling faces!" But the people decided he was trying to work them. There were a few older men in the audience who were more directly caught up by the young Hungarian's overt provocation. One person stood up indignantly and shouted—"Stop translating, all Germans understand English!"

Peter answered that understanding and hearing a text are not the same thing. This led to a lengthy discussion. Ieva saw that Peter was growing helpless in the face of aggression.

Ieva asked:

"Peter, irony is meant to create distance, isn't it?"

Peter turned his attention to her. He looked at her warily.

"In order to talk amongst themselves, Hungarians were forced to use subtexts—to read between the lines and beyond the jokes. By the 80s irony had become the official language in Hungary. If someone spoke seriously, it meant he sided with the regime—meaning he was lying . . . It's hard to joke around. If I tell a Russian a dirty

Transylvanian joke, he'd laugh for an hour. A Hungarian would laugh for half an hour. A German—for five minutes. It's just that the joke would be foreign to someone born in the Carpathian forest, where everything smells of blood and death."

"And now, when you travel the world? Do you maintain your cynical view of things?"

Peter shrugged.

"No choice. I grew up with irony. It's my second skin."

"And distance as well?"

He nodded.

Barbara pushed her way through the crowd with a CD in hand. She looked at Ieva, and Ieva smiled encouragingly and waved.

Barbara studied at the Konrad Wolf Academy for Film and Television under director Hans Foses, and Hans practically put the girl on a pedestal. Every time she'd met Ieva, Barbara tried to speak Russian. She gushed about Russia and her dream of traveling to Moscow. Ieva was too lazy to keep reminding her that the Baltics and Russia were two different places.

Once they had talked about Latvia.

"What's Germany to you!" Barbara had cried out. "Compared to the massive area of your country!"

When she saw Ieva's surprised face, she explained:

"I mean the steppes!"

Ieva had laughed, but said nothing. In the eyes of the international community Russia was irrational, but the romanticized idea Germans had of Russia was sometimes even more so.

Small and lithe with short-cropped hair, Barbara reminded Ieva of a teenager. Hans said she had style. And her film was amazing, Ieva would see for herself. That's how a director was supposed to act, Ieva thought—like a jackrabbit. White against the pale winter snow and brown against yellow summer reeds. So the world is never closed off to them. So they can get inside a foreign world and observe.

Meanwhile Barbara was presenting her movie:

"Last summer the cameraman and I filmed in Romania—in Bucharest. It was really tough, not so much physically, but spiritually. You'll see . . . Some scenes were staged—the ones filmed in the youth center—but the rest are documentary. We made friends with the Bucharest street kids. They live in heating ducts. We gave them a video camera and had them film themselves, in their world. For them it was a game, entertainment. For us—it was valuable footage. You'll see . . . What else can I say? Roll film!"

Peter sat down next to Ieva with a glass of wine and whispered into her ear:

"Thanks for the support!"

His shaggy hair fell forward onto her shoulder and tickled her neck. She drew back and laughed:

"Don't mention it! Have you been to Romania?"

Peter simply nodded his head in response.

"Japan?"

"No! Japan is the exception. And I never lie."

They were both overcome by fits of laughter as the rest of the hall grew silent and suddenly very serious.

The movie started.

It was powerful. Even for the students who had learned to emotionally distance themselves from the material used and evaluate a film's professional qualities.

Shaky scenes filmed with a miniature camcorder moved in time with the observer's breathing and heartbeat. Barbara was like a meticulous follower of Dogme 95, the so-called final film manifesto of the 20th century presented in Paris in 1995 by Danish director Lars von

Trier and his peers. This manifesto, or "Vow of Chastity," envisaged the creation of works that went against the manufactured glamor of Hollywood by:

–filming only in a natural setting;

–never recording the sound separately from the video, or vice-versa, and without using music unless it was actually in the scene being filmed;

–using a camcorder;

–making the movie colorful and prohibiting special lighting effects;

–forbidding the use of optical tools and filters;

–not having any actions in the movie that were impossible to realistically show (such as murder);

–prohibiting the alienation of time and geographic setting—the movie had to take place in the here and now;

–prohibiting genre movies;

–using only the Academic 35mm movie format (this rule was the first the new group themselves broke, by starting to use digital filming techniques);

–refraining from taking credit—the director's name would not appear in the credits.

Everyone knew that von Trier's self-irony was intact, and that the "Vow of Chastity" was more like a parody of a manifesto, but the scandal succeeded. Even though such bans were like a red cloth to a bull, they still encouraged them to consider the level of lies in filmed material: what's colored in by computer, cut out, lit up, made over, and then fed to an audience—like the whole thing had been calculated down to the last teardrop and dollar.

Ieva didn't think there was any need to discuss the topic. Everyone could tell plastic from glass and, if someone liked plastic, it was a matter of preference and knowledge. She enjoyed professional cyber-movies for their stylistic purity, but purity of style could hold your attention for ten minutes, no more. Even mistakes, if there were any, were interesting. In all other ways these movies were unbearably boring and predictable—like the human mind. They're for the viewers' entertainment.

No manifesto can make an artist out of a person. In turn, no artist can strictly adhere to a manifesto if he is truly an artist. Even if it's the one you've written yourself.

Barbara is undeniably talented. And she has a good cameraman. A delicate light stretched from the depths of the hall toward the screen.

The scenes revealed what was usually hidden from those who walked the earth—a shelter made of pieces of insulation covered in rags, faces stony from hunger and drugs—all of which light draws out from the darkness, like carving them from nothingness with a rough chisel, the naïve commentary of children. It was a physically visible hell.

The story slowly unraveled, highlighting the main protagonists. One of them was a boy who filmed the underground world. When he himself showed up on camera, people gasped—he was only eight years old, but he constantly smoked while talking to his counselor at the youth center. His opinions were rational and wise like those of an eighty-year-old man. It was terrible seeing this little person, this primordium of all mankind, who was destined to grow up in literal darkness.

But Barbara hadn't made the typical beginner director's mistake—pitying and adding emotion to what could already be seen. She gathered the teenagers and brought them to the seaside, filming their reactions to this never-before-seen element. The camera was and remained an observer. Letting the viewer think for themselves.

The movie also had a proper dramatic climax—it ended with documentary scenes in which some boys in the underground were judging the death sentence on one of their own—for some unclear, but in their belief, unforgiveable crime. A sawed-off barrel is aimed at the captive teenager, who at first squirms like a worm in fear of death, but then stands tall, puts his hands in his pockets and stares in challenge at the person taking aim . . .

. . . Ieva grows hot, and for a second she thinks she's going to faint. She doesn't know which tiny detail it is that suddenly rips open the storeroom of memories—the accused boy's stance, his sweater, the look in his eyes, or the barrel being aimed at him. But a scene of her and Aksels is there in her mind, clear, clear as day.

Aksels!

What kind of name is that?

It's so common!

Aksels and Ieva! She's the one taking aim. On the sunny day of January 15th.

Ieva realizes that it's been years since she's thought of Aksels. She remembers his face. See his eyes, but without any expression in them. Notices the small, birdlike silhouette at the end of the barrel. It suddenly seems to her that January 15th never happened to them. That it was a story about two other people in another life.

She lets out a low cry and rubs her hand over her face as if trying to wake herself up. Peter grabs her arm in concern, she pushes him away, gets up, and heads toward the back of the hall, where there are tables set with lunch refreshments. In one long gulp, Ieva drains a bottle of mineral water, then another. The movie has sucked the energy from her; she feels like all that's left of her is an empty shell.

The movie ends before the trigger is pulled. An open ending.

There are a few seconds of dead silence, and then there is applause. Barbara takes the CD out of the player and goes to her seat, searching for Ieva's face, but Ieva doesn't even wave. She's standing alone at the back of the hall by a white, cloth covered table, wolfing down some brown cake with whipped cream. She's cut off a huge chunk, loaded it onto a plate, and is wolfing it down.

Peter catches up with her at the park. He's standing in the wind— gasping for breath and his hair blowing around him.

"Maybe we can have dinner together tonight?"

Tonight, Ieva thinks. She'll pull herself together by tonight.

"Sure."

"I'll call your room . . ."

"I don't know when I'll be back. I was going to take a walk."

Peter shakes her by the shoulder.

"Then call me—room 311, on the third floor. You'll call? Around seven, eight? Promise? I'll be waiting."

He hurries back. Probably back to the café for yet another glass of wine to celebrate Barbara's movie.

It's still a beautiful January day.

The Spree River. Some school. Benches. The sun. Children shouting.

Wind and leaves. The anti-autumn. This is what April could be like in Latvia. Or Indian Summer.

I could be happy just to be happy, Ieva thinks. Happy about the river, or Berlin. Look, Möbelhaus Kern—such pretty, light-colored sofas and dark leather cushions! Except something has jolted her heart with such unease that she can't enjoy the cushions.

A Deutsche Post boy rides up to the furniture store on his bike with its yellow mail pouches.

"What's the date today?" she asks him.

"January 15th," the boy answers, and with one look Ieva sees herself like in a mirror—standing bewilderedly in front of a shop window with her dopey, lost-in-the-past eyes. She steps aside as if in apology.

Aside. Aside. Aside.

More than anything right now, she wants to be in this moment and in her skin.

She stands on the Alt-Moabit Bridge. The Spree flows under it dark and fast, but can't pull out to sea the handful of ducks and geese stubbornly fighting the current. On one of the bridge pillars, someone has written in graceful lettering—*Alla heisst Gott.*

The fresh air gives her strength to exist. When she gets back to the hotel she's exhausted, but calm. She spreads out on the bed and lays motionless hour after hour, enjoying the hotel's anonymous emptiness, the fact that there are so few of her things here, so little of her life.

To be alone. To not think of anything. To extract these hours from the flesh of her being.

Evening slips in unnoticed. She had dozed off from staring at the ceiling. She takes a cold shower, gets dressed and calls Peter. He doesn't pick up. After fifteen minutes she calls again, then decides to go down to his room. What if his phone just isn't working?

The soft, red hallway swallows all sound. Ieva knocks at 311. After a moment Peter opens the door—half naked. A towel wrapped around his hips.

"I was asleep," he said. "Didn't hear your call. Come in!"

Ieva clearly senses the hidden advance in his lithe, tan back, the crease in the material of the towel around his waist, and the provocative look in his eyes. The nature of woman is to inspire man. And what then? When there's nothing left to inspire, to satiate them?

The blood quickly rushes to her cheeks. She lowers her eyes.

"No, thank you! I'll wait in the restaurant," she says briskly and heads for the stairs.

It is what it is. A glance and a disarming spark that either happens or doesn't. And sometimes that spark flares up in a moment shared between two people.

But she doesn't need that anymore.

Peter clinks his glass against hers. The glass wall of the Arus Hotel restaurant extends along the edge of the river. The restaurant looks out onto the rushing Spree, the dark depths of which catch hold of as many reflections as there are stars in the sky.

He opens a packet of cigarettes and offers them to Ieva. She declines.

As he lights one he idly says:

"I'm not addicted to cigarettes! I just smoke them for pleasure."

"And pleasure? You're not addicted to that?"

They laugh again. It's easy to spend time with Peter because he is so damned confident, so bright and ironic.

And then he grins wickedly.

"I was in Latvia once."

Ieva asks:

"What did you think?"

"It was five years ago. I was looking for a translator for my book. I only found one Hungarian translator in the entire country—some old guy about a hundred and thirty years old, a complete Methuselah. I flat-out told him not to translate my book, and went on to Lithuania. You're like an Indian tribe—locked into yourselves, resolved to be withdrawn."

It's not exactly flattering. Ieva decides to fight back.

"Writers are more of a tribe," she laughs. "But you look pretty meticulous. You took care of the translations for your book yourself? You're your own manager, right? Y'know, Peter, I'd like to know—doesn't your life as a writer suffer from your life as a performer?"

Peter's dark eyes narrow.

"How do you mean?"

"I watched you when you read the fragment from your play. You calculate how many smiles each of your jokes will get. And if the audience doesn't react the way you're used to, you break down, feel out of place in your own skin. Don't you become the dependent one, then?"

Check.

Smiling, he draws on his cigarette and leans back in his chair.

"There isn't any writer's life or performer's life. There's only one life. Mine."

Then he serves up an unexpected question:

"What about you? I've been watching you all week. Are you happy with your life?"

And mate.

Ieva can't find the words.

"You're an amazing woman in everything you do. How come whenever you tell a story you always finish it by saying you wish it had been different? Does someone else make your decisions for you? And if not, why don't you do what you want to do? It just seems that the whole time you're living *this* life, you're thinking about a *different* one instead. So tell me, are you happy with *your* life?"

Luckily, Ieva's phone rings, granting her some time to think of an answer. It's Monta. Missing her mother and not at all surprised to hear she's in Berlin. They talk for a good half hour. Screw the roaming fees.

When Ieva looks back at Peter, her doubts have subsided. She won't stitch black and white together anymore. Only white with white. And black with black. The answer can already be seen in her face when she speaks:

"What was it you asked?"

"Are you happy with your life?"

"Y'know, our Latvian tribe has this poet, Ziedonis, who once said: Happiness is only the order of all things. I'd say that happiness is an open ending."

"Well put, and even a bit ironic. But how come your eyes look so sad?"

"Because today's January 15th. That's all. Let's take a walk along the Spree."

MONTA

THE TEMPTATION OF THE FOG

THE sunset is totally insane, Ieva thinks.

And where are they all going . . .

Tonight the sunset is pure madness, this is what she thinks.

And what she thinks has no meaning. The word "insane" hasn't meant anything special for some time now. People shout it in the streets when they want to make others think they still feel something. And she has no clue what madness or insanity really are. Just words.

So we need to get rid of them.

And that orange, flaming eye through the bluish veil of mist and the fragile claws of night reaching for the white, disheveled clouds . . . Something dramatic was happening there, something strange. Over the woods themselves.

How can you say it, what do you call it, how can you find the words?

She looks again a few moments later—there's nothing there anymore. It's extinguished.

That's a good word—extinguished.

Extinguished.

She looks out a different window. A group of kids runs around the courtyard in the half-dusk and calls for a dog to follow them. It's always like that—always following them. Her daughter did it, too, step by step. Going somewhere. But she had so wanted to protect them. The dog and her daughter. And everyone else.

There's no way she can.

Fog settles over the yard.

Maybe she should call these kids inside? So they can smear their muddy fingers on the walls and steps, eat cookies in the dark of the room, at the foot of the bed. So they can squeal and dance among the pillows, secretly play with her lipstick and, one after the other, suddenly grow up.

Like corn kernels exploding high over the midday heat.

When kids grow up, they instantly distance themselves. They become continuous even though, frankly speaking, it seems like just five seconds ago they were nothing more than an orgasm.

There are a lot of little deaths in life. Though no one probably thinks of these fragmentations like that. So what are they called?

She doesn't know.

Kids glide through their childhoods and continue being continuous.

It's wrong. Like all the grownups who carry the many lives they've lived within themselves, continuing and continuing on.

She could call them in—like recruiting an army—pass out chocolate rations for survival and smile bitterly at them, rewarding them for their nerve to come inside with their muddy shoes. But the dog will probably drop ticks, fat like overripe grapes, and the kids will trample them and smear them over the floor. She doesn't have time to wash the floor tonight; she has to protect her idea. A kind of basic task, egotistic. She has to be with herself. So trivial! And what's more—what a sunset! The shouts of the kids in the courtyard. They live in an entirely different world, a world she knows nothing about. That world will blossom when hers wilts. Every moment, thousands of worlds simultaneously blossom and wilt. A moment of chaos in your head—God, when am I going to have time to wash THESE dishes?!

What time did he leave? It seems like it's been forever. But no, just a few hours. Maybe, if she were someone ELSE, she'd be able to take a nap in the middle of the day? . . .

Where are they calling that dog over to? Where will they wander off to, where will they go with their unkempt, tangled hair and frozen, red hands? Wherever it is, there'll definitely be some kind of danger: a marsh, quicksand, a quagmire, a steep bank of sweetly flowering, poisonous Daphne bushes or something else equally alluring... Maybe she should protect her daughter, call her in, keep her under her wing? Once upon a time those kids had been her daughter.

At one time she still entertained the hope that she'd be able to protect all of them.

From everything.

But no. It's not possible. She has to be with her own self tonight. In a completely grammatically incorrect sense. A small task, because the goal is small. She is nothing more to the history of the world than an ant is to Mont Blanc. That's why it would be best to go, bless the dog and the kids, gather them up, and feed them or something. But her goal is minute, and her suffering will be great, because he who puts others before him is happy—only she still puts herself first more and isn't even ashamed of it. She's come to enjoy withdrawing further and deeper into herself. And someday she'll have to pay for all of it.

This fog!

One time at the Central Market, a gypsy woman had told her fortune: "You'll start from zero many times over, it's a gift you have. But only to a certain extent."

Marking boundaries. Building a wall? No use—she doesn't have the skill. You can't start anything by force. It's just—I choose to believe. Again and again from the beginning. Ieva looks around carefully. If there had been anything left over, even a grain of sand, she could cultivate a pearl out of it.

She could keep it together.

Everything is scattered. Live half your life and realize that every-thing is scattered.

But at night she can feel there's a river. Not a single time in her life, not a single territory through which this river flows, isn't a part of the river itself. The heart of the river is somewhere in the distance—there, from where the river flows, or there, to where it flows.

While she washes dishes she suddenly grabs a pencil and writes on a paper towel—Oh, this fog! How she'll wind up paying for this sentence! Half of her unhappiness is her imagination and curiosity. She'll withdraw from life with each letter, paddle away from existence, until she'll no longer be able to pave a path back to the simple scene beyond the window. Farther and farther away—like a stream down a mountain. Like the Earth from the sun. She'll continue. She'll be far. And wide. She won't tell her daughter how much she misses her, because she won't know how to find the right words. She'll spend days hammering out the same passages, struggling to formulate love in short sentences on paper until others will simply accept it. She'll spend her entire life studying, but never learn how to write the word "sunset."

It's insane—where did it all go! It was just there, she thinks, look-ing out at the grey sky. And the courtyard is empty. They're all gone.

MONTA

SHE gets in late. Nobody visits this late—it's unacceptably late. *Extremely* late. It's already that time when early evening is being ushered out by the night. The twilight pulls your thoughts under—and once twilight sets in you can't start anything. Tendrils of darkness snake into your mind. It's too late to talk. Everything seems to have already settled into itself, so why waste words?

It's a good time to drink tea and sit quietly. That may be exactly why she chose to come over so late, so she wouldn't have to talk. So she could spend the night and take off in the morning. Visit mom— just a date circled on the calendar.

Ieva opens the door.

"Hi!"

"Hey."

A quick kiss on the cheek and then a step back. Maintain some distance. The air around Monta carries a lingering haze. She probably stopped for a quick smoke before heading up.

Ieva makes tea. Monta wanders around the apartment.

"Can I use the internet?"

"Of course."

She sits at the computer. Her hair is in dreads—tight braids, thick and prickly like a bristle brush and the color of darkness. Her angular shoulders hunched, her slender neck tense. It's like her daughter is surrounded by invisible spears, cactus needles. A teenager; not to be touched.

"Do you want tea?"

"Bring it here."

Ieva sighs. The hope that they could at least have tea at the table across from each other—even if in silence—bursts like a bubble. Ieva puts the teacup on the desk.

"Thanks."

The screen flickers in the half-light. The lives of others. Her daughter's messages—concerns, losses, gains—Ieva has no clue about any of them. A silver stud through Monta's eyebrow. Small hoops and a few safety pins line her ears, spiked leather bracelets hang around her thin wrists, and her eyes are outlined in black. She's checking her friends' profile updates on Draugiem.lv. She's inaccessible to her mother—simply offline.

"How are you?"

"Fine."

Monta shoots her a look that clearly says "leave me alone." Ieva goes back to the kitchen. After a while she calls out:

"Want to go to the theater next week? I have tickets."

"No."

A few minutes later:

"Do you want to come see me at work sometime? We're putting together a new movie—it's really interesting."

"No time."

"How's school?"

"Fine."

"Where do you work?"

"Sky City."

"What do you do there?"

"Work with snowboards."

"Do you snowboard?"

"You see any snow around here?"

"We could go to Switzerland."

"Thanks, but I've got stuff to do."

"What was your boyfriend's name—Tomass?"

"Yeah."

"How's he?"

"Fine. C'mon, Mom, not right now."

Ieva sighs.

"Hungry?"

"No, thanks."

Ieva turns on the television. Something she hasn't done in ages. But she has to pass the time somehow while Monta's online. While she's visiting.

For a long time, one sits in front of the computer, the other in front of the television. Ieva washes up and gets ready for bed. Suddenly, she gets an idea:

"I'll draw you a bath!"

"What d'you mean, bath? I have a shower at home."

But Ieva continues:

"A shower's a shower, and a bath's a bath. I'll draw you one right now. I've got this new bath oil. It'll be the best bath you've ever had."

And she gives the tap a hard turn, so the water gushes out. So she won't hear Monta's objections.

Soon the bath is ready. Ieva sprinkles some jasmine blossoms into the bubbles and lights the candles at the foot of the tub. She puts a white cotton shirt on the chair.

"It's ready, go ahead!"

Monta doesn't answer. Ieva changes into pajamas, gets into bed and intently watches the hallway through the open door.

The teenager sits at the computer for several more minutes, then gets up with a sigh and goes to the kitchen to wash her teacup. The splash of water, the clinking of dishes. She comes to the doorway, looks at her mother as if she's about to say something, then turns and goes into the adjacent room, where a bed has been made up for her. Ieva starts to think Monta will just go to sleep fully dressed.

But she doesn't. She goes to the bathroom, then comes back into the hallway. She looks at the computer, then at her mother. Then she goes back into the bathroom and shuts the door with a bang.

The sound of belts and snaps hitting the stone tile can be heard through the closed door; the ringing of metal and sound of leather. Then silence.

It seems like Monta is in the bathtub for at least an hour. Finally the bathroom door opens again and a figure dressed in a white shirt tiptoes into Ieva's room.

"You asleep? Thanks for the bath. G'night."

"Maybe you can sleep in here tonight!" Ieva calls out sharply—too quickly. Monta starts and turns to leave.

"No way!"

"Then at least come sit with me for a bit!" Ieva begs.

"No!"

Monta goes into the hallway, but doesn't turn the light out right away. She moves around the apartment like a cat, inspecting photographs and paintings, flipping through magazines. It's already long past midnight.

"Please, come here, sweetheart! Can't you just sit with me for a minute?" Ieva begs again.

"No!"

But after a few more minutes, Monta does come in. She takes a book from the shelf and puts it back, looks at the flowers on the windowsill, then finally drags herself over and sinks down onto the bed.

At first Ieva is afraid to move, as if some rare bird has just landed in the room. Then she frees a hand from under the blanket and reaches toward Monta. She can easily sense her daughter's warmth in the dark, her pale face and long shadows under her eyelashes, her smooth and youthful skin. Ieva puts her hand on Monta's shoulder. So thin, so fragile. She caresses the shoulder once. And then a second time. Monta says nothing, but her breathing is anxious and her heart thuds in her chest—the beating is easy to hear through the blanket. Ieva keeps caressing her daughter's shoulder. She keeps telling herself the caresses are both strong enough and calm enough, the type of touch used to tame timid horses. Wild horses are tamed with a different type of touch. Monta is incredibly timid, not at all wild. She stays still. Ieva puts into these caresses everything she can't say with words. They're together again, sharing the same warmth; as if Monta were still only the hint of a person inside Ieva, as if she were still that earlier version—the three-year-old daughter Ieva could take into her lap. The harshness has fallen away, like the snaps and spikes in the bathroom. The imposing black leather and studs are gone. The makeup is washed off, all the foreign, abrasive scents scrubbed away. Monta smells like a child. Ieva's child. Even the acrid smell of cigarettes is gone. She's all freshness and warmth.

Her child.

This moment starts, lingers, and passes. Monta knows when it needs to end—she moves away.

"G'night, Mom."

"Goodnight, sweetheart," Ieva replies gratefully.

The next morning they dress quickly and drink their tea in a hurry. They steal glances at one another.

Each day is completely different from the last, each day is a lifetime. And the night is something entirely different from the morning or afternoon. They represent numerous and varied thoughts.

Today is very matter-of-fact, and the morning is full of promises. Ieva puts some money on the table.

"For the apartment and for school."

"Thanks, Mom . . . Mom?"

Ieva listens—something important is coming. Monta's voice has changed.

"I might leave school. Tomass says it would be good to work abroad somewhere."

She hurriedly pulls on her dark jacket and yanks the hood over her head, maybe so she won't hear the answer, even though her own voice sounds unsure.

"Location isn't important. If you want to do the right thing, you can do that anywhere. If you want to screw up your life, you can do that anywhere, too."

Monta gets defensive.

"Who says I want to screw up my life?"

"So finish school and then go do whatever you want. You've only got a year left."

As she rushes out behind Monta, Ieva feels like she's tracking a fleeing animal. The thud of army boots as her daughter disappears around the next flight of stairs, and then again around the next one—Ieva feels she won't catch up to her, like she'll never catch up to her.

And yet there's the next turn and then the door, and then the kiss goodbye. Life gives you time to catch up.

"You know I love you," Ieva tells Monta.

Monta's answer is unexpected:

"I'm not sure if I believe you because you've never had time for me."

"You think? Things were different way back then, it's not who I really am. Here, take this and read it later. I found it last night."

Ieva has given her daughter a page from her sixth-grade Latvian language workbook. The text is marked up and corrected, barely legible. Clearly a rough draft.

"Assignment #96:

Happiness! Sweet, dear happiness! Where are you? Why do you visit so rarely? I want you to visit me more often. Come visit when I'm sad, come when I'm having a hard day. Come straight away, dear happiness! Happiness! I want you to visit the orphans and the children who have nothing to eat! They also need happiness. If you, happiness, would go visit these children, then their faces would be all joy and smiles. Go, dear friend, go to those people who don't have money, so they aren't sad. Put smiles on their faces and love in their hearts. Do you know, dear friend, that each person and living thing needs happiness—if only a little bit?"

COFFEE AND CIGARETTES

MONTA sits with a friend at a café. Sunlight washes uselessly over the mud-spattered windows. It's a cheap place right on the corner of the street, and whenever a tram rolls by it feels like its wide metal body scrapes against the café door.

Monta cries, smokes, and speaks:

"Jesus do I feel bad for him. You can't even imagine. I was four when he showed up in the apartment—Aksels must've found him on the street, still a puppy. I remember they put him in some kind of box under the kitchen table, but I'd always sneak in and take him out, then we'd race through all the rooms. He was so cute and smart. I've never seen another dog like that . . . And then Dad shot Aksels— Aksels was Mom's boyfriend and Dad basically shot him out of jealousy or something, I don't know, it's a long story. And right after that we moved in with this old woman, Faniija, over on Ģertrūdes Street. I don't know why, but Mom took us out walking all the time—you wouldn't believe how much we walked—the dog and I were always starving, and I remember Mom was having trouble keeping jobs, so she couldn't even afford to send me to kindergarten. I was only five or six, and all we did was walk, all three of us. And I was so hungry. Along train tracks, bridges. It was crazy—all over Riga. We'd take a tram to some suburb or just wander through the city on foot. And you get so hungry walking around like that. Mom would stop to buy a small chunk of cheese for the dog and a bread roll for me, and we'd be on our way again. Five minutes later it's like the bread never happened . . . She was restless or something back then. I remember she'd carry me on her back when I got tired—I'd fall asleep, get some rest, and she'd just keep carrying me. Then she left for school in Moscow and said she didn't take us with her because that city was pure stress, but I wouldn't have gone with her anyway. I had a babysitter and my grandma Lūcija—Jesus, it's horrible to say, but if Mom died I wouldn't cry like if my grandma died. I swear to God. I was around ten when I first understood people die, and the first thing I realized was that my grandma would die someday, too—and I just burst into tears. I could cry again now just thinking about it. My grandma has been amazing, she's done everything she can for me. Mom visited often, but I just couldn't bring myself to really talk to her. I've never been able to and know for a fact I never will. There was this one time she yelled at me, I don't remember what for, probably something stupid, but later I went to her room and asked 'Are you mad at me? Do you think I'm worthless?' Because that's how I felt about myself then. And I hoped that she'd get up, hug me, and say 'No, I'm not mad at you, sweetheart, and that's God's honest truth.' And I never thought she'd reject me. But all she said was, 'No—how many times do I have to say it?' I got stubborn all of a sudden and stayed put, just stood in the doorway and kept repeating 'Why are you mad at me?' And finally she said, 'Just leave me alone for half an hour.' You can't imagine how I felt. We were all we had in the world, and that's how she reacts! I don't know, maybe I'd just pissed her off. That wasn't the first time it had happened, but after that there was definitely a sense of finality. I thought, 'Fuck, I could go forever without talking to you if I needed.' I didn't want to trust her anymore, I couldn't laugh with her or anything. I felt like at any second I'd be told to just shut up. After that time I went to sleep on the mattress next to the dog. She came over later and kissed me on the head, but then left me alone. Maybe she was tired of fighting with me. Maybe because she'd been telling me since I was little, 'Live your own life, I won't force anything on you. If you want to sleep next to the dog, that's your choice.' But she didn't consider that I might be lying there crying. Alright, fine, if she left me alone it was to leave me alone. Fine. After she got back from Moscow she acted like she was in heat. Always going out at night. She'd say, 'Go to bed! I'll be back in the morning.' But I couldn't sleep, just sort of doze until she'd get back around 4 A.M.—happy and smelling sweet. It seemed like she went through guys like she was flipping through the pages of a magazine. And all the massive amounts of drinking with friends—directors and actors—at the time I thought she was out of control, but I guess it also kind of made sense, and at least there was always someone around. And she's quiet by nature. She can go days without saying a word, just thinking about something. Then the next day she'll laugh like crazy and go wild, running barefoot through puddles downtown. And what always pissed me off the most is that she only ever talked to me about serious things in public when there were the most people around. We'd be in the mall or theater and she'd suddenly think of something and start lecturing me. Discussing aspects of *my* life. And at the top of her voice, like it was just the two of us. I distanced myself from her. Later I dropped out of high school. That set things in motion. I went to night school so I could get a job. Then I got my first boyfriend and we rented an apartment together. Of course I took the dog with me. Then last year the boyfriend left me. I took it really badly, it just destroyed me. It was right during spring finals week—I wanted to kill myself. And of course I can't eat anything when I'm depressed. In one month I lost sixteen kilograms. Can you imagine? Sixteen! Coffee and cigarettes in the morning, alcohol and sleeping pills at night. Just the two of us, me and the dog. Mom didn't know my boyfriend had left me, I just

told her she couldn't come visit. There was no reason to. I could go
see her if need be. She doesn't have any time anyway. Then Tomass
came along—last summer. That's how it goes with guys. Tomass is
great, I can't complain. But your first love is your first love, right?
I feel like the trouble always starts with the second guy—after that
things just get out of hand. There's the third guy, then the fourth. My
grandma once said, 'Life can give you one, or many.' Whatever, it'll
be fine. But I'll never forgive Mom for what happened with Dad. He's
sitting in prison, and she won't go anywhere near him. I think they're
even still legally married. My mom says it's her life. She doesn't talk
about it with anyone. Yeah, it's her life, but he's my dad. She won't let
me go visit him. Someday I will. Right now I'm still kind of freaked
out by the idea. Not of prison, but of my dad. Can you imagine?
He's basically a stranger. And what would we talk about? He's seen so
little in his lifetime, if you think about it—he grew up, got married,
shot Aksels. And that's it. Locked away in prison for years and years.
That's not a life. So what would we talk about? But the dog, he got
older and died. The vet came over this morning and had to put him
down. Then Tomass and I buried the dog down by the lake. That
dog lived for fourteen years, easy. That's pretty much my whole life."

THE ATTACK

AN ATTACK ON PLACES/THINGS,
OR THE SACRED RESOURCES

IEVA does everything with drive. Even life.

Because places and things are so passionless. "Created only for ourselves—no, not even for ourselves, but for some inexplicable need," as writer Matīss Kaudzīte once put it. And it takes time for you to understand what they mean to you. A morning on which you stand with your face to the sun in a glittering corner of a Riga microregion, the blowing wind, and the scent of crushed grass on a soccer field. You are alive and young. A night out with friends on the granite steps by the river. Ships and seagulls bob in the current. You are happy. A moment with your mother as she puts a cool hand to your forehead when you curl into the couch next to her and cry as meekly as a kitten, you're thirty or more years old, but it hurts so much, Mommy! Her cool hand on your forehead immediately melts the heartache. In your past remain the bend in the road, the tram tracks, a cloud of dust, and your time.

The first time Ieva travels to Milan for some European conference, she spends her free time wandering the wide, overgrown boulevards, listening to Austrian journalist Michael Schulter's monologue:

"And the main thing that left Western society speechless when the Iron Curtain fell was that there was nothing behind it! You have nothing! Everyone thought you'd all pull out these masterpieces from hidden drawers, just like the masterpieces of the people who were convicted as dissidents, driven out, or who emigrated by choice. You had those kinds of huge works, true, but it turned out you could count on one hand the exceptions in the vast majority that remained immobile and indifferent. How do you judge that? Where are the sacred resources of Eastern Europe? Maybe there aren't any at all?"

Ieva looks into his thin face and sharp eyes, which are partially obscured by his round glasses—in the stark daylight their lenses shine like scrying crystals—and she feels she has no opinion. She is the very immovable mass Michael is talking about.

And suddenly, without warning, a scene from her memory washes over her—Gran's footprints in the roadside sand, butter so yellow it's as if the cows were fed nothing but marigolds.

Why this memory? She shrugs. Michael doesn't get an answer.

But when the plane from Copenhagen breaks through the layer of clouds over the Baltic Sea and resurfaces over the eastern coast, Ieva glues herself to the round window. Piltene—a dark dot on the map. Mordanga—a fleck. The Venta and Lielupe Rivers—golden hairs. The absurdly tiny fir trees—thick combs with an occasional deer among them. What would they all be without the heat coursing through Ieva's veins? Piles of wood people call homes? Water? Pine forests? They're self-explanatory. Coldness, foreignness.

For some reason this morning, Ieva has the strong feeling that Gran isn't dead. That she's living with Roberts in their seaside cottage. Ieva borrows a car from friends to drive out for a visit. More than ever, more than a child is capable of, she believes it's possible to drive straight into the past. That there's an island somewhere where everything that once was is alive and well, where it's possible to go and see your past self draining a cup of milk at the wax-cloth covered table. Why not, if the taste of milk from your childhood is still on your tongue. The cows were milked early when the sun first rose, then the milk poured into an enameled, metal can, covered with the white saucer with the chipped, gold rim, then set in the front hall on a stone block. Outside a hot summer day lights up, covered with a dewy, sun-kissed glaze. There's no refrigerator at home. One cup of milk has already been poured and set on the table for you, the little one, live-culture milk at its natural temperature with a thin, sweet layer of yellow cream settling on the surface. As you start to drink it three small, brown pancakes are placed in front of you, and then the cow pokes its head through the open kitchen window. Gran places a "Selga" brand cookie on the cow's long, narrow tongue, and it disappears like fine dust on a wet grindstone. Oh, Ieva knows about this spectacle, the cow's tongue—lithe and scratchy, like an incredibly strong tentacle that almost always tries to pull in Ieva's little hand, tear off a hair ribbon, or drool all over her apron. As she's watching the cow, Ieva knocks her milk over with her elbow. "That's enough!" Gran scolds the cow, not Ieva, and pushes its darkish blue head outside and closes the narrow blinds. The cow heads toward the sea and Ieva catches up to it halfway. The morning has begun.

It could be that nothing has happened yet—it's still fall. The stove is lit. The big water kettle hisses. Gran takes a cast iron pan with a mustard-marinated roast out of the oven and goes to the pantry to get the apple wine. Ice blows in from the front hall. A white dog with a black head sleeps on the edge of the well-worn armchair, until it slides off and lands with a rustle into the pile of onions covering the floor like a thick rug all the way to the window. There's a porcelain sugar bowl on the table with one handle missing and a sprig of lingonberries painted on its side. And a silver spoon placed in raw cane sugar.

Later, the bed will be made for you in the other room, a scratchy linen sheet put down and a rag quilt on top, heavy as a person. You'll shiver for more than ten minutes in the freezing bed as you wait for it to warm up. The light will go out, you'll talk about this and that. Maybe you'll get a bedtime story, or a story from Gran's childhood. You'll warm up as you stare at the low, whitewashed ceiling beams. And the sleep you finally slip into will be a calm and welcoming return to a world that never ends.

You'll wake up around midnight, the heat of the inglenook against your cheek already cooled to a lukewarm breath. The scratching of mice behind the peeling wallpaper, the resin-like light of the moon . . . thoughts of nothing. A complete sinking into the heart of the night.

These, Michael, are my sacred resources. Behold, a sugar bowl, a silver spoon, a quilt as heavy as a person. Maybe they'll outlast us. But they'll never again live the life that I see through my eyes. Come, Michael, and look into the drawer of Eastern Europe.

KURZEME

THE rain has been coming down hard all night. Puddles form on the ice.

Wind blows the fog toward Riga. Ieva keeps on driving. After years and years she's gotten up the courage to drive out to the Zari house.

The smells of the Kurzeme region. Is it sentimentality that comes with age? Back then she had no idea what destiny had in store for her, a nineteen-year old waiting at the bus stop.

The Zari house. Andrejs's parents live there now. Rooms. Familiar smells. After so much time spent in lifeless offices and air conditioning where the atmosphere is dead—here it's fragrant. Curtains, the door, steps. Everything has a history, even the paint on the walls. The tears well up from the smells alone. Memories swim before her eyes, ghosts. Ieva standing in the big room with an iron in her hand just after Monta had been born, ironing tiny clothes.

Monta once told her about a memory she'd had of summers at the Zari house: "There's the road, the sun is shining, the wind blowing, and me and the dog." She'd said it with such happiness in her voice. What can a two-year-old possibly remember? But, see, she remembers.

Oh, sentimentality. But Kurzeme has a certain *something*. Rugged land. Wind from the sea. She's so lucky that destiny bestowed these things upon her.

Andrejs's father is napping in the cool of his room upstairs and cries when he sees her. He grows airier every year, like some kind of butterfly. And more gentle. He used to be tough as a rock. He ruled over everything—animals and people. Was the final word for the women, the livestock, the men. Ieva can't stand it. He's lighter. Soon the wind will blow him away like dust. She can't stand it. It makes her want to cry. Scream. But there's no point. There are no tragedies in Kurzeme. Everything here is self-explanatory. The tears stream like sap from birch trees in spring. There's no need to scream; this suffering is imagined. She has to say her goodbyes and go on with her life.

A young woman with large, naked breasts lies on the wide bed in the central room, nursing a baby. A hundred thoughts rush through Ieva when she looks at the baby. About Andrejs's father, sitting in the next room waiting to be blown away by the wind. About Andrejs's grandmother, still large and heavy in her grandson's absence, but whose eyes are as teary as all the rest, who squeezes Ieva's hand as she looks up at her and asks—what reason do I have to stay here? And she knows the answer already. To stay for the sake of staying. To live for the sake of living. To be happy for the sake of being happy. Even though just once she'd like to hear: Because you're needed. We all need you. Hang on until the end. In this network of hands and hearts. This network of touches and glances.

Smells and a brilliant sun. Andrejs's mother walks her out—they get in the car and drive over hills and muddy roads. They both cry. They both hide their eyes and know full well that they can't hide them. The sun betrays them. Skin, pores, wrinkles, wet eyelashes, bright eyes and pitch-black pupils like moving mirrors, wetness smeared across temples and outside over the fields—it glistens. They have to part ways. Ieva is ready to accept even a single word laced with reproach, but it doesn't come. Mothers are smart. They have to part on good terms. Andrejs's mother stays on the hill, wipes her eyes with her handkerchief and heads back. Goes her separate way. Ieva honks the horn a few times in farewell.

From the depths someone whispers: All is well. The seaside villages are dipped in the red March sun as it sets. Ieva loves Kurzeme. She can smell it. It nourishes her.

THE CROSSROADS

AKSELS

HE invites me to meet up with him.

We drink our morning tea on the terrace by the estuary. Next to us is another never-ending meeting—where the river flows into the calm sea. We drink strong, yellow tea that makes the blood in our temples sing like violins. We're alone, with the exception of a few birds flitting about by our feet.

The sun is already high in the sky, but the clammy cold of last night still hangs in the air. Dew glints on some of the stone tables. Flies rest motionless on the banisters, and the granite floor is still covered in the layer of sand blown onto it overnight. The server reclines in a folding chair he's put out in the sun, and smokes his first cigarette of the day while reading the paper. Now and then he pushes a hand back through his hair. The smoke that trails thinly up from his cigarette is carefree and winding, freely floating off into the great blue. I feel the structure of this city slowly course through me, saturating the cells of my body with its light.

I start to distinguish between the smells that hide shyly in gardens and those that aggressively rush in from the levee. I can visualize the shadow the black church steeple casts onto the central square, and how it always trips up the paperboy as he runs by with a newspaper bundle in his arms. I realize: if I lived in this city permanently, I'd

158

have to huddle under a blanket with a mug of tea in the middle of the day just to fight off the chills from the persistent blue and razor-sharp cold of the sea.

"More tea please," I say to Aksels, and in the moment the tea slowly pours from the teapot into my cup, a whirlwind of clarity rises up inside me so strongly that my chest tingles, almost like when you step up to the very edge of a cliff. I suddenly know that the dead come back to life and how they do it. I know how the living come back dead. I know what it's like to be a bird, a dog, and a spider, I oversee everything in this exact moment of time, a few seconds that last an eternity. The wind blows my hair across my bare shoulders and it's a loving caress. The city looks on with seeing eyes. I no longer have to count on the rare handouts from friends. From here on out, every new morning, every stranger will be a friend and an embrace—joyful and dramatic. We are all trapped in life.

The contour of the sea is wrapped in a haze. I can fly. And I can not fly, there's no difference anymore. There's no need to separate these concepts.

"Such a clear morning," I say to Aksels.

Someone's feeding seagulls from a barge and the water looks like goose bumps. The breeze surrounds us. Reflections dance on the surface of the tea.

"Like the one before you died," I say.

"Yeah."

"Do you think I described it well enough?"

I can tell he doesn't want to talk, just look out onto the horizon. He doesn't see any point in talking things out. But there's an excitement eating away at me like before a long-awaited vacation. I ask and ask. And finally he starts to talk. He tells me about what I haven't written.

Once he and Ieva had talked about making a life together, about moving into a house, about how they could someday actually live— with everything living entails—with tea in the morning, dinners, flowers on the windowsills, and kids. They'd been walking along the dirt road with the birds of summer singing around them. Ieva had gotten pebbles stuck in her sandals.

"The roof is leaking and one of the corners of the stove is broken," Ieva had said. "Where'll we start?"

This daily complexity surrounding a simple road.

"Let's make a deal—we'll live once we're thirty, but not until then," Aksels had answered.

"Life is too long for a single happy life," he says now. "Life always consists of many lives."

Back then Ieva had nodded and thrown her sandals with a whoop into the green fields. So long, pebbles! They both still had ten years to that looming thirty—ten years was a lifetime. They seemed a perpetual cycle of euphoric days and nights without an end in sight; an unbroken happiness.

We'll live after that. This terrifying phantom at the end of it all. After that.

"We believed that 'after that' would never come," Aksels says.

And it never did.

Aksels died. Ieva, on the other hand, has never loved life enough to want to live—to actually live. It's her own fault. You need to immerse yourself in life like sinking your hands into the earth, you need to concentrate. Sprout roots. Break a sweat to earn a vacation. Nothing ever comes easy, Ieva's Gran used to say. Yes, nothing ever comes easy.

"Why do people accept all these ridiculous rules as self-explanatory—only because they're subject to them?" Aksels asks.

"I don't know, I'm too lazy to look into it," I answer. "And it doesn't interest me. It's boring."

Ieva was the same way. She lived without living, and that's her weakness. She was a bird picking at crumbs with wise ignorance. Morsels of sun.

"But if you really think about it," I say, "the only reason we're sitting here is because she's remembering you right at this moment."

To a random observer this could look to be a strange kind of celebration—the sea, the morning, and seagulls. And two people sitting next to one another in silence. A little over ten minutes while drinking tea. To both of us, these minutes are the entirety of Aksels's life.

Aksels rests his chin in his hand and looks at me thoughtfully. He's stayed young. Beautiful, welcoming, and as cool as ice. My face already shows signs of aging. For a second I think about how different we are, but only for a second. All I want to do is turn my hands palms-up toward the sun and soak up this moment. To unfurl the flowers, shake out the pollen, let out the buds. Be like a sponge and absorb the impossible—the absence of time. With the scent of seaweed and the feel of another person's gaze.

I ask flat out:

"What do you think? Is a person given only one love in their lifetime, or several?"

"What's love?" he asks.

What's love? The hot hand of the sun slides heavily down the back of my neck. The wind whips the shorter hairs at my temples. This world is my home. Here I choose a person who will observe me for many days and nights—is that love? I'm tired. Happy. Then . . . sad. With disheveled features, ugly, and content. Young. Middle-aged. And old. And someone wants to observe me. Even like this. As everything. Forever. Love. Maybe that's an observation?

"Well . . . in spite of it all, we always find a way in life to be together for a few moments," I say.

"Destiny," Aksels jokes.

"The encyclopedia of life."

"The abridged version."

"Of pictures."

"For kids."

"What's the point of it all?"

"Nothing," I laugh. "Insomnia and lack of appetite. Movies and books."

"A good metabolism."

"Metabolism, of course. And that's a lot. I don't know about other worlds, but this planet only has one criterion—life."

After that I ask:

"Aksels, can art be a cookbook? The living teaching the living is like the blind leading the blind."

"Eh, that's not true—if the living weren't able to give the living any advice, there'd be a lot more dead people."

Aksels smoothes his blonde hair with his hands, then stretches. His beautiful arms cut into the sky like lightning.

"Thanks for the tea," he teases, feeling his pockets. He puts on his sunglasses; I'm clearly and starkly reflected in their black lenses. "I've got to go do my things."

"Of course."

He leaves, and in that moment the sun over the sea becomes slightly overcast. The sky grows muggy, as if someone has breathed onto a blue mirror.

Your absence. We're strong; we have to unravel it all piece by piece. Take care.

THE PRICE OF MEETING

IEVA'S TREE

THESE days Ieva spends a lot of time wandering the train tracks.

The tracks wind throughout Riga. Ieva likes the spots where they come together in thick clusters—by the Daugava Stadium, by the Matīss Prison, under the Gaisa Bridge. And she likes the spots where narrow, rusted tracks lead to nowhere. Where the buildings are falling apart, the factories are shut down, and the railway ties are separated by fields. There are a lot of places in Riga that look like World War II just ended.

Ieva likes them and isn't afraid.

She wanders.

It's a habit characteristic of living dangerously.

She has a dog and a child, and often gets into trouble with those train tracks. Because she takes the dog and her daughter with her when she goes walking. Her brother says no smart woman would do that. But Ieva isn't a smart woman, that's the thing. She's not even a woman yet. She's like a blind child with a seeing-eye kid and dog.

A blind child feeling around for a way out.

She likes to roam through desolation, where the city drops away—ditches, marshland, trenches, and construction sites. The outer limits. Where there are lakes like eyes and rivers like veins. Where the flesh of the earth is as thick as a fox's coat—rust colored reeds and white splinters. Her daughter snaps reeds in half. The dog sniffs at something. Ieva watches the current. Their trio makes her think of bird watchers, or geologists in the desert. No one's in a hurry.

They move as slowly as clouds that are seeing this world for the first time and don't understand its hierarchy, can't grasp what the most important things here are, what they should pay attention to.

Ieva wanders and doesn't think; she hopes that, while she wanders, her thoughts sit in a room somewhere in her head and patch the shreds of her life back together stitch by stitch. While her thoughts are busy doing this, she wanders.

And someday her thoughts, those seamstresses, will wake her and present her with a new suit—her fixed life. Then she'll finally settle down and stop wandering.

On their way back downtown, Ieva, her daughter, and the dog cross the iron bridge over the canal. So they don't have to take the boring route to the Vidzeme highway. The water churns far below the beams, and her daughter throws pebbles into it.

At that moment a train crawls out of the woods just outside the city. They're right in the middle of the bridge when the conductor sounds the horn. Ieva looks back. There's no place to run. Her daughter is too young and the dog clueless—they won't know how to flatten themselves against the rail for the train to pass.

Ieva doesn't remember much more after that. She hoists her daughter under one arm, grabs the dog by its scruff and gallops toward the end of the bridge, leaps over the beams. They make it.

Then all three of them sink into the grass on the embankment. Her daughter reaches out to break off the tip of a reed. The dog, a little offended, licks the fur on its back.

As the train rushes past, its wind tears at her hair and clothes. Her thundering heart settles only once the train is out of sight.

Idiot! Who are you to cross over that bottomless pit and drag others along with you? Where's your lighthouse, your beacon?

It's died out.

Ieva rents a room on Ģertrūdes Street in the apartment of an old woman; a room with a view of absolutely nothing.

What is nothing? The airless shaft of the courtyard and the sagging windows of the adjacent building. A few clotheslines crisscross the sky. By turning a crank, you can raise your laundry up there, into the sun. And at night you reel it back into the dusk—dry, lightly cured by smog and the smell of car exhaust.

Now and then a man's naked white ass comes into view in the brown frame of the window to the left of the central stairwell.

So is that something?

It reminds her more of nothing.

And Ieva's room doesn't have any luxuries like a clothesline with a crank. The bathroom is in the hallway. Her daughter pees in the sink. Some nights she gets the urge to do the same, but overcomes it.

The dog stands with its front paws on the windowsill between the flowerpots and freezes like sorrow in frost. He watches the birds.

The birds are crows. So are crows birds?

It reminds her more of nothing.

Ieva talks into a cellphone. Her hair is cut short. A lean, boyish face. She looks out the window at the once ornate, but now run down balconies of the building across the courtyard.

As she listens to the voice on the other end, she takes a dark violet men's dress shirt from the back of the chair. The shirt has pale red stripes. She puts the phone down on the bed for a second. Presses the shirt to her chest and looks into the mirror on the wall.

She shakes her head as if she doubts her reflection. Then she picks

up the phone and puts it back to her ear. There's nothing but a disapproving silence. Then a voice firmly says:

"But you're not even listening!"

Ieva says:

"Stop, Mom, I'm listening. I know it all. It'll be fine."

Her voice is carefree, but her face forms a painful expression as
the last words leave her mouth. As if she were screaming in despair,
howling without a sound.

"Stop," Ieva says into the phone. Please, God, so her mother won't
pick up on it. So no one finds out about this facial expression. A non-
expression of a non-creature. A living face of a living thing. It's not
what she is. This desperate plummet in an anti-gravity room.

Phones are a wonderful thing—communication without a face. All
you have to do is calmly say the words "it'll be fine, Mom," and you'll
believe it yourself. The tension in your mouth fades; only the veins at
your temples throb for a long time after, like the adrenaline rush after
committing a crime. Emotions are supposedly closely connected to
mimicry. Relax the muscles in your face and the rest of you relaxes as
well. The only downfall is that mimicry, in turn, is closely connected
to mimicry.

Pretending. But how else can she adjust to the rat race beyond
the window? Nature is fascinated by Ieva's species—humans. May
there be the continual births of girls and boys, a balance—half and
half, may they procreate, and may they die when the time comes. But
nature has no interest in people as individuals. It's up to each person
separately to determine how he spends his time here.

The relaxation of facial muscles is enough for Ieva.

But the eyes? When she relaxes them her eyes betray her in the
tenth of a second and fill with tears. She tips her head back as if her
eyes were two dark, glass bowls filled to the brims, and she has to
take them somewhere.

Take them to safety.

She's successful. Doesn't spill a drop. The moisture slowly re-absorbs into the inner corners of her eyes. It's horrible, tell me, my dears, where am I? On the blade of a knife, on the cusp, in a foreign territory? Something could happen at any moment. It scares her to think she could one day start screaming with sound. And somewhere where it would be completely inappropriate.

Ieva returns to the conversation. Resurfaces from her inner silence with the phone to her ear.

Her mother is saying:

"What others want, he does. No pretenses, and that's the problem. Some people can walk that fine line without crossing it, you know? But he's a criminal element. I studied his astrological chart, his Moon is in Leo, what can you do."

Silence.

Ieva sits on the bed and focuses on the worn paint of the floor. The dog comes over to her and rests its head on her knees. She pets him mechanically.

"You're not listening again," her mother says after a pause.

"I am, Mom, but . . ."

"He's that type. Sitting in prison only because prison is like death."

Ieva asks:

"When will he be free of me?"

"He'll be free of you once he learns to love life. It could happen one day. Sometimes it's important to just live for that day."

Ieva thinks for a moment.

"And when will I be free of him?"

"When your mind frees itself from him. Did you do what I taught you last time?"

"No," Ieva lies.

"Well! How can I help you when you won't even try? I can't do it for you. On the night of a full moon, sit at a table, light a candle, tie a red thread around it, hold the ends in one hand, then cut the thread with scissors and wish him all the best. Wish him good health, freedom, and happiness—but without you! And for yourself, wish for your mind to free itself from him. You'll see, you'll feel better. The moon can do amazing things."

Ieva remembers the night the full moon floated large and dull as a ghost ship through Fanija's kitchen window, melting the curtains with its icy glow. The white windowsill and lace curtains shone in the dark. Everything the moonlight touched turned black and white, even the candle she had lit, the red thread, and Ieva herself. She murmured a prayer and cut the thread. The two ends remained in her fingers.

What small results, she had thought.

All these years with Andrejs.

And two thread ends in her hand.

It didn't feel better.

"Fine, Mom, I'll do what you say. I just have to wait for the next full moon. But today I want to drop Monta and Dārcis off at your place."

"You're going to go see him?"

"Yes."

"Idiot. He's using you—when'll you finally get it?"

"Thanks for the kind words. Bye!"

Ieva cuts the conversation short and throws the phone onto the bed.

She takes off her T-shirt. Looks at her breasts in the mirror. Nothing wrong with them.

Her face still looks good, too. When we're young our faces are like uncharted maps—smooth, flat. As they age they acquire Bermuda Triangles, underwater territories, landslides, avalanches. Her mom's face doesn't show signs of wear, or stress, because she never blames herself for things. But Ieva will definitely get wrinkles, 100%. Ieva is a single, black splotch. She's sick of it, but what can you do? She's got that kind of personality. Everything she does is a result of inspiration, nothing else. She works in an office supply store, and the other saleswomen are always surprised at how much of what she does comes from inspiration alone. "Some days you're so creative, but others you're totally out of it," says Gunta. Gunta is young, pretty, and—most importantly—always cheerful. Cheerful people are never out of it, and it's a good thing if you meet someone like that in your lifetime. When everyone else has a heart full of sorrow and complaints.

Ieva puts on the violet dress shirt. She's also young and pretty, so what. Sometimes it kills her.

A disheveled head of hair emerges from under the pile of blankets on the bed.

"G'morning," Monta says. "Where are you going?"

"We're going to Grandma's because Mommy is going to go see your father. Time to get up and brush your teeth."

Monta runs to the window and hugs the dog, who is once again frozen in vigilance.

"Dārcis is coming to Grandma's?"

"Of course! Put his collar on."

The south-facing side. Pigeons scrabble on the outer windowsill of the small, sunny room.

Their landlady Fanija sits on the edge of the bed among pillows covered in crocheted slips. She looks like an amber mummy, in her white blouse and the same wavy grey hairstyle actress Zarah Leander wore in her prime. Fanija looks at the peeling floor paint with great interest and occasionally pokes at it with her cane.

She says to Ieva:

"Come look at my country house, Ieva—here and here. And there, too. And this one here, look, an old man with an upturned nose, two white dogs . . . and this one's a map of Latvia. Where are you headed, Ieva? That shirt looks good on you, it's a nice men's dress shirt, isn't it? You don't see that much these days, women going with this kind of extravagant style, but it really is an extravagance, isn't it, Ieva? What's more—winners aren't judged. Can I call you Eva? Y'know, I was once lucky enough to fall in love with a boy a lot like you . . . yes . . . it was in Paris in '37; my mother was an actress in Baty's theater . . . *Theatre Montparnasse* . . . That won't mean anything to you, but if you'd seen the old façade of the Montparnasse theater, believe me, it would change your life... Baty was staging Flaubert's *Madame Bovary* . . . It was a good show. They played pieces from *Lucia di Lammermoor*. Donizetti . . . My mother was one of the four beauties who voiced poor Emma Bovary's thoughts . . . like a Greek chorus. The boy played Leon—he was a very beautiful man, and how he sang! I was seventeen, he was my first love. I almost went insane, but I couldn't show it . . . When Emma shouted 'love is not better than marriage' on stage, I always started to cry. She stood in a cheap and dirty hotel room and screamed—love is not better than marriage! Imagine how awful it was, Ieva! . . . I think his name was Charles, the boy. He came to our place for lunch."

Fanija sinks into her thoughts. Ieva waits. Until Fanija finally stirs, like she's wriggling out of a bog of memories.

"You're not in the least bit similar to him, but there's still something . . . a gesture . . . a look, when you come in."

Ieva looks at the veins on Fanija's hands. Ieva doesn't have time to wait.

She says:

"I want to pay in advance."

Fanija looks at her blankly. Old people can sometimes suddenly flare out mid-sentence—like a candle that's been tipped over. Ieva puts her money on the table.

"For the room."

Fanija nods, but Ieva doesn't know what for. She backs up toward the door.

"I'm going now. I'll be back tomorrow. I'm going to visit my husband."

As she reaches the door, Fanija speaks, surprising her.

"Don't take this the wrong way, Ieva, I find you incredibly nice. Just remember to always put the bathroom key back in its place. I don't have a spare."

Ieva, Monta, and Dārcis stand in the front hallway of the apartment. Monta leans against the wall and holds Dārcis by his collar. Ieva puts on the necklace Andrejs gave her—the Virgin Mary hanging from a woven cord. We're all set to go with our collars on, Ieva thinks.

"Let's go!"

And they go.

She drops her daughter and the dog off at Pērnavas Street, where Monta is quick to fish her mother's white guinea pig from its sand-filled aquarium and drop it on the ground—much to Dārcis's barking delight and the guinea pig's mortal fear. Ieva listens through her mother's complaints and suggestions, then heads back into the street after a wash of goodbye kisses from Monta. She puts on her headphones and turns on her CD player, listens to Laurie Anderson's album "Bright Red."

> *Remember me is all I ask*
> *And if remembered be a task forget me.*
> *This long thin line. This long thin line.*
> *This long thin line. This tightrope made of sound.*

This music is like a frosty glaze forming over an oppressive heat. Over life's distorted faces, broken-down by the black ice of passion, over the fire-filled bodies, markets, sales, weddings, births, and funerals. The music climbs over the dusty streets and freezes these things in moments, echoes, reflections. It fits in perfectly with Ieva's own Ice Age.

She turns the volume up as far as it will go and shrinks into a corner of her world. Her mother just told her, "Read your life like a book, and with pleasure! It's your privilege and yours alone." Ieva skips ahead few tracks and watches as the city shifts in crystalline arcs.

All of these faces, her species. Ieva is able to participate when the music plays, to once again breathe in the air so many others have breathed for millions of years.

Watch your life as if it's a movie—with an aching.

You had that rusty old car
And me I had nothing better to do.
You picked me up. We hit the road.
Baby me and you.

We shot out of town
Drivin' fast and hard
Leaving our greasy skid marks
In people's back yards.
We were goin' nowhere.
Just driving around.
We were goin' in circles.
And me I was just hanging on.

In the Central Market Ieva breaks through the hundred-headed mass and thinks about Monta. Her soft, silk-like skin, her clear eyes, the warmth so newly ignited in her heart! The way she looks along at the road ahead.

Stay with Grandma, be good, don't give Grandma any trouble! Mommy's going to go see your father. To visit.

For now Monta doesn't have any questions. It's what has to be done, obviously the entire world works like this. Mommy has to go see Daddy, who Monta doesn't remember. She doesn't know where he lives; all she knows is that she has to wait for him to come home. A priori love. She has to wait for Daddy like she has to wait for Santa Claus. But even Santa comes around more often—once a year.

Now and then Monta throws out a question that's like a slap in the face—she asks Ieva about Aksels. She still remembers Aksels.

Where's Ocela?

Ocela's in Heaven.

There's no use waiting for Ocela.

Ieva fills her prison-visiting bag with things from the Central Market. Black tea, the simplest kind, loose, granulated if possible. Bacon. She spends a lot of time looking at the hanging hunks of pig meat at the stand; she'll miss the train if she doesn't hurry. But she has to hope the bacon will be the real thing, smoked in alderwood, not chemically dyed brown. An entire kilogram of onions. Herbs, cheese, mineral water. Candy—thin, chocolate-filled wafers coated with a sugary glaze.

And the most important thing—cartons of cigarettes. She won't buy them at the store, but at the market pavilion at the intersection where they're cheaper. Where under-the-table merchants with raw and weathered faces shout into the crowd: *Spirt, vodka, sigareti!* Ieva gives one of them twenty lats, takes the cigarettes, and waits for her change. The man turns his back to her, as if she didn't even exist.

When he starts to walk away, Ieva grabs his sleeve.

"What do you want, lady?"

"Ten lats."

"You nuts?"

The man swears and shakes Ieva off, but as he turns to leave his eyes flick to the opening of her shirt above her breasts.

Ieva automatically brings her fingers to her chest.

The tin pendant Andrejs had given her, the Virgin Mary on a woven piece of string. Warm from her body heat. The merchant most likely has a similar one around his neck—and if he doesn't, then someone he knows definitely does. A pendant made in prison. A class marker.

The man mumbles something, gives Ieva her ten lats, and then they're parted by the flow of marketgoers. You don't touch your own. Don't screw over your own. Who were you planning on cheating? One of your kind? Have you completely lost it?

Eagle bites the weasel.
Weasel bites back.
They fly up to nowhere.
Weasel keeps hangin' on.
Together forever.
And me? I'm goin' in circles.
And if I open my mouth now
I'll fall to the ground.

Ieva pushes her way out of the pavilion. The sweat-drenched stench makes her dizzy, nauseated. She closes her eyes and breathes deeply through her mouth. Beads of sweat form at her temples.

She just has to get through it.

Summer has finally relaxed the muscles of its face.

If it rains, it's torrential, sudden and unruly. If it's sunny, the light is open and raw. The fields are cleared and filled with scavenging birds and dust clouds.

Ieva settles in the diesel train with her bag like she's planning on being there for life. For four hours she stares out the window, as if she could absorb the future through her pupils from the mute lips of the scenery outside.

The moon can do amazing things, her mother had said.

Ieva remembers the last time she visited Andrejs.

He'd given her his shirt.

Ieva remembers herself in the prison's hotel room, in front of a female guard. They stand face to face, both silent and with feet slightly spread apart.

Ieva unbuttons her dress.

For a moment their eyes meet. The female guard looks down. She puts her cool hands on Ieva's shoulders, then slides her fingers down over Ieva's collarbone, around her bra, and down her ribs.

Thighs.

Knees.

Ankles.

As she stands Ieva looks down at the wellspring at the back of the guard's head where her dark hair forms a small whirlpool. The axis of the skull, Ieva thinks offhandedly. Children are born with open wellsprings, and then the skull grows shut. Then they build schools, churches, and prisons. Someone has to do it.

The guard is squatting and inspects Ieva's sandals one by one. One winter, when it was ungodly cold, Ieva had lined her boots with folded newspapers. She remembers the female guard who had unfolded and skimmed over each newspaper in annoyance.

Someone has to do it.

Ieva buttons up her dress.

178

While she does that the guard prods the loaf of bread with a long needle; then the needle is dragged through the block of butter. The needle is put down and the guard opens the bottle of mineral water, puts it to her lipsticked mouth and tastes the contents.

The guard sits next to one of the nightstands. She methodically opens the carton of cigarettes, takes out each one and puts it back. Dumps the contents of Ieva's backpack onto the bed.

The guard flips through Ieva's journal, then tosses it onto the table.
The guard says:
"You can't bring that."
Ieva nods. Thoughts are a scary thing—grenades, guns, narcotics.
"They'll come get you tomorrow at ten," the guard says.
She gathers up all the items to be temporarily confiscated and leaves. Ieva sits down so her shaking legs don't betray her, and waits. There's a knock at the door.
Another guard brings in the prisoner and leaves. The prisoner is dressed up in a suit. He stays standing by the door, grinning stupidly.
He approaches her cautiously, stands for a moment, then pulls her into his lap. Her smooth cheek against the bristly roughness of his.

They lean with their elbows on the windowsill because there's nothing to really talk about. The window is open and sunlight streams in through the bars. Andrejs moves close to the bars and calls out—kss, kss, kss! A cat is walking along the meticulously raked strip of sand between the prison hotel and the zone fence. The cat freezes, looks up at the window, then walks on with purpose, its tail twitching.
Andrejs turns his head.
"Tell me what it's like out there."
Ieva gets flustered.
"I can't."
"Why."

"It all changes so often. You'd have to see it for yourself."

At some point the room is finally filled with the gentle shadows of twilight. Flies buzz around the final rays of sun over the strip of sand. These rays are so curious, so full of magic and freedom, that Ieva can't think of anything better than what those flies are doing—dancing for the setting sun. Except the window is barred.

Andrejs hands Ieva an icon stitched into a plastic slip.

"I wanted to give you this."

Ieva reads it:

"'Be not afraid! Open your heart to Christ—the Lord . . .' John Paul . . . Do you believe in God?"

Andrejs answers:

"Don't know."

Ieva reads on:

"'Fools—this life was meant to given away, and nothing more . . .' To who?"

"What do you mean 'to who?'"

She asks:

"Who are we supposed to give our lives to?"

Andrejs scratches the back of his head.

"Like I know . . . It was written in a book. Here we call those things icons. I make them myself. Got nothing else to do."

Night. Light from the watchtower searchlights moves diagonally across the ceiling of the prison hotel room. Ieva and Andrejs lie in bed. Bodies rigid, naked, without touching. It's hot. Now and then the guard alarm sounds outside.

Ieva asks:

"Where'd you get the suit?"

Andrejs answers:

"From donated clothes. Norwegian."

"It looks good."

"Thanks."

Silence.

Andrejs's hand moves and rests gently on Ieva's chest.

"You've gotten pretty fragile. Like a skeleton."

Ieva laughs.

"Like a skeleton!"

"Don't do that. Eat more. You'll get ugly."

Silence.

Ieva says:

"I've got to save up. I've eaten nothing but water for a while now. It's got nutrients in it, too, for real. Just have to get used to it."

Ieva's eyes in the darkness. Andrejs also pretends to sleep.

Then she suddenly sits upright in bed.

"Something was here! In the dark. Something evil! What's that noise?"

After a brief silence Andrejs answers:

"The alarm outside."

Ieva shouts:

"No, no! Here! There was something evil moving around in here."

The massive May moon fills the window—an agitated red, and completely dead. The air is alive and pulsates with the chirping of crickets.

"This is a prison, Ieva. And you're sleeping next to a murderer, by the way. Or did you forget that?"

Ieva leans on her arm and looks into his face. The moon shines through her eyes, her forehead is white in the glow.

She says:

"Stop reminding me all the time! I'm sleeping next to a person. That's how I want to see it."

Andrejs doesn't know what to say, and just waves her off like he would a fly. Ieva sinks back against the pillow and continues:

"We have a daughter. A daughter, Andrejs."

"I want you to bring her with some day."

"She'll never, ever set foot in here!"

Morning. Ieva lines dishes on the shelf. All that's left on the nightstand is a watch. Outside it's pouring rain and thundering. Andrejs sits on the bed, smoking nervously.

She sits across from him and picks at the corner of the blanket. He gets up and starts pacing the room.

He says:

"They've forgotten. It's already five after."

Ieva forces a laugh:

"That would be just perfect—to forget about us in prison!"

Andrejs asks:

"How'll you get to the bus stop? It's pouring and cold—take my shirt."

Ieva pulls the shirt on over her dress.

He says:

"Just think, my shirt'll be free in a few minutes."

There's a knock at the door.

Andrejs looks at Ieva.

"Everything that's happened, and prison—but I haven't turned into some kind of animal, Ieva. You hear me?"

A guard with a wide, official face comes in.

They're taken away.

Prison hallways.

A maze of hallways, the door that opens and shuts with a bang. For a brief second they're able to see each other through the glass door.

The prison gate.

They return Ieva's passport.

She steps out into the rain, right into the core of it, this mess of intoxicating freedom, water, and sand. It won't even let her breathe in—just exhale. Endlessly exhale as she looks back at the white fence, then back out toward the city and the future, which slowly but surely draws closer through the slanted torrent of water from the heavens.

The moon can do amazing things, her mother had said.

Ieva snaps back from the window when she hears the station announced over the speakers, her stop. She turns the Virgin Mary pendant from Andrejs over in her fingers, and then she's on the platform. Dingy piles of leaves litter the concrete under the green benches, stray cats laze about, and everything is surrounded by a slow, small-town calm.

This is how I'll get lost, she thinks. I'm already lost, disappeared, a rat among rats, a grey cat among grey cats, that alcohol merchant at the Central Market gave me my change because I already belong to a class, I'm one of them, one of the imprisoned, who'll forever feel their scars and pain against the ones who imprisoned us.

Ieva gets into the only taxi waiting on the other side of the station.

"To the prison?" the driver asks, studying her and the bag.

All she has to do is nod.

You count my vertebrae when I light the stove. Loved by the touch of your fingers, they ignite one after the other and glow in the dark like embers.

Later I'll walk you to the station and you can warm your hands in my embrace. Dig deep into the ash to the embers, to the spine-like fire.

Look at the stars up there!

So high.

You'll take out a burning ticket.

The train will come, sputtering and cold. There's a terribly cold emptiness under my heart; it counts your steps to the train stairs. Look out the window before your view is blocked by the grey bridges! A cat warms itself by a fire on the platform.

Wave goodbye.

"Here's your prison, honey!"

Ieva presses five lats into the fat, hairy paw of the taxi driver and slams the door. She didn't see anything—not the road, the church, the overpass! Not even the pretty sandy clearing before the prison.

There's a new broad, ugly staircase leading to the prison accounting department waiting room, and a large window at the landing. Ieva's silhouette is visible in the sunlight as she heads to the second floor. Everything smells strongly of whitewash.

After that is a long hallway with many doors—all on the left-hand side. The hallway looks robbed and forgotten. Ieva tries every other door, but each one is locked. Only the second to last door opens.

The room is filled with light. The outskirts, clearings, the second floor. A Soviet-era building with gigantic windows. A coffee cup sits on the windowsill; curls of steam rise from the black liquid, feeling their way upwards and forming condensation on the edge of the blinds, backlit by the sun.

Three women raise their heads from where they sit at their desks. One of them is eating a salad from a plastic container.

Ieva says:

"I need to pay. For a visit."

"Ludmilla!" the women call out.

The one eating carefully wipes her fingers in a paper napkin and opens a ledger.

Coffee steaming away on the sunny windowsill. The smell of mayonnaise from the salad.

The woman by the window turns, takes the coffee cup, blows on it, and drinks. The woman by the door turns a radio knob; a jumble of sounds as the signal jumps from station to station.

Ieva counts out her money for the woman at the middle desk and signs the ledger.

Ten or so people are waiting in the prison yard for visitations. A guard comes out to them, loudly calls a name, and the person called goes inside. Ieva and an older woman with two fully-packed plastic bags remain outside. The old woman fishes hard candies out of her pocket, tosses them in her mouth, and grinds them like a horse.

A group of flushed men runs by—young guards in army boots. They run, buttoning up their jackets, their guns dragging on the ground. Ieva watches them.

The guard comes back outside and calls Ieva's name. She follows him to the passport window, holds out her passport, but then quickly pulls it back and puts it in her pocket.

She mumbles:

"I . . . no . . . I have to go somewhere else!"

A stern-looking officer brings his freckled face close to the glass.

"You're here for a visit?"

"I—just—I'm dropping something off."

"Next window!"

She goes to the next window, takes off Andrejs's shirt, folds it as best as her trembling hands will let her, and places it on top of the groceries. The official stares in surprise at the half-naked woman in front of her. Let her! Ieva catches a whiff of the bacon. She feels sick.

She pulls her coat on over her bare skin.

Then she rips a page from her notebook and writes: "Everything's over for real now. Ieva."

She walks along the sandy road toward town. Now and then she glances back as if she can't believe it—back at the prison where she's left Andrejs alone. Ieva walks on, letting go of something close with each step she takes, violently cutting the ties that would otherwise take forever to untangle painlessly. She makes it to the merciless core of freedom—traitor!—the chaos of air, fire, and earth. Don't describe it as beautiful, that's what Andrejs would have said, but how else can she put it? That second in which, despite everyone and everything, you take those first steps on your path, in your own moment of being? Because Ieva can't go on lying anymore.

So long, marriage! Take care, church, and the words of the pastor—in sickness and in health, for richer or poorer, until death do you part! So long, love—where did you go? Time, come judge me! But no one else is going to do that. I have to judge myself.

And you shouldn't lie to yourself, shouldn't lie to anyone—freedom is always right there with you. You just get up one morning and go.

Freedom is always within arms' reach.

The trip home lasts twice as long because she tries not to think about anything. And when you think of nothing, time drags on. The wheels of the train clang, the thick, grainy August air thumps in the open windows, nothing is happening.

Ieva doesn't seem aware of herself or others—she stares at the window. It's growing dark.

Now she's alone. She'll have to figure out how to live on—naked, without Andrejs's shirt. But she wants to put off that train of thought.

People look at her, study her face. People see everything. That's what the species is like.

She puts on her headphones, "Bright Red," cloaks herself in the icy fringe of the music. One by one, the passengers break down and dissipate, frozen in frosty crescents. All that remains is the darkness, the darkness, the darkness, and the inviting red eyes of the semaphore, so trustworthy and present along the entire road of life.

> So here are the questions: is time long or is it wide?
> And the answers? Sometimes the answers
> just come in the mail. And one day you get that letter
> you've been waiting for forever. And everything it says
> is true. And then in the last line it says:
> Burn this. We're in record.

Ieva gets out at the Central Station in Riga and keeps walking along the Railway Bridge, crossing the river. Her fingers feel for the Virgin Mary around her neck. No one stops her; she doesn't think about whether or not she's allowed to cross here. She wants to throw the Virgin Mary into the deepest part of the Daugava River. Let the stream weave her into the sand and sediment. The Virgin Mary is most definitely on Andrejs's side, Christ is on his side, and both of them—Mother and Son—look down on Ieva disapprovingly from the heavens.

The Railway Bridge.
Riga shines evenly on both sides.
A black river down the middle. No sweet little Daugava here, friends. It's a massive current, wide and threatening.
It's raining.

Trains move in both directions on the bridge. Ieva presses closely against the rail when they go past. The conductors look at her in surprise.
Over the middle of the Daugava Ieva sees a dark figure walking toward her. She slows her pace and crosses to the other side of the

bridge. The figure crosses, too. It turns out to be a uniformed Railway Bridge guard with a nightstick on his belt.

"Your permit, please!"

Ieva answers:

"Permit? I don't have one."

The guard orders:

"Then you have to go back! You can't walk on this bridge."

Ieva looks over his shoulder, the river once again throws the rushing sound of her own blood back into her ears.

"No walking?"

The guard is annoyed:

"No! Like you're from another planet . . . No one can walk on the Railway Bridge. Turn around! And fast. Otherwise the police will get involved."

Ieva goes back, and on the way she rips the Virgin Mary from around her neck and throws her over the rail into the water. Ieva falls into the wet grass next to the bridge supports and pounds the ground with her fists. Why can't she live to honor this beautiful, thick grass?

A thought suddenly comes to her that has her immediately on her feet.

What if she's? . . .

Pregnant!

She trips and stumbles as she moves and only now realizes that she's completely frozen, hanging around the bridge with just her jacket and no shirt, and in a downpour no less!

She buys a pregnancy test in a 24-hour pharmacy and races across the wet sidewalks to Fanija's apartment. The city smells like it never has before.

Thank God she's at least able to be alone tonight!

Ieva goes quietly into her room, closes the door, and opens the window. The coolness of the mud in the courtyard rises up between the buildings to meet the night sky. It's so rare she gets to be alone. She melts with the dimly glinting creases in the curtain.

Morning. She has to wait until morning.

She sighs heavily and undresses, puts on a soft cotton t-shirt, and falls asleep clutching Monta's big stuffed bear.

A yellow-green and bright sun shines through the maple tree and draws a shifting, trembling design on the staircase. Fanija opens the bathroom door on the landing. Ieva stands and studies the pregnancy test, which slowly reveals a single line.

Fanija speaks:

"Ieva, I already told you to make sure to put the key back. I couldn't get into my bathroom all day yesterday!"

Ieva answers:

"I'm sorry."

Fanija asks:

"What's that?"

Ieva:

"A test. I'm not pregnant."

Fanija tries to understand the situation, then dismisses it with a wave of her hand and says:

"So no miracle, then."

Ieva asks:

"Miracle?"

Fanija answers:

"Sure. It would've been a little angel sent to the rescue. But no."

She continues:

"You know, it's been two years since my son disappeared—I told you once already—he went out one morning for milk and just never came back . . . yes, Ieva, let's go . . . and you know, after that a large bird landed on my windowsill and tapped on the window a few times, clearly, slowly, with a pause between each one! And then I understood! I understood everything!"

Ieva offers Fanija her arm, and they slowly head back up the well-worn stairs. Fanija continues:

"Thank you, thank you! That bird, you know, it tapped maybe three times. And, quite frankly, I understood. I've already waited two years. I have to wait one more, Ieva. My son'll return in a year. A miracle, right? But I understood."

Ieva asks:

"How old are you now, Fanija?"

Fanija answers, a bit short of breath:

"Eighty-four, Ieva. I'm bored of waiting and paying a pretty sum for this apartment, but what can I do? Think about it! But I'm doing well. I found a fifty-santim coin on the stairs today. How d'you like that?"

As they go up, Ieva listens to Fanija's words, understands what she says, and asks questions. But at the same time she feels with every cell in her body how much she misses Monta's smell and face, the dog's energy, her mother's unsolicited advice, the playground and store, shopping and trains, and the sky—wide open one morning and closed the next.

And she manages to see Andrejs—it's a tenth of a second, a scene from her memory of one spring morning at the Zari house—maybe it's the flicker of the sunspots underfoot that triggered it? Ieva remembers a similar morning with sun, she sees Andrejs, how he looks as he stands in the apple orchard next to the stone rubble of the barn, where all the trees are blossoming. There's a chainsaw at his feet and, as he looks at the twisted sweet cherry tree in front of him, he says to it:

"Your turn."

The tree looks back at him.

He picks up the chainsaw and checks the gas level.

He glances at the neighboring tree, a maple sapling.

"Don't look so smug. You're next."

At that moment Ieva calls to him:

"Leave me the maple."

Andrejs looks intently at Ieva, who is kneeling in the shade under a silver yew-tree, and reminds him of a large, talking bird.

"What do you need it for? It's not even a fruit tree."

"Leave it. Please."

Her voice sounds so strange.

And that tree is still in the yard today. You can touch it if you want.

Ieva sees this scene and immediately forgets it because her phone rings; it's her boss calling to tell her that they ended up finding another intern to take her place, she causes too many problems—her kid is sick, she's got to go who knows where to see her husband. Got it, thanks. Ieva manages to think it's the hand of fate. She has to find a school, she wants to study something. Before she gets completely lost in the fray. And she has to finally go see a doctor. How much longer can she lose weight and walk around feeling sick to her stomach if she's not pregnant? And at least she paid this month's rent in advance; she's got an entire month—she's rich with time!

Then a thought rips through her mind like a bullet: that it hasn't been made official in any church, that anything could happen, and that this book called her life is still without an ending—it's not good and it's not bad, and yet—it's her life, this uninsured, death-bound expedition, this unrepeatable morning full of pigeons and the shadows of trees, the sun, and Fanija's stories. Full of future get-togethers and laughter. This book—the privilege of reading it is hers, and hers alone.

JANUARY 15TH

THERE'S nothing good about a 200-plus-pound black guy emerging suddenly from the shadows and jumping you. Ieva's happy for anyone who hasn't had to experience that.

At first Ieva doesn't understand what he wants, he just comes at them. In the moment his heavy hand comes to rest on Ieva's shoulder, when she catches a whiff of his hot breath, acrid from eating Latvian garlic toast, and when she understands the true consequence of trouble—this is the moment he first sees Aksels. Aksels stands next to her in the biting December wind, and the white light by the entrance of Polārs Bar sways, pulling his face from the framework of the night. The black guy immediately shoves Ieva to the side and lunges for Aksels.

Ieva lets them fight. She senses that something awful could happen right then, but god dammit, she can't do anything about it. Ieva screams out something, but her voice drowns among the sounds of the slush-covered street.

The black guy throws Aksels down onto the ice. The puddles on the sidewalk are frozen over, dark as onyx. Shit, Ieva says to Ningela, the gypsy or Indian woman who materializes in the Polārs doorway. Shit, Ieva says, see what the Āgenskalns neighborhood has become!

Blacks and Indians! But Ningela doesn't understand. Ieva's speaking Latvian, but Ningela only knows a few words of the language.

Ningela pushes back a few nosy people who flicker like shadows in the bar's entrance, and then slams the door. Enough, Ningela shouts out at them in Russian, enough!—but the black guy doesn't hear her. Tell him to stop, tell him that's enough, Ningela screams, hoping Ieva will put an end to it. The black guy's boot flashes in the light of the weak lamp. Aksels is there, in the dark, on the ground, on the ice, or who knows where. Ieva grabs a board leaning against the wall and hits the black guy across the back. It stops him for a second, and Aksels manages to get away. It's what Ieva has been hoping for this entire time, that Aksels would run if anything ever happened. Ieva doesn't know why he didn't run when he had the chance that night. Maybe his pride was at fault. Ieva had underestimated him—Aksels, it turns out, isn't someone who runs.

It's only when Ieva slams the board into the black guy's back that Aksels clambers awkwardly across the ice and into the darkness. Right then his fate was already sealed, he just didn't know it yet. Ieva takes off after him.

Then she yells at Ningela for a while longer from the darkness at a safe distance, while Ningela stands on the steps of the bar, her white slippers reflecting a weak glow in the never-ending curtain of snow. Ieva understands enough of what Ningela is saying to know people think Ieva and Aksels snitched to the cops. That the cops busted them for 30 grams of marijuana. That Ningela's daughter was arrested and that they now blame Ieva and Aksels. Ieva doesn't know who told them that bullshit. While Ieva and Ningela are shouting at each other, Aksels stands behind Ieva, she feels him against her back—his mute presence, his support. The black guy leans against the front of the bar, short of breath and seething, spitting dark drops of blood from his split lip onto the white snow. He pulls a joint out of his shirt pocket. A third of it has already been smoked, and he slowly and calmly lights it up again. He's even blacker against the falling snow and the cold glare from the bar. Ieva can smell the heavy scent of weed, even through the mush of snow and rain. Son of a bitch! Where did he come from! Fuck! Ieva and Aksels leave. Empty-handed.

Nothing changes much after the night that black guy kicked Aksels. Ieva goes to work, but Aksels sits around at home. A friend pays back a debt—homegrown marijuana from the countryside, and a bit of cash. Aksels jokes that you can't have the bad without the good. Every cloud has its silver lining. He says this, Ieva's pigeon-grey love with a silver lining. This lining shines all around him—in his hair, his skin, fingertips. A glimmering vein around his dark rainbows.

That's how they spend the last night of the year—pressed close together on a mattress. The first morning of the New Year arrives and Ieva looks intently at his eyes when they open. At how they move, his eyes, at what they look like. It's so wonderful, life. Liveliness. The life, the liveliness that hides in Aksels.

Aksels doesn't contemplate life.

Ieva is the first to wake up and watches Aksels closely, resting on her right elbow as he lies half awake. He rubs his forehead, then his face contorts as he untangles himself from his dreams, and his eyes fly open. His eyes search, they're in the moment, they find Ieva, and they clear. Ieva freezes, afraid to breathe. He looks at her silently for a moment, then smiles and reaches for a cigarette. Nothing out of the ordinary. This is how their mornings start. For two years Ieva has had no greater secret than the man next to her.

A week later he can't even get up if he's sitting, or sit down if he's standing. He says Ieva's being ridiculous and has her go buy weed. Ieva smokes less so that he can have twice as much. The usual kindness toward everyone and everything that comes from smoking up. The thrilling generosity. Ieva doesn't say a single negative thing to

Aksels. They almost stop talking completely. When they eat dinner, Ieva knows to go get a fork, or glass, or knife, even if he just looks at her. Until he tells her—enough. He's sick of seeing this warmhearted nurse everywhere, stop it, Ieva! And she stops. And just looks at him with wide, frightened eyes.

She's scared of how shivers run through her bones when she looks at Aksels. She can't avoid it. Countless times she'll go to kiss him, to simply and lightly touch her lips to his; Ieva does this every time he starts to say something, or when he watches TV, or when he quietly smiles to himself. And he'll impatiently wave her off, but not reprimand her. Aksels knows—if he reprimands her at a moment like that, he'd cut her to the depths of her heart. But he also knows that when Ieva kisses him, she's trying to hold onto a part of him, and that cuts him a hundred times deeper. I haven't even gone anywhere yet, he thinks, hope dies last, don't you know that, dear Ieva? He can't bring himself to say it out loud.

Ieva looks at him and now and then runs a hand through his hair. Touches her lips to his eyebrows, eyelashes, ears. Ieva loves Aksels. In this exact moment. In this exact moment.

That black guy wrecked Aksels's hip while they were fighting on the ice. One night Ieva wakes up to a stifled cry in the pitch-black room. Terrified, she feels for the lamp. When the light bursts harsh and bare into the room, she sees that Aksels's face is covered in sweat and he's barely able to catch his breath from the pain. In the kitchen, the refrigerator lets out a loud whir and falls silent. Ieva rummages in the shelves for all the stashes of weed she can find. Aksels asks her to turn off the light, it's hurting him. Ieva opens the curtains and turns out the light. They lie in the reddish glow of the city. Hold each other by the hand and wait for the drugs to kick in. They don't. Ieva carefully frees her fingers from his and feels along his side downwards, even though he tries to stop her, pushes her hand away. But Ieva keeps going, even forcefully, while she stares unblinkingly out the window where the evening wind ferries light and shining clouds. Aksels's hip is hot and swollen like a chestnut about to burst.

For a second Ieva pulls her hand away; she sees the true extent of misfortune.

The following morning they go to the clinic. Ieva sends Als a text message saying he shouldn't expect her at work. Als answers she shouldn't expect to have a job tomorrow. And if that wasn't enough, the eggs burn in the pan, and Aksels starts making excuses. Says he doesn't want to go to the clinic, Ieva should just go buy more weed. Like a geezer asking his old lady for his morning dose of vodka. Then Ieva flares up. A few plates shatter against the peeling kitchen wallpaper. White shards rain down on the strange and silent rusty fragments that lay about their kitchen like sleeping goliaths, these things that barely resemble an old gas stove, small propane tanks, and cast iron radiators. It's a new January morning outside—a chilled aquarium bubbling with the icy greens, reds, and blues of the sky.

To get weed, Ieva screams, to get weed! She snatches the lit cigarette from Aksels's fingers and smashes it into the sink. Always with this disgusting smoke, I can't breathe! I can't breathe, Ieva screams, but Aksels smirks in confusion. You dick around here day after day, or go drinking downtown, but I have to work in the market and freeze while I watch picky old women paw mandarins with their chubby fingers and ask—Where are these from? From Latvia, I tell them, from across the river in Mārupe! They puff up like pigeons and swear at me, then go away. Als writes down everything I say behind my back, in a black notebook. He hates it when I upset the customers. Then he docks my pay, sneering with his stupid Chechen—or whatever he is—face. Minus ten lats, he says, or minus five. Depends on the day. But all the while Aksels sits around in front of the TV and smokes the weed bought with the money Ieva earned! How do you think Ieva likes that!

But all she really wants to say is that he needs to go to the clinic. He gets it and pulls on his jacket. And for that she loves him. For often respecting her seriousness. For the simultaneously simple and painful gesture with which he finally gets to his feet and pulls on his old leather jacket.

Ieva looks in every possible place for her passport, finally finds it in the hallway under some dusty bicycle parts. Aksels, it turns out, has a different name written in his passport. Ieva decides the name Aksels suits him much better. He looks at his passport as if in wonder. He's sweating just from waiting. The stairwell reeks of piss. They're both twenty-one years old.

Ieva remembers—they're taking the tram. She doesn't remember which line. Aksels stands opposite her and looks out the window. He's dealing with the pain. His face glassy and his eyes steel.

They sit next to each other at the clinic. Rest their hands on each others' knee in this strange world; the background whines with the sound of a dentist's drill and the foreground is full of patients struggling to find a seat on the long benches lining the halls.

Aksels is called in and Ieva goes with him. He doesn't have a patient card, he's not registered and has never been to this clinic. They're sent from one office to another until they find the right one. A good amount of money is spent to get him registered somewhere. Destruction whimpers quietly in every corner: pensioners sputter and curse, sweating mothers sigh heavily as they hold their babies.

They need to X-ray Aksels's side. He undresses and lies down on the table. Ieva stands back a bit like his escaped shadow and watches silently. The nurses try to position Aksels's hips in the right angle. He digs his mouth into Ieva's palm and screams noiselessly in this dark, warm abyss. Ieva glances fondly at his hips. They're as beautiful as they always are, so slim. The skin of his groin like light velvet. His penis darker, regal, and haloed by golden hairs. She's happy the nurses get to see it, too. She cries out of pride. Everything happens at once and doesn't want to stop. They can't X-ray his hip. He screams through her hand, bites her fingers until they bleed. The doctor decides to administer anesthesia. A needle sinks into Aksels's vein, and his body instantly goes slack, as obedient as a ragdoll. His hips are positioned into the right angle. The lens moves toward the only place on his body that is void of beauty, the place that has opened the door to chaos.

He's out of it for a long time, laid out on a brown, pleather couch. His body is wracked by chills, he's freezing. Ieva covers him, wraps him in a blanket. She sits next to him on a white stool, motionless, while Aksels is broken by the nightmares of narcosis. It's hell for both of them—Aksels's convulsions and Ieva's motionlessness, their mutual isolation. Finally they both come to in the same world; Aksels opens his eyes, but they're not his own. They've switched him out from where he used to be.

Ieva helps him dress. The nurse comes in and hands Ieva his hip X-rays and a referral to the hospital, then anxiously asks them if Aksels doesn't want to wait here longer for the anesthetic to wear off. They shake their heads "no" almost in unison.

Outside the city has snowed over, ice crystals crunch underfoot, children run around with red cheeks and lips shiny from sucking on icicles. Tires creak, the tram tracks sing, street sweepers clear snow with silver shovels. The sun burns the piles of snow along the sides of the street like fire. No road has ever, nor will it ever, seemed so long as those few hundred meters to the tram stop. Now and then the wind pushes loose bricks of snow from the clubbed branches of the linden trees. Aksels supports himself on Ieva's shoulder—rather, he's slumped against it. He feels so heavy, waterlogged. A few times he falls onto a pile of snow and wants to rest there. Ieva doesn't let him. C'mon, let's go, she says, c'mon, c'mon! Ieva isn't thinking of anything, not even the tiniest thought. C'mon, c'mon, c'mon.

In truth, Ieva has nothing more to say. She asks Andrejs to take them to the hospital tomorrow. The sun shines brightly as Ieva smokes at the gate of Andrejs's mechanic shop, and he looks at her with lazy, half-lidded eyes. Of course I'll help, he says, when have I ever not helped you . . .

The icy wind blows the smoke back into her face, the contours of her lips are red and raw. You've totally wasted away, Andrejs says. Of course, Ieva says and looks away, it's from the stress.

Andrejs asks:

"Why are you smoking?"

Ieva answers:

"To calm my nerves."

Andrejs smirks.

Andrejs shows up on time. They're already waiting in the court-yard. Aksels gets in the back, stretches his leg out on the seat. Ieva sits up front next to Andrejs. She shows him the X-rays—a couple of dark and mysterious landscapes—and the long bones of Aksels's legs through the fog of flesh. As they drive they pass cars, high-rises, bridges, and streetlamps. The sun is shining again and the fields of snow glitter blue and violet.

Ieva says:

"Can I smoke in the car?"

Andrejs asks:

"Why do you need to?"

The wind whips at the smoke through the open window together with strands of Ieva's hair, pulling them into the open sky.

Ieva repeats:

"To calm my nerves."

He asks:

"You really believe that?"

She nods.

Wide, smooth hallways of stone stretch in all directions at the Cancer Research Center like forgotten czarist-era cavalry arenas with their high ceilings. The sun is unbearable. Its destructive power comes through countless windows, its rays of light dancing with tiny particles of dust in the air as people walk past.

The doctor examines the X-rays, shakes his head, and asks Aksels to undress. Aksels takes off his clothes without a second thought; he's spent most of the last days doing the same thing. Ieva doesn't budge an inch. When the doctor asks the nurse to shave Aksels's hip so they can run tests, Ieva takes the razor from the nurse's hand.

He stands in a spot of sun like a slim, careless being. Ieva kneels down and shaves the front of his hip. The hollow under his hipbone around the ugly, swollen thigh. The fine, unruly hairs burning in the soft light. One by one they fall to the ground, where the cold shadows instantly extinguish them like sparks. Ieva wants to kiss his hips, but her despair has robbed her of feeling, she can't feel her own face. A minute later they sink a thick needle into his leg. Aksels grabs onto the edge of the table and grits his teeth so hard his lips turn white.

The doctor asks to speak to Ieva out in the hall. He says something about bone cancer, the fastest of the slow deaths. Asks if Aksels has sustained any injuries. Tells her to call in a few days to ask about the test results. He disappears back into his office as Ieva turns to run.

She runs, no, she goes, but the air lifts and carries her until she can't keep up anymore—galloping from one end of the hallway to the other. The air washes over her and slams into the walls like foam, smearing against the window blinds. Andrejs stands at the window opposite of where she finally stops. Ieva chokes on air, is out of breath, and goes to him. Andrejs looks at her long and hard and says he loves her. Can you honestly not shut up, Ieva says, if only for a second, please, for Aksels . . . Andrejs can't. He hurts her with his heavy and endless love even when she's sobbing and gasping into his sleeve, even when Aksels emerges fully-clothed from the doctor's office and walks over, his crutch tapping against the cool tile floor. He walks toward the two of them with infinitely drawn-out, long, uneven steps, cool and indifferent, right up to the two of them, who are looking at him as if he was limping straight for Heaven's door.

Back at home Aksels says to Ieva:

"So what now?"

Ieva answers:

"I don't know."

He gets angry:

"You do too! You talk to the doctors, so please, enlighten me!"

Ieva says nothing. Aksels knows. He's only pretending he doesn't get it.

He tries a different approach:

"How long do I have left?"

"At most—two months. We have to call back January 15th for the results."

Silence.

"Hey," he says. "Don't let them take me."

Ieva doesn't know how it happens, but people acclimate. That fascinating acclimation mechanism when faced with the unavoidable—no, what is she saying—when faced with anything that lasts more than a few hours. She remembers that first night: they're both smoking on the balcony, and it's briskly cold. When they sit with their backs against the wall all they can see over the concrete-block railing are the stars, which are truly glowing. Between them is the small birch tree, white with bare branches—it grows on the balcony through a crack in the bricks. Below them is the city center, the laughter of pedestrians scattered over the icy sidewalks like red, crystal apples, and the shining reflections of billboards on the cobblestones. Thank God the Christmas market carousel has quieted down. It's hard for Aksels to sit, he folds his jacket under his leg and stretches it out toward the horizon. He's on clonazepam to override the pain and anxiety. He's pale, weak, with bright feverish eyes, and smokes cigarette after cigarette and rambles on. It seems he's talking about how important it is for people not to hurt one another. Expands on the topic. And then he's plowed down by sleep, like slipping into a coma. Ieva drags him back inside. Holds his head in her lap and suddenly hates whoever wants to take this beautiful, warm doll away from her, this doll she can never get enough of. She starts to cry, even though at moments like this tears usually avoid her like she's fire. Ieva and Aksels love movies, run piles of them through their old Panasonic the way other people run loads of clothes through the wash. It takes away the ability to feel anything. Any time she starts to suffer, she remembers some actor or actress in a similar situation and the way they handle it. Contort their faces while the cameraman mercilessly milks the moment with his lens, drawing out the tears, screaming in terror—she has no doubt that the actors are experiencing instead of acting. But it's not the actor or actress that drives her crazy, it's the director and cameraman, and all of these gigantic industries, machineries, the desire to run dry and scan sorrow onto a screen for all to see, to not turn away from the vein that has been brought forth and torn like an oil line. And after that, when something happens to you personally, you're just not able to cry anymore.

But, Ieva says, fuck all of that. Precisely because on that night with Aksels at the balcony door, Ieva cries. She cares fuck-all about the movies. Even if hordes of gorgeous, magnificent actresses had pornographically poured their tears, snot, and spit in front of the camera, knowing that the lens was capturing every movement of even the tiniest movement of the muscles on their faces—even then, Ieva would have cried one more time. All she thinks about is how someone wants to take the heavy, slumbering head in her lap away from her.

Of course anything can happen in life, but not all because of some shithead black guy! Not because of that idiot Ningela, who puttered around behind the counters at Polārs, wrapped in her sickly-sweet renditions of Indian perfumes. Not even because of the bar itself—the shittiest of all bars, the dregs of the Āgenskalns barrel, that dump. Spending time in there, no matter the season or time of day, always gave you the overwhelming feeling of sitting deep underground. Or rather—at rock bottom. The stale smell of cigarettes, worn-out couches, a TV somewhere in the background soundlessly playing MTV while the audio system up front blasts something entirely different . . . The stale, cigarette-like regulars, who call themselves artists or life artists, but who are really just broken clocks, each bullshitting and babbling about the time they were actually meant to stop in.

All she wanted to do was buy some weed from Ningela's daughter, but that black shit had come out of nowhere and thrown Aksels down onto the ice. Well, and then his hip got banged up, and then misfortune quickly started to fester. It's so stupid! Not like this, not like this—Ieva begs as she cries, her tears rolling down her face in the dark and into Aksels's hair.

The next morning Ieva cries differently, but again about Aksels. Then the next night about something else entirely, but still about Aksels. But on the next night—she doesn't even cry anymore, just sits thinking nothing, shot up on diazepam, and grinding her teeth. Making a game of it, tensing and relaxing the muscles in her jaw.

This is acclimation, you get there without even realizing it. And already thinking ahead. Thinking ahead. It's a horrible betrayal. To think ahead about Aksels. Who's left on the side of the road like a broken clock, while the tram whips past and carries her farther away. Away.

Ieva says:
"But what do you mean—don't let them take me?"
Aksels smiles crookedly:
"Remember Sid and Nancy?"
Aksels's idea slowly crystalizes in Ieva's mind, and when it finally hits her it scares her beyond reason. Her eyes go wide:
"You want—ME to?"
"Yes, you. Who else? Listen, Ieva, I haven't lived long, but I've lived how I've wanted. Seriously. And I want to die how I want."
Ieva leaves the room and slams the door.
"Forget it! What are you thinking? I'm not capable of murder!"

The pain wakes Aksels up in the middle of the night. He's convulsing like he's been thrown on high voltage wires. After he takes all the medication he can, he lies limp and moaning. Ieva changes his sweaty shirts and sheets, four sets over the course of the night. They're soaked through.
Toward morning Aksels says:
"Please, shoot me with a shotgun. From fifteen paces."
Ieva cries.
"I can't shoot you like some animal!"
"Please. If you love me."
Ieva screams:
"Then I've never loved you!"
Aksels screws up his face. Maybe it's a smile. He stares at the ceiling and says:

"Make anarchy your mother. Create as much chaos and confusion as is in your power, but don't let them take you alive."

Ieva presses her hands over her ears.

Eventually Aksels convinces her to drive out to the countryside.

Sid and Nancy in room 100 of the Hotel Chelsea. An eternal secret only for the two of them. This time Sid will die. Sid fills Nancy's head with words, about how he wants to lie down by the birch trees at the far end of the pasture, where the first buttercups of summer always bloom. No one will know. It'll be their secret.

Ieva has never been able to imagine this kind of helplessness, hasn't even been able to feel it. She doesn't want to accept Aksels's illness. She should, because there's no way out—no way out! There are moments when Ieva's mind blazes magnificently clear and fierce like a newly sharpened knife. She understands that there's no way out, just a life continued without Aksels.

Life hasn't asked for Ieva's thoughts on any of the coldhearted things it has to offer. It is what it is. And that's that. She's never wanted any of it. Aren't they fantastic, elegantly sadistic gifts for a single person who has nerves, feelings, a mind, and heart? How can she accept all of them, she doesn't have enough hands! Generously, lavishly, life—thank you for showing me your real face so soon.

If all this was about her, Ieva would care less. But the life of one person, a whole person, stands before her. Like something untouchable has caressed her, something flowing out from an icon and through the stained glass windows of a church.

She has to accept it.

Crystal clear winter days hold steady in the skies, blue as seals with numbers on their haunches, slowly digesting time, my forehead is hot, Ieva thinks, thinks, thinks. She can't think of anything.

Ieva senses that she could find salvation in faith, and watches the sky. Sunsets are amazing, but nothing more. The sky is silent.

And Aksels is still here beside her. They have to get ready. Ieva's forehead is hot. As long as she keeps busy she can stay calm. But when she's by herself, she cries.

Aksels says:

"You're too attached. That's your flaw."

Ieva's so offended she doesn't know what to say. She even blushes. She cries:

"Flaw! Flaw?"

Aksels says:

"You actually enjoy suffering. You have a thing for it. You're happy now that you have something to suffer over."

He says:

"Me, I'm not attached to anyone. There's no one I'd cry over if they died."

It's an unholy nightmare, all of these conversations. Chaos. Lies. Carelessness, fleeing. Pretending the whole time like they're talking about someone else, not about themselves. Ieva's bloodshot eyes and the worry that she feels nothing. Everything's happening so fast.

One night when Aksels has fallen asleep on the couch, Ieva sneaks over to him with scissors. She looks at his face for a moment. Then she gathers her courage and quickly cuts a lock of his hair. She thinks she's pulled it off, and turns quickly to leave the room. At the door she looks back—Aksels is watching her. He sees her, silently. The only movement is in his eyes as his pupils contract and dilate.

Ieva opens a window.

"What fresh air!"

The air downtown is terrible, but Ieva thinks it's good enough just because it's air.

Aksels wants weed.

Ieva doesn't give it to him, hides it. He gets angry.

Ieva asks:

"Do you even know why you're dying?"

Topics like these bore Aksels, he doesn't want to talk about them.

She says:

"You're dying because you've lost your mind. From all this shit."

Aksels shakes his head.

She says:

"Yeah, you lost your mind. There's nothing worse than losing your mind. And now you're dying."

Aksels says:

"It's my choice. Give it to me."

"I'm going to be all alone!"

"You're only thinking of yourself!"

Ieva's eyes bulge from their sockets in grief.

"And you're only thinking of yourself!"

Aksels says:

"Everyone thinks only of themselves. It's how it should be. Give me the weed. It numbs the pain."

Ieva calls Andrejs:

"Do you still have that old shotgun?"

Andrejs says:

"Yeah."

"Does it work?"

"Yeah. I shot a wild boar with it yesterday."

"Where are you?"

He says he's at the Zari house. Trying to saw firewood.

That's bad, Ieva thinks. Sid and Nancy's plans are in danger of falling through. But Andrejs says:

"Come on over. I'd like it if you did."

"Will you help me?"

"Of course. When have I ever not . . ."

It's morning when Ieva goes into Aksels's room and says—Ready?
Aksels replies—Ready.

An idea needs time to grow, like an oak needs time to grow from
an acorn into a tree.

There's no reason to worry about being late. At 4 A.M. an invisible
caress on her shoulder and a whisper—now! And it begins. The road
forward. Or the backtrack. Or something entirely different.

But first you need an idea.

It's the afternoon of January 14th. Ieva calls Andrejs.
She says:
"Hi, Andrejs."
He answers:
"Hey, Ieva."
Silence.

Ieva finally speaks:
"We've got a few more things to take care of here, and then we'll
be on our way."
Silence.
Then Andrejs answers:
"I love you, Ieva."
Ieva shouts angrily:
"Cut it out, will you! Come pick us up at the crossroad tonight.
Aksels can't walk."
Ieva's ready to announce Aksels's name to the mailman, the police,
Andrejs—to anyone, one hundred times and more in a row. Aksels's
name is smooth as a sea pebble that she can turn over in her mouth
and caress with her tongue.

"I'll be there."

Andrejs hangs up.

Ieva has a brief vision of Andrejs hanging up the phone and looking out the kitchen window. She's seen it so many times before. Over the wood panel table covered with a white tablecloth; the kitchen is filled with the brilliant light reflected by the snow-covered pine trees, the blueness of the sky, and the glistening sun over the wintery fields. It's unbearably cold in the kitchen, the winter dust collects on every dark-stained surface and rough wooden shelves.

Even back then, Andrejs never kept the house warm enough when Ieva wasn't home.

She doesn't pack anything to take with and dresses for spring, even though outside is a bright January morning. Aksels says something about anticyclones. That they're mountains, invisible mountains, radiant and bursting with sun—with diamond surfaces.

Surfaces shift, golden ridges collapse and crumble into little ripples in the windshields of passing cars, in window blinds. Yellow sparks melt in the whites of both their eyes. Ieva asks:

"So what are cyclones?"

To Aksels cyclones are the depths of the sea, rolling streams, and fertile dampness.

They're sitting in the kitchen. Before, Aksels never ate much because he smoked weed. Now he's nauseated from the pills and drinks just a bit of coffee with milk. Ieva's nauseated from life. From everything that's happening. She stopped eating when Aksels stopped eating. Not on purpose, no. Just—it's the two of them. And in a way Ieva is Aksels. When he stopped eating, so did she. It's simple, really. Now they're like bony scarecrows with only a little straw left. Monta is plump and energetic, she knocks over her cup of milk and lets out a squeal.

Ieva says to Monta:

"Why does Monta knock her milk over every morning?"

"No! Mommy knocks milk over every morning!"

"Monta does!"

"Monta doesn't know!"

"Then Monta has a bad memory!"

"No! Mommy does!"

It's hopeless to argue with Monta, especially on the mornings she wakes up terribly happy.

Ieva dresses Monta. Monta grows suspicious.

She whines:

"No wool tights!"

Ieva says:

"Monta isn't going to daycare. Monta's going to Grandma's! Grandma has cold floors."

"No Grandma's! Spiders!"

It's strange with Grandma. Sometimes Monta's happy to go to Grandma's, but other times she sees spiders when she's there. Today is a spider day. Monta protests and squirms, but Ieva finally gets her dressed.

Ieva's also dressed; she turns to Aksels and says:

"I'll take Monta to my mom's, and then we'll go."

Her voice catches in her throat when she sees his face. How he's watching her and Monta. He's caught them being full of life.

In the moment she was dealing with Monta, Ieva forgot. Forgot everything else in the world, Aksels included. She lost herself in the action and became the action herself. The sun plays on the ridged icicles behind the window. Ieva holds Monta's scarf in her hand and can no longer find words. There'll be many more scenes just like this one after Aksels has died.

Aksels is sitting in a chair with his bad leg stretched out in front of him and is intently watching Monta. His expression belongs to him and him alone, and God only knows if he's even aware of what lies behind it. It's some kind of great vibration, the nature of things, that pulls him in. He watches Monta run through the hallway and for a moment sees the turning of the world's gears. Like some incredibly old toy, a teddy bear handed down from child to child and loved to the point its worn, plushy seams suddenly burst, spilling dust and stuffing and sand—and you can see that the bear's voice box still worked, crackling as it forms the words: I love you, you love me, I'm alive, you're alive . . .

These words gather in the gap, the distance, the space between them. Aksels touched by death, and Monta touched by life.

And what Aksels has asked Ieva to do—wasn't it in actuality a childish thing to ask? Wasn't it something a monarch would ask? Death wanted to take him to that faraway pasture, but Aksels had Ieva, thank God, he had Ieva. He could count on that even in death. And now he will walk ahead like a lord, Ieva will follow behind him leading Death by the reigns, that greyish horse with the dark, ugly muzzle of a hyena, she'll lead it and saddle it, and Aksels will get up in the saddle instead of being tied up and dragged behind . . . Aksels will get up in the saddle. Yes, it really was free will.

Ieva calms down and wraps Monta in the scarf. She's realized that she constantly continues the dialogue in her subconscious—is it right, the thing Ieva's promised to do?

Like a clock—tick tock, tick tock.

They hadn't done anything yet. Everything could still change. And yet—nothing could change ever again.

Every few moments there had to be an affirmation, a contribution. And if a moment came and the affirmation wasn't there, it could only be undone by a hundred other moments that did have affirmations.

It was a massive military draft, and Ieva had been called up.

Ieva says to Monta:

"Give Ocela a kiss!"

Monta goes to Aksels and gives him a kiss. Ieva's scared—Monta will say something, something that will make him realize he's seeing her for the last time; today and tomorrow will be the last time for scenes and observations.

"Hurry up, Ocela, she'll overheat!"

Aksels throws her a surprised look—she's being pretty harsh! But he immediately understands that it wasn't out of place. Ieva is organizing his death, that harshness is clearly to be expected, so he says nothing. Ieva doesn't apologize, not even with a look. Better to be harsh than to break down.

Ieva and Monta head out the door.

That evening Ieva and Aksels go to the bus station. Ieva is ready to say to everyone they pass—hey, look at Aksels! This planet will disappear tomorrow! A star will fall! You can look at him and make a wish, and he'll make it all come true! Aksels looks at her disapprovingly, as if she's stupid. But there isn't even a hint of irony in Ieva as she buys two outgoing tickets knowing full well that she'll only be buying one for the trip back.

The bus is warm, narrow, and dark. A strip of tiny blue lights lines the sides of the aisle. Aksels isn't able to find an empty seat that would let him painlessly position his bad leg. He sits on the raised floor at the back of the bus; rather, he lies down on it and leans on his elbow. The other passengers stare at first, but quickly forget their surprise and doze off. Not a whole lot can be seen in the dark. Ieva crouches down next to him.

"Even the tiniest bumps are like earthquakes," Aksels says.

Ieva touches her lips to his forehead, which is damp from the pain.

Another hundred and twenty-four kilometers.

When they get off at the stop for Zari, at the intersection of four roads, Andrejs is already waiting for them. The car is thumping with music, and when Ieva sees his face through the window she grows annoyed. Aksels stands with his body twisted sideways and breathes in the night air.

"Greetings, kids," Andrejs says. "Hop in!"

There are two gypsy hitchhikers already in the car.

The kitchen at the Zari house is warm when they get there. The rest of the rooms are unkempt and cold. Andrejs and the gypsies drink champagne and talk about the forest. Where they can get wood, and how much money they could make sawing lumber.

Andrejs says:

"I want to go back. I'm sick of that city. Ieva, what d'you say we move back out here, to the countryside?"

Ieva sits next to the stove warming her hands, seething. She drinks a glass of champagne and waits for the gypsies to get out. Aksels sits at the end of the table and drinks nothing. Just answers if someone asks him a question.

"You're alright, guy, just kinda quiet!" one of the gypsies says and claps Aksels on the shoulder. Aksels breaks into a sweat from the pain.

"What's that face for—you disrespecting me?"

Aksels shouts back:

"You shit!"

They both jump to their feet and stand face to face, each with an arm raised back and ready to strike. Andrejs gets up and pushes them apart.

He says:

"Enough! There'll be no fights in this house!"

After midnight, after the gypsies have left and Aksels is asleep on the mattress set up on the floor by the big window, Andrejs and Ieva sit and talk quietly by the last of the dying embers in the open mouth of the stove.

Ieva pleads:

"Give me your gun and teach me how to shoot it."

Andrejs gets his gun and while Ieva's inspecting it, asks:

"What're you guys up to?"

"He's dying."

"He looks fine to me."

"He only looks it. We have to call tomorrow for the test results."

Aksels's voice comes from the direction of the big window:

"We don't have to call anyone. I know what the results are."

A thousand giant stars shimmer in the window when Ieva finally takes off her top layer of clothes and curls up next to Aksels.

Aksels whispers into her ear:

"Why'd you bring him into this? He'll turn you in."

"Him?"

Ieva even laughs:

"He'd never."

The full moon is shining on the other side of the house. But it can't be seen from the kitchen. Andrejs sleeps on a cot next to the stove.

The morning of January 15th arrives.

A brilliant sunny morning. The blue of the sky, the green of the fir trees, the snow, and the coastal sand join to form a braid. Aksels has been listening to the tendrils of wind knocking against the windowpanes since midnight. It's a new day second by second.

Ieva and Andrejs wake up. Andrejs lights the stove and makes tea.

Ieva gives Aksels a shot of diazepam so he can get up. She also gives him painkillers and a glass of water, but talks with Andrejs over her shoulder:

"Give me the gun and then leave us alone."

Once Aksels has gotten dressed and had some tea, Andrejs gives Ieva the gun and walks out of the house.

Aksels asks:

"Where'd he go?"

Ieva says:

"Don't know. Away."

There's an awkward silence. The forgotten teakettle whistles on the stovetop, a sharp line of steam shooting toward the ceiling. Aksels looks helplessly at the teakettle.

"Well then—be good!"

"I'll try."

Again, silence.

"Don't cut your hair short—it looks bad on you."

Then he starts to tease her:

"You're totally going to get fat once you turn thirty."

Ieva scoffs:

"No I won't!"

"Let's bet on it!"

"Forget it, I'll never get fat!"

"Let's bet a fur coat. A great, big, shiny fur coat you can hide in. I'll send you that coat from the other side when you're a big fatty."

With that his energy is spent. Silence.

"It's hot in here," he complains, once again sweating from the pain. "Let's go."

They find the birch trees at the far end of the pasture. The blinding ice crystals of snow are melting under the sun. Aksels limps over to the thickest birch and puts his hands on it. Looks up at its slender branches. Then looks at the ground.

He stands under the birch. Looks to Ieva, his eyes squinted.

"Well," he says. "I'm ready!"

Ieva says:

"I'm not. Haven't kissed you yet."

She goes up to him and looks him right in the eyes, searching for his like a falcon hunts a swallow.

She asks:

"You really want me to do it?"

And then in an instant she's embarrassed because she sees that her doubt cuts him deeply. She kisses him quickly on the lips and steps back from the tree, fifteen paces.

Andrejs comes out from the cover of the pines.

"Don't drag the barrel on the ground!"

"Ignore him," Aksels warns.

Andrejs says:

"Think about what he's making you do! It's ridiculous!"

"Ignore him, shoot!" Aksels shouts.

Ieva lifts the shotgun to her shoulder to take aim and keeps backing up.

"Wait for me! Wait for me there!" she shouts and can't shoot. Aksels stands with his hands stuffed in the pockets of his coat and watches her. She looks at Aksels down there at the tip of the barrel, he's no bigger than a bird. Ieva stumbles as she keeps backing up and backing up, Aksels waits, watches her intently, starts to panic. Ieva can't shoot.

A great force steals the shotgun from Ieva and swings it hard back at Aksels. Ieva knows what's coming and turns to run, her hands pressing hard against her ears. She runs and screams. Doesn't even know herself if it's out loud or internal.

Then—externally, or who knows, internally—there's a mighty crack. A cry.

Ieva trips, falls to the ground, her hands grab at the snow. She hears absolutely nothing; then a distant hum in the sky. She looks up—an airplane.

Andrejs comes over to her with the shotgun. He offers her his hand, then pulls her to her feet. He's stunned.

"I'll go get a shovel."

Ieva staggers after him. They get to the kitchen and sit down at the table. Andrejs pulls a bottle of brandy from a cupboard and pours two glasses. Ieva drinks. Andrejs drinks.

For a moment Ieva gets dizzy, as if someone has clubbed her over the head. She screams:

"You shot him? Aksels? You?"

Andrejs goes to the shed to get a shovel. He says:

"Bring the green blanket with you when you come back out."

Ieva follows after him in slow disbelief. Andrejs has been digging hard and is already up to his waist in the ground.

Aksels is lying by the birch. Slumped over onto his once painful side. A small, red mark has formed in the white wool of his sweater, right on the chest.

Ieva looks at his face and screams in horror—it's not Aksels anymore. Strangely limp, shrunken, small. A thing. An object. Aksels isn't here anymore.

Ieva hands Andrejs the blanket. He wraps Aksels up in it and says:

"Otherwise he'll get sand in his eyes."

Ieva takes the red wool scarf from around her neck and wraps it around Aksels's head.

Andrejs says:

"Don't do that—they say you won't be able to move on with your life until the scarf rots away."

"I don't want to move on without him anyway!"

Andrejs says:

"I'll close his eyelids."

"No, not you!"

Ieva leans over Aksels and draws her fingertips down over his eyelids. Accidentally touches his neck. His head is still warm. Ieva screams:

"Why did you shoot him! It was our thing!"

Andrejs carefully buries Aksels's body in the yellow sand and says nothing. Ieva has never seen anything so yellow before.

"It was supposed to be different! You ruined everything! Now it's God knows what!"

Andrejs stays quiet.

"I didn't want it like this," Ieva digs her nails into the cold ground in horror. "Come out, Aksels, it's all wrong!"

In this moment, Andrejs thinks Ieva's lost her mind. Her brittle nails break quickly, red bursts forth from her fingertips against the rocky soil. Andrejs grabs her under the arms and pulls her away from Aksels's grave. She kicks and claws at the ground.

In this moment, Ieva has not lost her mind. Her mind is clearer than ever before. She only thinks that what happened in the snowy field is a lie. That it's a game in which Aksels is smirking and watching from the sidelines, winking his left eye in his usual way.

Ieva strops struggling in Andrejs's arms. She musters all her seriousness and calls out meekly in the direction of the grave:

"Aksels, come on! That's enough."

Nothing happens. Andrejs lowers Ieva to the ground.

The ground is wide open.

Ieva runs over to the shotgun, picks it up, and aims it at Andrejs. "Get the hell away from here, go very far away," she says to him.

"Oh please," Andrejs answers coolly.

He turns to leave, but remembers his shotgun and takes it away from Ieva without another word.

"I never loved you, never!" she screams.

Then he really leaves. Gets in his car and drives away. Warm air swirls around the roof of the car, but the car itself is a dark, brown thing that slowly melts into the hot chaos of pine trees and glaring snow.

Ieva heads back to the house, now and then looking over her shoulder as if to mark an unseen point on a map that she'll have to remember for the rest of her life.

Once inside she's immediately overcome by a sadness so piercing it could break through her skin. Look, the knife Aksels touched last night, and the bread loaf; look, the curtains that were put up when she and Aksels still lived here that summer. The heat of the full summer moon that she doesn't want to think about. Summers like that often involve something that destroy happiness—a fight, depression, or ignorance—but every memory from the time they spent together seems happy.

His grave will always be visible from the kitchen window.

Andrejs will never be able to sell the house to strangers.

Ieva leaves the house for a bit, leaves the weighty sadness behind her.

She takes a pencil and tears a page from her notebook and sits down by Aksels's grave. Sunlight foaming on glossy stones. A coolness that hangs over the white plane of ice. Damp, rich earth. Ieva writes a poem in memory of Aksels. In Russian, for some reason. The poem has lines about how every angle here is straight, but you're twisted into a circle.

She writes and feels like an idiot. Behold, there lies Aksels. Shot dead. Here. And she's writing a poem.

Aksels, forgive me!

But she doesn't know how to comprehend Aksels's existence without the poem, what he meant to the world. Right now Ieva is as exposed as topsoil in the middle of January. Ieva is a raw piece of meat. She doesn't even need to work up to it, the poem just spills out.

Words have almost no meaning. Aksels's meaning isn't in words, isn't in content. Ieva senses Aksels's existence in movement, in the stream that has been set in motion by his death, that flows away through bodies. The sense of this movement seems to erase every moment of betrayal and weakness in real life.

A stupid poem. Consolation for the weak. Pointless.

She has to live on somehow. A Judas.

Aksels, forgive me.

A mare and her foal come into the pasture not far from her. Both animals stop at the barbed wire fence. Ieva watches the foal as it nurses. It's a hefty mare with shaggy legs. Her foal is also strong and healthy; its broad back is like a yellow tray carrying bits of hay and the tip of a fir branch. Ieva walks toward the foal. It comes right up to her and nips at her wherever it can reach, just like a lively foal would do.

Ieva pushes it away.

"You're biting!"

The foal gets angry and nips at her even more, and Ieva has to get away from it. No velvety lips, no pensive, violet-colored eyes. The foal is biting like crazy, full to the brim of spiteful life, so full of boiling blood that it could burst.

The things Aksels will never see again.

At night Ieva wakes up to the sound of a quiet movement in the distance. As if the wing of a guardian angel had slipped over her shoulder in the black darkness.

She lifts her head and listens to the night.

Silence.

But through the silence—a siren. And glaring lights in the window.

She throws on her clothes, yanks on her boots and clambers down the stairs, tripping on her laces and almost falling headfirst into the cement steps.

Morning is just dawning in the wintery fog. She sees the dim headlights of a car and dark, stooped over silhouettes. She runs into the illuminated circle. Aksels has been dug up. One policeman is smoking, the other is unwrapping her red scarf to uncover Aksels's face. Andrejs sits hunched up on a rock, holding the shovel.

Her eyes meet his in the glow of the yellow light and she immediately starts to cry. It's as if someone has hit her over the back, knocked her to her knees, grabbed her by the hair and commanded—cry!

Only one sentence revolves around her head—What are you doing, Andrejs!

He came back! He dug up Aksels and confessed to the police!

One of the policemen takes down Ieva's name, last name, and address.

"Your husband shot your boyfriend out of jealousy. We'll need to question you. Get in the car."

Ieva can't speak. She feels the massive force that suddenly stuffs your life into a drawer, a folder, a system, or a file—it always flows out from questionnaires, forms, transmitters, the worn-out codes hammered into your brain in a poorly lit room. It flows from these officials; the night and their uniforms turn them into giants made of a different, more noble stuff.

They push her into a car that reeks of cigarette smoke. The door slams shut, the headlights bounce over the mounds of snow and the thawing road. She continues to cry for Andrejs, who is waiting with the two remaining police officers for the coroner. The policeman driving the car looks at her with sympathy and fishes an already-opened bottle of brandy from under the seat.

"Take it—a time-tested aid," he says. "There's nothing you can do anymore."

Once they've finished questioning her, Ieva is brought back to the Zari house and released—like a young, domesticated wild animal that now has to learn how to survive on its own in the woods. She doesn't have the energy to go back to Riga. And that's a good thing because, and Ieva doesn't really know why, the next night they bring back Aksels's body. No one says anything about the morgue, doesn't even hint at it. Maybe because it's winter and Ieva is penniless?

Aksels is laid out on a stretcher. Ieva has them carry him through the warm kitchen, where she's been sleeping on the cot, and place him next to the wide-open window of the far room on the second floor.

People say they're afraid of the dead. It doesn't even occur to Ieva to be afraid. It's her Aksels! So beautiful and pale. Now and then she caresses his head. His jaw is set in a stubborn expression. Eyelids fine as silk, frozen to his irises. The stubble on his face and his hair keep growing. His hands are positioned in a ridiculous way, Aksels never held his hands like that! Ieva discovers that the index fingers of his hands are tied together with fishing line. She carefully cuts it away because she's convinced it's hurting him.

They've done an autopsy. The front of his sweater has been cut open and then sewn up with surgical thread. Aksels is flat as a board—they probably took a lot of him for themselves. Ieva hopes they've left his heart untouched.

She spends each night with Aksels. Touches his cheek, lights a candle she found in a kitchen drawer. Drinks brandy straight, pulls it into herself like fire.

There's a full moon. It flashes its white face over Aksels. During the day there's sun. A few flies crawl around Aksels in the morning light. But January flies are so groggy that they don't even think to feed on him. They just bask on him in the warm sun.

Gran shows up, sits in the kitchen and cries, forces Ieva to eat something.

Andrejs's father drives out and slaps Ieva across the face and calls her a whore who's ruined his only son. Andrejs's mother and Gran cook together, and the kitchen fills with thick steam and sniffling. Andrejs's father drinks Ieva's brandy.

Later that night everyone goes looking for Ieva and finds her lying next to Aksels, her eyes strangely bright. She's running a fever.

The next day Lūcija arrives—as usual, whenever Ieva truly needs saving. She's brought Monta with her. Monta showers her mother with kisses, then climbs into the bed next to Aksels, pokes his cheek with a finger, then immediately pulls back and starts to cry.

"Why is Ocela so cold?"

Lūcija says:

"Why are you keeping him here? Are you out of your mind?"

Ieva answers defensively:

"They brought him here."

Nothing here is as it should have been. This mess, this commotion, it's ridiculous. Aksels wanted to rest in peace. And now it's the exact opposite of what he wanted.

Aksels is taken to the morgue, but Ieva is taken to the hospital—her toes are frostbitten. Two days later there's a beautiful funeral at the old manor house. Aksels is buried in the local cemetery next to his mother, Stase.

The sobbing is an intangible sea. When a wave hits, Ieva cries. It's not a voluntary action—not in any way. It's as if she's standing in the water with a large, open wound, a sore. When a wave hits, it carries salt with it and it hurts, and the tears come. It's easy to cry when washing the floor. Then Ieva is bent over and the tears fall straight down instead of in her sinuses, or her throat, or elsewhere. Her tears grow heavy right there on her lashes and drip down. Ieva washes the floor with them.

Ieva works like a scientist in a submarine of tears, matter-of-factly executing the necessary functions for survival—she eats, sleeps, pees. Aksels watches from everywhere. Ieva is embarrassed.

From then on Ieva starts every meal by silently offering the first bite to Aksels. She eats inside of Aksels. Ieva herself is Aksels.

Aksels is also the full moon. When is stands silent and large over Earth, he's there. At 4 A.M. on the night of every full moon. Before his death, silence was silence. After it, silence became woven with thoughts. If she listens carefully, Ieva can sense Aksels is contemplating there in the silence. She lies in bed, afraid to move, and takes part in his thoughts. It doesn't have a definite form or direction; Aksels, streaming through the moonlight, contemplates in every direction, intelligently and achingly.

Dung flies—big, fat, active—that's what real life looks like!
You can only keep something sacred in an abstract form. And put it in the left chamber of your heart. Any icon placed in the picture frame of life looks blasphemous, even though blasphemy is really just

life itself. When you cry, someone somewhere is definitely laughing. That's the way it is and there's nothing you can do about it. Except store Aksels's flat, helpless body in your memory.

Helplessness. That's the second thing Ieva can't stop thinking about. A child's helplessness, an animal's helplessness, a sick person's helplessness, and an elderly person's helplessness when faced with an intelligent and capable mind. When faced with strength. Maybe that's where all faith, hope, and trust hide?
Whose hands will you wind up in when you're helpless?

From then on time splits—time before Aksels's death and time after it. Text messages received *before* and texts messages received *after*. The date on the packaging of a dried up loaf of bread is *before*, and Ieva shudders even before she's read it, even before she knows what she's read.

And what can she do now that she's left alone without Aksels? Hope that some day she'll be overcome by that somber valley to which he took off like a bird with a broken wing? Ieva would know how to die right then and there, but she wasn't convinced that she would die in the same place as Aksels. Ieva looks for Gran's Bible—it was supposed to be the book meant for the times fate separated two people and they needed a guide to find their way back to each other. The Bible was in old print, and nowhere did it explain how to die with another person.
Ieva went to church. The services dragged on, the pastor talked about the rich and the poor, and who had a harder time getting into Heaven than threading a camel through the eye of a needle. Everyone repented their sins together, the pastor forgave them in the name of the Lord, and then fed the hungry in two lines with the body and

blood of Christ. Ieva swallowed it all and believed, but no matter how achingly she sang along, cried, prayed, and ate, she didn't see Aksels anywhere in this place. She left while the pastor ground out his last phrases about Christ, whom the pastor obviously loved. What was Christ to Ieva when she loved Aksels? Aksels wasn't here.

Ieva also searched in the forest. In the trees, in the sky. Aksels wasn't there.

He wasn't in the cemetery, either.

He wasn't anywhere.

Only in as much as his body lay those few nights next to Ieva, completely dead, cold, and beautiful. And in as much as his soul appeared at 4 A.M. on a full moon like a thought weaving through the room.

And maybe not even that was true.

Ieva suddenly understood death.

She understood—there simply wouldn't be anything more.

The world would never have another person like that.

Somehow she had to live on. Ieva had heard stories about Buddha who, when he saw his first dead body, was unable to go on living and sat under a tree, where he had a revelation that eased suffering. Ieva didn't have a revelation. She burned a few of Aksels's things, put his photos and documents in envelopes, and didn't know which envelope held the meaning of life. The reason to be.

The thread of substance had broken. Ieva continued to exist in body, but only so Monta wouldn't be left alone.

And every now and then she told her daughter a little story about the time when Ocela had still been with them.

Tell someone about your dreams.

Always, definitely tell someone about the dreams you've dreamt. Once you undress the dream with words, you'll discover the meaning of it.

Explain the dream using the shortest possible words.

Once you undress the dream with words, you'll see your delusions in the words.

Explain the dream using the simplest words possible.

Be alert.

A few years go by, and then one day Andrejs's mother calls her up:

"Dear, if you hold any part of life to be sacred—go visit Andrejs in prison."

THE NINETIES

RIGA

INITIALLY Ieva, Aksels, and Monta stay with Ieva's parents in their two-bedroom apartment in a Khrushchev-era building in the outskirts of Riga. Ieva's brother Pāvils is studying in America and his room is empty. "It's a nice room, on the sunny side!" Ieva says in earnest joy as she sits on the floor among the clutter, watching the sun reflect on the rust-colored roof of the building across from them. The room is too small to fit three beds. Monta sleeps between Aksels and Ieva. She often shifts to an angle in her sleep and Ieva and Aksels have to fight to keep from being pushed out of bed.

During the day, Aksels and Ieva look for jobs. Ieva's mother Lūcija babysits Monta because Monta is still too young to send to kindergarten.

Ieva's father Pauls still works in an office; despite the changing times, every morning for the past thirty years he stands at the mirror tying his tie, then takes his briefcase and heads to work. He was never in the Young Communist League and has never been a member of the Communist Party—something that's considered a huge plus in these times. Possibly because the members of the Communist Party who were quick to switch sides are now Pauls's bosses. A hard-working person will be hard-working no matter where he is. Pauls and Lūcija have never taken sides, unless you count the time Pauls burned his Soviet passport at the Freedom Monument during the Awakening Manifesto. After that Ieva and her father went to vote in the first election of the newly independent Latvia. The officials didn't let Pauls vote, he didn't have a passport. I burned it at the Freedom Monument!, he had shouted, but they still didn't let him vote.

"An official is always right," he later joked about his bad luck.

I'll place a dream about my Fatherland under my pillow,
one day I'll meet with it again and be happy,
and sleep as soundly as a baby in its mother's arms—
even in the suffering of death.

This poem by Jaunsudrabiņš, "For the Deported," is always written on the first page of Pauls's day planner. A free Latvia has always been his dream. He was disillusioned rather intensely at a young age—the deportation of his loved ones and the suffering of legionnaires.

Like every child who grew up during the war, the most important thing to Pauls is safety. He doesn't seek out confrontation, doesn't alter decisions, is careful with his finances, and always has a little pocket money for Ieva.

"But in moderation! There are sprinters and there are marathoners," he'd say. "Speed is the death of a marathoner."

Pauls is a marathoner, but very upbeat. Ieva thinks he could have been a fantastic actor had he wanted to. But even actors have to cross the line now and again, and that was something Pauls could only do in his dreams.

Even the theater pales in comparison to the streets. People don't go to the theater—what's happening in the streets is more interesting. The founding and collapse of banks, political parties, governments. Office workers are plucked like reeds by the raging storms of political powers. Many nights Pauls comes home from work completely withdrawn and sits in the small kitchen emptying a half-pint bottle of brandy.

"So I don't have a heart attack!" he explains. "Today I had to explain again to the new minister why the last one made such a mess."

Aksels lucks out and gets a carpentry job at the Academy of Music. It's easy enough. Ieva sometimes goes to visit him in the academy's basement—to make love, since they can't at home. They put a blanket down on the floor. The dark vaults are warm and smell of wood glue, and dusk is filled with the sounds of the academy students' nightly practices.

Ieva isn't as lucky in finding a job. She diligently looks through the want ads in every possible newspaper. For the most part people are looking for secretaries—young women with a high school education, good Latvian and Russian language skills, and computer skills. English language skills will be considered an advantage. Ieva's young—she has the necessary education and even understands some English. But she has never in her life seen a computer.

One night Pauls says:

"No problem! Come see me at work tomorrow!"

The next day Ieva trudges up the huge staircase of the Ministry of Finance and watches the young women strut confidently through the plush-carpeted hallways. That's what a secretary has to look like in the capital—long blonde hair, a thin gold necklace, and an immaculate suit.

Ieva's father sits her down at his desk. Hm, Ieva thinks, so that's why he likes his job—the centuries-old oak desk asks no questions and embraces you in its sanctuary, which smells lightly of warm paper and sealing wax.

"Look!" her father says. "This is called a mouse. And that's the monitor. Did you really not have a computer class in school?"

There were, they did have classes like that, where the teacher sat with his droopy mustache hanging over his desk and made them fill notebooks with writing on the basics of programming, showed them photographs and once took them on a special trip to the teacher's lounge, where the school's only computer sat under a cover in a locked cabinet—a real monolith! At least that's what her classmates had told her; Ieva had been home sick that day.

Now she puts her hand on the mouse and moves it across the desktop. And the movement of her hand is reflected on the monitor: a white arrow moves around the screen. It's complicated, but at the same time so simple. Something in Ieva's mind is good at connecting her hand with the screen. Her father teaches her how to boot up and shut down the computer, how to open a new Word document, and Ieva heads home in a good mood. All that's left to get is a suit, and she'll be a secretary!

But it's not that easy.

The first job Ieva gets is in some automobile club owned by twin Armenian brothers. Ieva's diligent, writes press releases, and handles commercials for the radio and television, issues membership cards. Until one night when she stays to practice with the computer and she notices some flat-out lies. It's advertised that the automobile club has a couple thousand members, but she can see on the computer—there aren't more than a couple hundred! The following day she tells Olga, the office manager, a prissy Russian woman with long, buffed red fingernails. It's just some kind of mistake, Olga says. The next day the Armenians fire Ieva.

Now a bit smarter, Ieva tries out a position at a construction firm. The director, a small and chubby old man, never misses an opportunity to pinch her butt. For a while Ieva pretends not to notice, but one morning when the director asks to recite some poems he's written for her, she loses it and starts laughing hysterically.

The repercussion comes soon after. The office hosts an associates' evening—Ieva fills bowls with fruit, lights candles, gets a fire going in the fireplace—if a secretary wants to get her pay on time, she has to be capable of more than working with a computer or speaking English! The director calls Ieva into the room with everyone else and offers her a glass of cognac.

"But you know I don't drink," Ieva says.

The next second the director throws the cognac into her face.

Ieva even tries placing an ad—*Looking for secretarial work.* The next day the phone at the Eglīte apartment rings non-stop with calls from what are basically pimps. A gruff voice breathes into the receiver:

"Are you interested in work over the phone?"

"What kind of work is it?" Ieva asks before she gets what's going on.

"A certain way of talking over the phone, you understand?"

Ieva understands and yanks the phone cord out of the socket. There'd been no sex in the Soviet Union. Now the city was full of so-called escort clubs—cropping up like mushrooms after the rain. Sex over the phone and in saunas, escorts, strip teases, massages. Once she was approached in the square facing the National Opera by a man with a pathetic droplet of perspiration at the tip of his nose. He'd said:

"Do you want to be a model? You've got a great rack and long legs."

Ieva grows tired, but doesn't give up. Everyone in this insane city needs a job—but does that mean she won't find one? Riga swarms like the entrance to a beehive in the spring, and pulls Ieva along with it—young and with her hair in the wind. Each new day brings hope, but each night brings dark defeat.

She applies for a job at an advertising agency. They need advertising agents for the publisher of the largest illustrated magazine. Her interviewing director is a lean, bearded-type in a plaid jacket who dozes lazily in the rays of sun falling across the large desk. Ieva tells him outright:

"Hire me. I'm done with being a secretary who gets cognac thrown in her face."

The director opens his eyes, smiles, and draws a checkmark next to Ieva's name.

She goes to training, where she and the other blank canvases listen as a well-rounded and advanced advertising agent lays out the rules of the game and gives them secret tips: how to handle their victims, how to conquer and win a seat at the table. Shamelessness, tactics, obstinacy—he more or less spoon-feeds these things to the silent group.

And then they're let out into the world with contracts in hand. Their salaries depend on the price of the deals they sign on.

The first place Ieva ends up is in the office of a car dealership. The front room she's told to wait in has a table, a chair, and a dark glass wall. Ieva walks around the room, looks out the window. Sits down in the chair and thinks—about nothing. The minutes go by; her half hour has already come and gone. She hears quiet music coming from behind the door. Ieva remembers that she'd almost ripped her only pair of stockings that morning. Do they have a run in them now? She stands up, checks her nylons and carefully straightens and smoothes her skirt back down over her thighs.

She's finally called in. Ieva goes into the adjacent room, and it's like there's a small party going on. A low stone table is covered in bowls of fruit and bottles, there's music playing, and several men in suits are sitting on the leather sofa. One of them asks her:

"So, what did you want to tell us?"

They're all grinning at her. Ieva turns to face the thick glass wall and sees that it's only tinted black from the outside. For an entire half-hour, it's like she's been in the palm of the collective hand of the men sitting down behind her. Like a live movie on a giant screen.

"Thank you, but I'm all set." She blushes and leaves the room to the thunderous sound of laughter.

She lucks out at the wedding shop. The store's management hears her out and has her prepare an ad series for six magazine issues. Ieva's almost walking on air. Finally, this hopeless running around until her heels are rubbed raw will yield some results! She showers kisses on Monta, Aksels, her mother and father, is up late sketching drafts and coming up with slogans. She won't say anything at the agency, just show up and drop the signed contract on the table; she has brains, after all, and she'll come up with a marketing slogan so amazing it could inspire anyone. Your wedding dress—the caress of a silky summer night! A velvety autumn dream! A luxurious wintery mist!

The management at the wedding shop like her suggestions, Ieva is overcome by excitement and the store director just smiles as he looks at this blustery and passionate advertisement agent.

"The way you look right now, I'd marry you myself," he says. "But first I'll have to consult with our accountant."

Forget the accountant! It's a fantastic offer. Ieva slides the contract over to his side of the table. All the director has to do is pick up a pen and sign it. Still smiling, he watches Ieva float out the door, the valuable piece of paper clutched tightly in her hands.

Yes! Ieva really is walking on air. A five-hundred-lat contract! She'll finally be able to buy something for herself, Aksels, and Monta. Take a trip to visit Gran by the seaside. Being poor is something you can only deal with for so long. Constant poverty can wear down even the strongest spirit. Ieva dreams of one day going into a store and just buying things. Without mentally tallying her remaining santims.

Back at the agency, she finds Zane smoking in a sunspot in the hallway by an open window. They'd already noticed each other during training. Zane is pretty, with an honest face and honest eyes. She used to be a TV journalist. She looks over as Ieva runs up to her with sparkling eyes and gives her a big hug.

"Good news?" Zane asks.

"A five-hundred-lat contract!" Ieva says proudly.

"Oho! Me, I'm sick of it. I'm quitting. I go to all kinds of companies, see all the people I used to film pieces on, and they all laugh at me when I try to convince them to advertise with us. 'Do you seriously have nothing better to do?' they ask. Guess I'll have to go back to television."

"Why did you leave in the first place?"

"Lost my husband and kid in a car accident. For two years after that I was totally wrecked. Now I'm trying to bounce back."

Ieva bites her lip and lowers her eyes. She doesn't know why, but she feels like the wooden floor of this hall, the color and boards worn down smooth by hundreds of shoes, will stay in her memory for years to come.

The advertisement agency tells Ieva that her contract is worthless. The director's signature is there, but there's no stamped seal.

"Did you honestly not know that you also need the stamped seal?"

Ieva remembers the smile of the wedding store's director. He knew—Ieva's sure of it.

And it's true. No one lets her in to see the director back at the store. An elderly, owlish accountant sits at the desk; a cast iron creature with a heart of lead.

"Young lady!" she glares at Ieva sternly over round glasses. "Do you want to bankrupt us? Do the math—do you know how many dresses we'd have to sell to break even on this kind of contract?"

Fine, fine. Ieva doesn't sleep that night, but she also refuses to give up. All the books say that success is the most important thing of all. And the face of Fortune could turn toward Ieva at any moment—she can't give up hope.

A new store for fancy designer jeans has opened up downtown. Walking down the street, Ieva sees a sign in the window saying they need a sales associate and heads right in. She's got nothing else to lose.

The store is clean, classy, and quiet. There aren't many people in the city who have the means to shop here. The sales associate hands Ieva the storeowner's business card, and Ieva calls him. His voice is calm and polite. He asks her to send a photo first.

If they need a photo, she'll send a photo. Ieva gets her picture taken for the first time at a photo shop. With the exception of a few pictures from her time living with Gran at the seaside, she has no other photographic proof that this Ieva person has ever existed. She's pleased with the outcome. Before she sends the photo, Ieva looks at it and wonders what people would say about the girl in the picture if they saw her on the street. Dark hair, a delicate face. Narrow eyes like she's Icelandic. Ieva remembers Jonsy and decides right then—even if she dyes her hair later in life, she'll never be like that.

The owner of the jean store apparently liked Ieva's picture; he calls her the next day. Tells her to come for an interview at Hotel Riga.

The red-carpeted hallways of the grand downtown hotel knocks Ieva's courage down a few notches. But she gets to the owner's office and finds him to be good-looking and kind. And all smiles.

"Have you ever worked in sales? Do you have any experience working with a cash register?"

Ieva tells him she's worked as a waitress, a secretary, and an advertising agent—but never as a sales associate.

"I think I'll pick it up pretty quickly, and I'll definitely have the time. No one ever goes into that store!"

The second she says it she bites her tongue. She's said too much again, and it shows: the owner's smile is gone, like someone hit a switch inside his head.

"Thanks, we'll call you," he cuts the interview short.

They don't call, of course.

Her job search takes her farther and farther from the glossy center of downtown. One day Ieva ends up in a neighborhood of Jugendstil buildings. She finds a fabric store that needs a sales associate. Ieva gets the job and can hardly believe she's finally working.

The director, Boris, only asks:

"Have you ever worked at the market?"

"No," Ieva says.

"Good. The market teaches people to steal."

That Ieva has zero sales experience doesn't bother him. Boris even gives her a certificate that permits her to work with a cash register. And learning to use the register is so easy a dog could do it.

They're a group of several cashiers, and they giggle all the time. There's a phone on Ieva's counter, and her duties include answering it the several times it rings throughout the day and explaining that the milking machine store has moved. The director's apartment and office are above the store. He's bought a part of this beautiful building; however, the façade is the only truly beautiful thing left about it. It used to house the apartments of Soviet Army officers, but those are now abandoned and have peeling wallpaper, battered stoves, and sawed-off radiators. The following winter is as cold as death itself; the cashiers walk around in fur coats and the loaders' breaths come out in puffs. They're brought a shipment of dry firewood once a week, and it's the unspoken responsibility of the cashiers to bring it up to the fourth floor and into the empty apartment. The director and his wife host parties at their place on those days. Afterwards Ieva heads home in a cold tram, her insides burning with vodka and her skin all tingly. They don't get Saturdays off, and there are more and more little things to take care of in the stock rooms on Sundays. Shifts from 8 A.M. to 7 P.M. are swallowing up Ieva's time like a giant alligator. Sometimes she sees herself from the side—standing at her counter and using her spare moments to catch her breath and giggle with the other sales associates, who have become like sisters to her. And what do they laugh about? About nothing. It's exhausted, meaningless laughter. They're young, true, but work devours youth. Who does Ieva give up her days to? Her daughter barely knows her and sees her only late at night. Ieva's mother complains about her health and that it's hard for her to babysit Monta. The worst is that Ieva sees Aksels less, too.

Who does she give her time to? The store manager? What did he do to deserve such a valuable gift? The girls say nothing. Doesn't matter which corner of Latvia they're from—they watch what they say. It's hard to find work. The director knows this and doesn't pay them much.

Ninety lats a month for Ieva and almost the same for Aksels still isn't enough to look for their own apartment. There's no time to look, anyway.

One night as Ieva gets off the tram and heads home through the mess of drizzle and car headlights, she's stopped by a pedestrian. Ieva looks at the face in front of her and her eyes suddenly connect with familiar features.

"Andrejs!" she cries out.

For a split second she feels nothing but pure joy. She even almost throws her arms around his neck to hug him. But Andrejs's hunched shoulders and hands stuffed deep into his pockets quickly remind her of some things from the past; things that are near and dear, but at the same time as disgusting as an amputated limb now teeming with disease.

"What're you doing here?" she asks, surprised.

"Waiting for you," he answers and looks around for a place to get out of the rain. They go stand under the roof of the newspaper kiosk. Cars splash down the muddy road in front of them, tires blend snow with water, pedestrians jump over puddles.

"This is for Monta," he hands her money. "Take it, just don't spend it on that jackass."

Ieva takes the money and counts it mechanically. Sixty lats. Andrejs is holding a business card in his calloused fingers. Ieva puts it in her purse. Her husband's telephone number. Like a secret she has to hide from her lover, the thought comes to her.

"Have you been out to Zari?"

"I drive out now and then. Nothing's changed."

Ieva remembers the quiet forest surrounding the pasture. Even when they're all dead and gone, the forest will be just as silent.

"So, how's your little genius doing?" Andrejs sneers. "Do you read books at night, too?"

"More and more," Ieva fights back tears. "Why did you even come if you're just going to be mean?"

"How can I not be? What a love. Actually your mom called, said you're not doing good at all. But that's none of my business anymore. See ya," he says, and heads off into the night.

Ieva trudges past storefronts. Her tears mix with the rain; no one will notice in this wintery mess. Everything's messed up, nothing's as she'd hoped it would be. So many useless quotes written in letters to her brother. Books are something different, something removed from real life.

Ieva doesn't understand why she's stopped in front of a bookstore. Very strange. It seems so long since she's read something. Doesn't even read newspapers anymore, only the bits of articles used as kindling for the stove in Boris's office.

In spite of Andrejs she goes into the bookstore and slowly browses the shelves. Books have always been there, within arms' reach, she realizes. They don't impose themselves. Just wait.

She picks one up at random—Roberts Mūks. *Eastern Religions—Meditation—Cyclical Time.* Picks it up and opens it.

Cyclical time.

Ieva has no idea how long she's been standing and reading. She doesn't understand the text, only barely grasps what it's about. The book is about something that has absolutely nothing to do with her life at that exact moment: the fabric store, money, her daughter getting sick, cold trams, cheap sausages, and bankrupt banks. But strangely enough, the text moves her, as if it was being read by someone whose existence Ieva wasn't even aware of.

She quickly buys the book. It doesn't matter that the money was meant for Monta. Ieva can skip her own dinner tonight. It's only a few lats, yet at the same time—a fragile inspiration, swirling over the black streets like the Northern Lights.

Back at home, Ieva traps her mother in the bathroom. Blackish foam churns in the washing machine; her mother picks articles of clothing from the foam in a trance-like state and tosses them into the bath to be rinsed. The washing machine is probably as old as Ieva, and it's finally broken down. When you turn it on it just churns and churns . . .

"Mom, why did you call Andrejs and talk to him about me?" Ieva confronts her mother in a threatening whisper.

Her mother looks at her. At this moment she is an old, ancient woman. Ieva's heart even skips a beat. Her mother says:

"It's late. We'll talk tomorrow."

"No, now! I'm living in your apartment, I'm grateful, but all I ask is that you never butt into my business again!"

Lūcija straightens up with the last of her strength and presses her fists into both sides of her lower back. The front of her robe is dark, soaked with water. The bathroom is as narrow as a test-tube—full of damp steam and the ineffective hum of the washing machine motor—an uncomfortably small space.

"Then pay me. What's that look for—you think it's not hard work? Then find someone who'll watch your kid for free from morning to night."

Ieva is so shocked that she starts to sputter:

"And I thought . . . out of kindness . . . that you guys . . ."

"We'll never not support you, even if it would mean living in a box ourselves. But it's not easy. It's not easy."

Ieva considers what she's heard. It's not easy on her mother, she has to admit to that. But—it's not easy for any of them.

"Listen, Mom," she finally says. "You're right, but I don't get what that has to do with you butting into my life. I asked you a specific question—why did you call my husband?"

Lūcija gets angry and plunges both hands into the mouth of the washing machine, throws the clothes into the bathtub with such force that water splashes up onto the walls.

"Because you need money! You have only one set of clothes, and if you weren't able to dry them overnight you'd have to go to work naked!"

At that moment Aksels sticks his head into the bathroom.

"I'm really sorry, but could I get in here for the toilet? Oh, Ieva, you're home, too? Great!"

They give each other a kiss and then Ieva and her mother go into the hall. As soon as Aksels is behind the closed door, Ieva whispers harshly:

"Thanks for your great advice, but I don't need it!"

Her mother calls after her:

"Take the money from Andrejs if he gives it. Monta is his daughter, too! Don't be so prideful!"

Life on Pērnavas Street ends with her mother's relative from the countryside who can no longer take care of himself.

One Sunday Ieva notices a gaunt, nearsighted old man in large horn-rimmed glasses wandering the apartment with a cane. Monta has just woken up and is riding her tricycle around in reckless circles and getting stuck in the narrow doorframes. She rides into the old man's legs and honks her horn. He starts to shout, spittle flying, and bangs his cane against the floor.

"Don't run me over! Don't run me over!"

This repeats several times. Ieva kisses Aksels and goes into the kitchen to make coffee. Then, hair disheveled and half-asleep, she takes her mug and goes to stand in her parents' room. Her mother is sitting at her desk reading the Nature Calendar, her father is watching Formula-1 on TV.

"Morning! Who's the old guy in our apartment?"

"Oh him! My grandmother's brother, Uncle Alfrēds. He has high blood pressure and sought refuge with us."

Ieva takes a long drink of coffee and thinks Uncle Alfrēds's blood pressure is probably not going to drop while he's here.

"Where is he staying?"

"Here. For a week already, if you haven't noticed."

Her mother points to a mattress next to the bookshelf.

Her parents watch her closely. Ieva senses what they want to say. Another of Uncle Alfrēds's moose-like bellows comes from the narrow front hallway.

Ieva picks up Monta, tricycle and all, and goes into her room. Aksels is still asleep, his bare arm slung over his eyes.

"Let's go for a walk!"

"Don't want to."

Ieva dresses Monta, then suddenly says:

"We can't stay here anymore, Aksels. Think about it."

She and Monta go to the park, where there is an abundance of fresh air, sun, and pigeons. Ieva is jealous of the pigeons. Everything for pigeons is always higher and freer.

Ieva watches Monta swing and thinks about Andrejs. That Monta is his daughter.

Monta is Andrejs's daughter.

Andrejs's daughter.

Suddenly she gets an idea—she finds a phone booth and calls Andrejs:

"Hi! Can you lend me two hundred lats?"

Silence on the other end. Then:

"What for?"

"That's not important. Can you help me or not?"

"Of course I can. When have I ever not helped you?"

With a secretive smile, Ieva buys a newspaper on the way home that's filled with ads for apartment rentals. She'll tell Aksels that the money was an unexpected bonus.

Their next home ends up being a long communal apartment on Blaumaņa Street. Aksels has gradually made friends with the eccentrics of Old Riga, and this apartment is the ghostly mirror of their world. It houses all types of people and it's a miracle if they can stay in their own rooms for more than a few minutes.

It's right in the center of Riga, and from the outside the building looks pretty respectable. But if the odd passer-by were to look at it longer, he'd see its hidden bruises and open wounds. The stone balcony of Ieva's and Aksels's fourth-floor room slopes dangerously low like a droopy lower lip. A small birch tree growing through the cracks in the balcony scatters reddish leaves right onto the sidewalk. The beautifully carved stone faces under the building's eaves are crumbling and eroded by moisture.

There's no door code to get into the stairwell, so it's used by both bums and cats as a place to sleep. Their apartment starts with a large kitchen, which, among people looking for something to eat, is cluttered with old appliances—a gas stove, a pile of rusted radiators, and broken refrigerators. The kitchen is always full of people and they use the broken appliances as tables. A long hallway leads into the body of the apartment. It's accented by cement beams, almost like a windpipe

245

with rings of bone leading into the stomach of a sleeping beast. There are nine rooms across from each other—the last door is the bathroom, with a shower and toilet.

"There is nothing new, we can only try to coordinate our lives with everything that has existed since the beginning of time," Ieva sits in her room reading Roberts Mūks. She likes this time and everything it brings with it—like a tumultuous river that overflows with silt during the rainy season. She likes the birch tree on the balcony and the high ceilings. Andrejs's money was also enough for two beds. Aksels made two pretty bookshelves at the carpentry shop. And then there was the old Continental typewriter that had been waiting for them in the empty room—like a gift—apparently left behind by the previous tenants. Ieva puts a sheet of paper into the black frame and slowly types out letters with one finger. Vowels and consonants, with and without the diacritics. Capital letters. Lowercase letters. She explores the typewriter like a traveler in a new country. Only Ieva has nothing to write about. Might as well copy Mūks. Ten times: "There is nothing new, we can only try to coordinate our lives with everything that has existed since the beginning of time."

She copies Mūks and then starts to form her own, simple sentences: "The fir tree is growing." "Monta is growing." "Monta is my daughter." "Aksels and I will be together forever." And she's fascinated by how the words, once they're typed out, suddenly take on a public format. Whether she wants them to or not. Accidentally or on purpose. Like a carpentry shop turns a fir tree into a sample display door. So that's the hidden secret of writers! They just write with a typewriter! Put their words into a concrete format. They command words.

In the meantime, Monta explores the apartment. She goes into each room, and the residents of each room eventually bring her back to her mother. It becomes a reason to have a cup of tea and start up a conversation. Their neighbors include art and philosophy students, punks, the singer of an underground band and her boyfriend, a German-language instructor, and provincial poets.

The most interesting person to Monta is Ilmārs, who lives in the eighth room.

Ilmārs is an antiques dealer with an inclination for photography. In his spare time he hangs around the apartment in his sweat suit and drinks a lot of green tea, which is why you'll almost always run into him in the kitchen. He has a ruddy, goatish face, grey beard, and watery green eyes. Rubbing his bare belly, which always pokes out from under his short T-shirts, Ilmārs inflicts listeners with horror stories from the lives of the Riga elite.

He brings Monta back to Ieva and gushes in appreciation at the typewriter.

"Oh, you're a poet?" he whispers and brings Ieva's hand to his lips. "It's a pleasure to meet you. Ilmārs."

Ieva explains that the typewriter had already been here, but Ilmārs shakes his head in disbelief. He's never seen it before. From that moment on Ieva was carved into Ilmārs mind as The Poet. In other words—a Muse.

"Come," he says. "I'll show you what life is! All you'll have to do is write it down."

He puts his finger to his lips and leads Ieva into the dim hallway. Germanic shouts come from the half-open door of one room—some boys are watching a documentary on Hitler. The shouts mix with passionate and heavy breathing; the singer and her boyfriend are probably having sex in their room. Ilmārs motions for Ieva to listen at another door—the Art Academy students are fighting, a plywood stool splinters against the door and Ieva escapes back to her room.

"You didn't even see the bathroom—an extremely fascinating creature spends all morning sleeping in there!" Ilmārs calls after her in disappointment.

Some time later Ilmārs brings home and gives his Muse an *Ērenpreiss*-brand bicycle. Incredibly old and heavy, but in working condition.

"Extremely valuable! An antique!" Ilmārs boasts.

She keeps the bike down in the courtyard, locked up with an iron chain to a maple tree. Dragging it up and down the stairs would be suicide. The bike opens up an entirely different Riga to her; it glides easily and lightly, relaxing the hectic streets, smoothing the nervous lines in the city's face. The bike reminds her of an old coal iron or the first pair of skis in the world—broad, substantial things that would let life could coast along without change. The stores, cafés, people, even the sky and the trees, even the river is wide open—all because Ieva herself is open. Her thumb poised, ready to ring the bell. Her lips ready to smile, her heart ready to answer.

Monta starts attending kindergarten. She's still little, but they have no other choice—Lūcija refuses to take her, says it's still too tiring for her to babysit.

It doesn't seem like kindergarten bothers Monta too much. She's a social soul and very independent, the kindergarten teacher says to Ieva with a reassuring smile. She has cause to smile—Pampers have finally secured the market in Riga. The teacher won't have to change any more cloth diapers. Even Monta is dropped off at kindergarten with a stack of Pampers in her bag.

Sometimes Ieva stops by the cast iron fence and watches the kids play in the green oasis set in the middle of the muddy, cobblestoned city. So loud and happy, as if the world were without war, sadness, defeat, and victory . . . They've only just come into the world, but have such wise eyes, such age-old stares. But with all the bitter memories extinguished in their mothers' wombs. Like freshly washed clothes bleached and dried in the sun and wind, they're once again ready for fun and games, fun and games . . .

God help me understand what a child is—and that I have one.

This is what Ieva prays for from the other side of the fence.

She knows full well that it'll come to her sometime later in life. She'll find out.

For now it's all the same: work or home. Work or home. She doesn't get any of it.

Now, of course, she's got a different job. Boris and Ieva never had the same idea of a work schedule. During the time they moved to the new apartment, Boris felt Ieva was asking for too many days off.

So it's without worry that she goes to the Central Market to find work. They always need sellers there and they work in shifts. She even gets days off! It's a luxury in this madness. And what's more, their apartment is fantastic! They have their own life—it is what it is, but it's their own.

And Pampers aren't the only thing that have taken the city by storm—the first cellphones have arrived as well. Als, the owner of the mandarin orange stand, ceremoniously presents her a giant Benefon, a brick with an antenna. So I can always get a hold of you, he says. After only a few minutes of use the receiver heats up like an ember and electric jolts start to course through your brain.

Ieva's parents also have cellphones. Ieva takes a black permanent marker and writes her mother's number directly over the kitchen sink. They have a great relationship now. But when was it not great? Love is the foundation of everything; it just gets forgotten sometimes in the commotion of the day. Even a mirror fogs over if you look too closely into it; the image becomes distorted.

Aksels has grown very secretive. He's stylish, he likes taking risks, he's polite and brave—all reasons why he's eventually gained the respect of the Old Riga party-crowd. Strange, almost underground literature-type books start showing up in the apartment—Indian mystic

Osho's *Diamond Sutra or Perfection of Wisdom* in a black hardcover, ridiculously battered Russian-language copies of Castaneda, Kerouac, Hesse, Camus, Flannery O'Connor. Some nights he gets home very late and brings a loud group of people with him. Ieva joins in, why not?

They smoke marijuana.

Everyone smokes marijuana.

Ieva tries it, too.

At first nothing happens. Ieva laughs and takes a deep hit, never skipping her turn as it's passed around. After a while she realizes that even when she's not laughing, all the muscles in her cheeks are tensed. She tries to fight it, but can't. Her head feels clear and filled with happiness, and she's the reason why. Her body stops listening to her brain. The room does the same—the walls aren't listening to the ceiling, and even the door has bowed out like the ribs of an animal.

With a silent scream Ieva runs into the stairwell and crouches down by the banister. Down below is a roaring, smoldering abyss that reaches for her little by little like waves in the sea. The walls are crashing in on her from the other side. Peace and safety exist only in the cramped space where she's crouched. When Aksels comes to get her, she murmurs in terror:

"Don't! Don't touch me!"

You can't mix alcohol with weed, Aksels tells her matter-of-factly later on. Some people react that way. From then on Ieva is always hesitant to smoke up.

Ieva also discovers something much worse and more ruthless than weed—jealousy. As she sits at home with Monta in the evenings, she tries to imagine what Aksels is doing out in Old Riga. With his friends. Ieva knows he's with his friends, but why so late?

Oh, Aksels says, I ran into so-and-so—well you don't know them anyway! What's the point in explaining?

One Saturday, when Monta is at her grandmother's, Ieva heads to Old Riga. Aksels and his friends usually hang out at the bar M6; she goes in, but it's dead and quiet. The only people there are Aksels and some extremely drunk girl. They're sitting at the massive wooden table; Aksels turns around suddenly and addresses Ieva—Hey! It's too late to run, she's been spotted.

Aksels widens his eyes in surprise.

"What're you doing here?"

Then he introduces them:

"Dace! Ieva!"

And he orders Ieva a drink.

Ieva slowly takes off her jacket and doesn't know how to act. Aksels just smiles, then goes to chat with the bartender. She can tell by how he walks that he's either had a lot to drink, or a lot to smoke. Dace turns her whitewashed face to Ieva. She has a shaved head, black liner around green eyes, and ears full of silver studs.

"He said," Dace whispers secretively, "that I have horrific eyes. Do I?"

Ieva doesn't respond. She can see that Dace is excited and concerned by what Aksels has said.

Aksels comes back, packs a small amount of weed into his bowl, lights it, and immediately passes out. The bartender whistles patiently and piles bananas in a bowl.

Dace has to get going. She muscles on her leather jacket, kisses the sleeping Aksels on the cheek, and leaves. She has long, deer-like legs that end in black lace-up boots. She has a free gait. Ieva definitely doesn't. If only Ieva knew herself, she might know what kind of gait she has. Right now she doesn't know anything about herself.

Except that she has become addicted to Aksels. It's a terrifying revelation. She leaves him in the bar asleep, dead to the world, and sprints through the streets toward home. As she runs she shoves people out of the way, apologizes, trips, and wonders—what's it like to be a man? To have a spear instead of a cave? With which to invade caves meant for spears, acquire them, inhabit them, conquer them, and then move onto new conquests. How, for example, how can you tell another human being they have horrific eyes? And to say it in a way that makes the other person ignite like a brush fire and burn so long that the point of ignition bursts straight forth, breaks through the layers of blood and bone. What does it feel like to have a spear instead of a cave?

Time is slowly running out—at least that's what it feels like to Ieva. She sometimes confronts Aksels when he comes back home toting an entire group of Daces, or when he doesn't come home at all.

"You get some rest," Aksels says. "Don't worry about me."

"How can I sleep when we live together, but you're never home? Maybe we should live separately."

Aksels laughs:

"Don't be stupid. I can't live without you! Come out with me at night if you want to be with me."

"You're the one being stupid. How can I go out? I have Monta."

At the end of the summer Aksels becomes a punk. He finally finds his religion. Where there used to be all sorts of music at home, even the stuff brought in by Aksels—Laurie Anderson's "Bright Red," Nina Hagen, Boris Grebenshchikov, Tsoi, Odekolons, Brian Eno, Nine Inch Nails, or even good old Pink Floyd—now they've all been replaced by the Sex Pistols.

A September evening flutters over the city streets like a starched linen sheet. Ieva puts on "Yesterday" by The Beatles. Piano and vocals. Clarity. Music that lets you exist without having to touch the ground.

When Aksels gets home he takes the cassette out and throws it behind the bed.

"Why'd you do that?"

"It's shit."

"Why . . ."

"Listen, let's cut the small talk. Come here, I'll tell you about Sid and Nancy."

They lie down on the bed very close together—shoulder to shoulder, breathing in unison—and for the umpteenth time Aksels tells the punk legend about Sid Vicious and his girlfriend, the blonde, curly-haired Nancy. The punk Romeo and Juliet. Monta is right there, crawls up and settles between them and quietly twirls a strand of hair around her finger. She also listens to the nightly story about that day in October, when in room number 100 of Hotel Chelsea the police arrested Sid for the murder of Nancy, stabbed to death with a hunting knife.

"When he was let out on bail on February 2nd, he overdosed on heroine. And since then, February 2nd has been Sid Day. He once said: *Make anarchy your mother. Create as much chaos and confusion as is in your power, but don't let them take you alive.*"

"Anarchy in the UK" is playing, washing like waves over their still bodies.

Aksels calls Ieva his Nancy, but she's not a real Nancy. She has too broad of a horizon. For example, try as she might, she can't understand why Tsoi, or The Beatles' "Yesterday" have suddenly become complete shit this fall.

"It's like you've switched on some kind of tunnel vision," she tells him. "I can't do that."

Dace understands Aksels a lot better. She's also become a true punk—wears black, torn fishnet tights, short skirts with studs and a red silk blouse. Aksels and Dace can talk about the things that interest him because Dace doesn't respond critically.

One warm, dark evening Ieva rides her bike home from work and suddenly notices them in a crowd. They're high, drunk, doped up on something else, and are staggering down the sidewalk, leaning against each other for balance, and holding hands as passers-by move out of their way.

Ieva holds her breath as she follows them, slinking after them like a tiger—slowly, secretly, but her heart threatens to hammer a hole through her ribcage. From this perspective it's clear that Aksels and Dace are a real couple—two Riga punks, not some MTV punk wannabes with their rich parents' credit cards in their wallets and CD players clipped onto their belts. Not some bored and spoiled dumbasses who stand in the streets at night drinking beer in their tattered leather jackets, but spend the mornings sitting in offices in white button-down shirts drinking coffee—no. They're real street punks: unshowered, shaggy, young, and wonderful. It's like they're on the edge of a blade, always on teetering on the fence, and their gentleness is their fearsome cries in the face of the world, and their challenge is the timid call to see how full of love and strength they are—useless invitations!

They stop by some hedges and Aksels disappears into the dark to pee; Dace waits under the wind-rattled streetlight—a delicate, black gravestone for Aksels's and Ieva's love. Ieva stops torturing herself, gets back on her bike and rides home. An hour later Aksels and Dace show up, along with a few friends they met on the way, Ieva makes tea, breathes in the smell of the weed, and when Aksels passes out Dace tells her:

"Do you know what he said to me today? I asked if he'd kill me if I asked him to, and he said no—never!"

Dace cries, smears mascara down her cheeks, tears at her tights with her black-painted fingernails. Ieva says nothing, just thinks. She's suddenly become very calm—of course, my dear, that's how it has to be because I'm his Nancy. In spite of everything, I'm his Nancy.

So sometimes Ieva finds Aksels in the bar by himself, they have a drink, talk in the basement of M6, and then Aksels looks intently at her and says:

"I look at you and you know what I think? I want you, I want you so badly, always."

He's high and distant, he doesn't use tissues when he has a runny nose, just turns away, pinches his nostrils and blows, he's a real punk, and Ieva isn't even disgusted by it. He's real. That's the thing—Aksels is very real.

He gets on the bike, Ieva walks next to him in a wild, flower-printed dress. It's evening, and Brīvības Boulevard is full of people, busy with cars. Aksels rides in the street, isn't able to keep his balance, swerves dangerously, and rides in circles. Buses line up behind him, forming a chain, but don't honk their horns. People look back at them and shout—a punk on a bike, look! And Ieva is next to him in her flowery dress and orange flats on her feet.

Such a peaceful evening, filled with happiness.

Aksels asks Ieva to dye his mohawk red and black. He sits on a stool in the middle of the room and looks at the birch tree outside. His hair is beautiful: light and slightly wavy. Ieva can't dye it.

"Think it through! It'll look bad on you."

"Who tells a punk what he can or can't do?"

Aksels winds up in a bad mood and comes home the following night blackout drunk. His hair is a stiff, black crest. He slurs that Dace did it for him.

"Where did she do it?"

"At the carpentry shop!"

At the carpentry shop! Ieva hasn't been there in the longest time. Maybe Dace lives there now! That's why Aksels only ever comes home toward morning.

Insane jealousy, spite, and exhaustion crash simultaneously down on Ieva like sudden blindness. She can't see anything anymore, nothing real, no future, and no light at the end of the tunnel.

Aksels explains:

"Stop freaking out! It doesn't matter because I only love you, you're my Nancy. Everything else is just something secondary."

Before he falls asleep he reaches for Ieva, forcefully grabs her thigh, latches onto her like a bear clawing into her side, tearing at her, then he mumbles something and passes out. Ieva watches his exposed face, unveiled by sleep, deformed by drinking. Then she watches the flies circling the light bulb above the bed.

Outside the rain is coming down hard.

When Ieva was little, Gran was always fighting the flies—she'd put screens in the windows, go after them with a fly swatter, and poison them with chemicals from a black and white mister. Here the window facing the street is always open, you can watch flies in their natural state. They congregate in the room, dance, listen to "Love Kills" by the Sex Pistols, and then disappear as quietly as they came.

Ieva checks on Monta in her bed, straightens the blanket, goes to the kitchen. Right now it's mostly empty. A strange guy is sitting in his underwear on a stool by the wall—he has his arms wrapped around his body and his legs crossed. The curve of his ribs sticks out on his back like sharp swords under his thin skin. Probably some student. Ieva searches the shelves for a bottle of red wine—and she finds one, thank God! The white wine is always the first to go.

"Ahoy! How's it going?" Ieva asks the guy.

"Can't complain," he answers.

Ieva nods to him, pours him a generous glass of wine. There's no further conversation. Ieva drains the remainder of the bottle in one go.

She goes back to her room, turns on the small wall lamp and looks at the remains of Aksels. With anguish in her face, she gets a pair of scissors and cuts off his mohawk. The black, foreign pieces litter the pillow. After that she opens the scissors wide and resolutely drags them across the veins of her left hand.

Odd, there's almost zero pain. Only that horrible anxiety where you feel like a bowl with a crack in the side and the contents dripping out. The awareness that hangs in the chamber of your skull like a bat flapping its wings wildly—soon enough it will be washed away, too. Solder it shut, sew it up, fix the hole!—her brain screams. Ieva looks at her arm—it's such a thin arm. With such important blood. She would've never thought that blood itself was the content. And when it drops to the ground, you can't gather it back up again.

Then that warning, hot throbbing starts up in her ears, throat, temples—who knows where it comes from. The last thing she remembers is the half-naked guy in the kitchen and his terrified expression when she wakes him up to hand him her cellphone, pointing to the phone number on the wall above the sink and repeating: Mom! Mom!

Her left arm was so tightly bandaged that it felt like it was made of wood. They gave her a small pill and, when she woke later that night, she felt she had grown distant from herself. On the second morning they gave her two even smaller pills, and she crashed down onto the bed like she'd been knocked out. But her conscience wandered the ceilings, sadly observing its reflection down there on the mattress. Time dragged on like a giant rubber band, people came, undressed her and put her on a gurney, covered her with a blanket. Gave her a shot of something. Riding through countless, light bulb-lit tunnels, she felt she was exhausted to the point of death. They wheeled her off to the side; listening to the surrounding activity, the rustle of the greenish-grey cloth, she wants eternally peaceful sleep. But it's not possible because her essence was removed from her and broken apart. Then they brought her under lights, there were several people who cut into her bare arms—all she could see were their eyes. These eyes were calm, but she was so tired. It took them a long time to find her vein and they told her it was alright to scream because it would definitely hurt, but she was so tired that she wasn't able to tell pain from non-pain. It didn't worry her anymore. Her only and slightly hazy desire was to reconnect with herself, to become whole again. Instead, someone gripped her face between strong hands and looked into her eyes, saying: Your heart is going to start beating faster now and you'll get dizzy, and then you'll fall asleep—can you hear me, Ieva, Ieva, Ieva?

One face slowly solidifies in the fog. It's her brother, Pāvils.

He's shaking her by the shoulder.

"Pāvils? How'd you get here?"

"I'm visiting on vacation. And you've scared the crap out of me my first night back."

"Sorry, I didn't mean to."

"I'm happy you're alive. They had to redo the surgery—they hadn't stitched the tendons up the right way. You—when you do something, you do it with such drive that not even a team of doctors can deal with it!"

"You'll stay in Latvia?"

"We'll see. We'll have time to talk about it. Rest for now."

"I'm glad you're here."

Monta didn't see any part of what happened. When Ieva gets back home, she's loving and gentle as she hugs her mother's neck. Aksels has changed, too. He's grown more serious, darker. It doesn't suit him.

"Hey," Ieva says. "Cheer up! It had nothing to do with you. I just got lost in something."

Aksels doesn't smile, but hugs her tightly and shudders as if he's fighting to hold back tears.

"Aksels, love, please, be like you were before," Ieva begs, terrified. "I won't do it again."

Aksels is never the same after that. Some time later Ieva learns from his friends that Dace died. Overdosed on some kind of unknown pills. Had a heart attack.

Ieva's own heart feels a small twinge. What was she to you, Aksels? And what am I? I'll never know. The heavens are silent.

Aksels has become more of a homebody. Plays with Monta, reads to her, even takes her to kindergarten. He doesn't cut his hair into a mohawk anymore, lets it grow out thick and light and short. It's an almost unbelievable transformation, but Ieva hopes it's for the best. If only she didn't have to see the look in his eyes—even more hopeless than before, almost indifferent, and simultaneously shy. As if he's waiting for fate to take away his final plaything.

THE BUS

IEVA and Aksels head to the bus stop for Riga early one morning. An icy wind tears over the countryside. Aksels picks up Monta and buries her face in the warm crook of his neck. He never has mittens, Jesus! The cold is merciless, the first warning to all living beings that winter is on its way. Ieva looks back and sees his frozen, bare, and bluish hands locked around Monta. And she is grateful.

They wait at the crossroads where four roads come together. The sky is black, the land around them is covered with a light dusting of snow. Their fatherland. From the leeside of the hill they can hear the roaring of fir trees in the gully by the stables. Ieva wants to hold onto this sound forever and can't believe she's leaving.

A lone milk truck rounds the bend and turns into the driveway of the Branku house. A dog barks, milk cans clank, the glare of sunlight, the squeaking of the milk cistern lid. Then the milk truck comes into view again and slowly drives off up the hill. Again there is darkness and wind. The road to the Zari house stays empty. There aren't any more cows or people; not a single living sound can be heard coming from there. Only the grass will grow up through the threshold come spring.

Finally, a pair of headlights reach out from the pine forest and a bus approaches the crossroads. The driver has picked up a lot of speed, but sees them and tries to brake. The bus slips along the road like a giant fish and eventually stops a ways down from where they're standing.

They hurry toward it. The door opens. Warmth. Tickets. A few sleeping passengers.

The driver gives them an apologetic look over the rims of his glasses.

"It slides like it's on ball-bearings. This is my first time on this route."

They drive through the village, where cows will roam the streets in the morning fog in summer.

Then the turn by the lake, where the shoemaker Mārica's house stands. When the shoemaker died, he'd given his blessing for the house to be turned into a *točka*—a trade-house for distilled spirits.

In the darkness, the headlights of the bus reveal a thin old man on the side of the road hugging a white rucksack and a crumbling pretzel to his chest. The bus driver brakes hard again, and this time he succeeds and stops right in front of the old man.

The doors open.

A dirty parka, a bare and absurdly skinny neck, a drooping mustache, and a red nose. Surprised at the unexpected attention, the old man stands staring like a fox caught red-handed in the henhouse.

The driver says:

"Hop on board, sir!"

The old man rubs his knotted, red fingers over his knit cap and then waves them at the bus driver as if in farewell. He turns sideways and continues his way down the path to Mārica's house, bumbling:

"No, no, I'm headed there, y'see . . ."

"Pff, you!" The driver shouts and shuts the creaky bus door. "Why're you hanging out like some ghost on the side of the road?"

The bus drives on and a dark veil once more falls over the landscape. But the dawn has already torn a red seam in the east.

Why am I not going back to the seaside and Gran's, to the west? Ieva thinks. What's pushing me in the opposite direction? What will I find there? I don't know anything.

All I know is that back is back there and forward is up ahead. Right now it's time for the road ahead. Life's desires have fermented in my veins and formed strength, much like birch sap will ferment in a bottle to form a champagne that can shoot out even the strongest cork. The time will probably come when I'll spend summer sitting peacefully in a lawn chair finding joy in the flowers, and I'll use the long northern winter nights as a black cover, a hiding place, a fen, so I can regrow my clipped wings.

The time will also probably come for low tide. When I'll skulk back to Kurzeme, to my birthplace—in the dark, along the sandy dirt roads, by smell. Along the seashore, the manure, the blue anemones, the fragrant paths of thundering storm clouds, clutching my last, crumbling pretzel to my chest. And some early morning bus driver will notice me, pull me out of the eternal night with glaring headlights, blind me, stop and open the doors in welcome.

And I'll say to him—No, no. I'm headed there, y'see.

KEEP YOUR FINGERS CROSSED FOR US, BROTHER

Pāvil!

Hello, hello, hello! The college that accepted you doesn't even realize yet how lucky they are!

You're going to fly for the first time—and all the way to America . . . Hm . . . You're going to starve to death because, if we're brother and sister, then we have a lot in common, and I can tell you one thing for sure—I CANNOT eat in planes! Hopefully it'll be totally different for you, you'll stuff yourself full of hamburgers one by one.

I know you're getting ready to leave, so I won't bore you with a long letter. Just one juicy quote—yesterday some of the local women were teasing Roberts when he looked at them: Roberts is so old that the only sexual organ he has left is his eyes. Hoho!

Also—I went to a Student Symphony Orchestra concert, Inguna's friend played first flute. And in the "style of Gershwin's Rhapsody in Blue!"

Really, really hope to hear back from you!

Ieva

P.S. I think Troyat's *Les Eygletière* is an <u>awful</u> book. There isn't a single protagonist! It's the first time I've noticed one missing. Maybe my realization is to the book's credit?

P.P.S. The meaning behind our initials: I—tension, emotionality; P—shyness, distance, loneliness. Does that fit?

Greetings, American!

How are you? Are you already placing your hand over your heart when you hear the national anthem?

"When the euphoria of a first meeting fades, you must quickly find a new acquaintance to maintain happiness and so life doesn't lose its edge. Year after year passes by in smiles and tired jokes, and the road is littered with hundreds of temporarily—for a week or two—amused people."

As you can see, I'm reading the ocean book again. Doncho and Julia. All alone in their watery wanderings.

If Gran and Roberts were to finally kick me out and I'd somehow have to get through life on my own, I don't think the results would be good—I'd make it to the bottom of the front steps, and that would be it. I don't know anything about the world! So many people know what pain is (right now the time is 13:10 and the radio just started to play Dārziņš's "Melancholy Waltz"—how perfect!), what misfortune is, but they live on and shine, and are happy. I'm spoiled rotten. I have everything, but I'm always depressed. Sad. Brother, it's awful. I want to understand: what's wrong with me, who am I, why is this happening?

". . . people are not limited in their abilities, but are rather limited in what they demand of themselves. In a moment of need, or even if we've made the conscious decision to, each of us is capable of mustering the kind of strength we never even thought we could possibly possess."

Hm . . . It's a nice thought, I'm waiting for that moment of need. I could even get angry at myself in the end. If I could . . . The book has answers to all of my questions, and simultaneously reprimands me for them. Because I believe books. Maybe unnecessarily?

"Fear is a product of either nerves that are shot, or a stupid upbringing."

I don't want what I immediately write down, but my hand moves like a sailboat across the paper, on its own accord. I think my fear comes from somewhere deep down. From the day Mom and Dad decided to split us up and left me with Gran and Roberts. I can't imagine a better childhood than what I had. Books, books, books, the sea, and Gran with her muddy boots and white handkerchief in the potato field.

But each time I see Mom and Dad I suddenly feel a horrible emptiness tearing through me somewhere deep, deep down. Like in a desert. I'm not condemning their decision, I know about Mom's illness and your condition, but I still can't entirely understand the separation. We're polite, but say nothing, and I'm really scared that I'm not loved. So be it, I think, it's not within our power to end it. I'm glad you got in touch with me, and were so sincerely and from the bottom of your heart able to convince me there was no reason to be afraid. The desert sprouted plants. Now you're my flower, my brother. A wonderful gift.

I hope you're not tired of reading all these whiny letters—I can't, I don't want to, I don't know how . . . The only people who I respect are probably you and Gran. And Jonsy, the woman from Iceland who I met on my trip to Sweden. She's so courageous!

"Man is a curious creation. I've observed a close connection between my mood and the wind. Today, with a fresh trade wind blowing, everything in my body rejoices."

Across the Atlantic with Dju—yaha! Where does one find a trade wind in Latvia?

Write me!

Ieva

⟋

Hello, my dear brother!

Life is horribly complicated, or else horrible and complicated. I've suddenly realized—everything is happening to me and it's awful. I can't avoid it anymore, I'm not as flexible as I was as a kid or a teenager, I'm stiff as a pole, and each splash of mud lands right onto my soul. I must be destined to live the life of a lightning rod. Right now I'm just one big compromise. In my mind I want to boss everyone around. Let them call me mentally incompetent! Out of the box and without boundaries. But on the surface I'm so quiet . . .

. . . the meek will be spit out . . .

Oh but I know, I know already! But I can't let loose, because I'm not alone anymore.

. . . if my life was just mine and mine alone . . .

My boyfriend is a gloomy person with an entirely wrecked world outlook and with a cruel relationship—scores to settle—with this life. And I don't understand why this life has chosen him for me. And I agree with him on everything because I don't have the heart to hurt him ("E tu, Brute?"), I stand silently by him and hope for peace, but . . . I at least learned one thing during my short time in Stockholm— always look at everything from both sides. A shitty trait! It'll never let me just be.

. . . he who comes first, to him I shall belong, and adorn him with chrysanthemums . . .

. . . a lone crane flies among the clouds, completely alone, without friends it lets out a strange and fearful cry . . .

Brother, I want to see you so badly! Please, please!

When will you be back in Latvia?

I'll call you.

Ieva

Hello, brother!

I've finally worked up the energy to write to you. I got everything you sent—even that lovely little note. I knew I'd write back to you, because I really want to see you, but threshing time ruined a few of my plans. True—you sometimes only need a minute to write a letter, but for me to write to you, I also need to be in the mood.

I don't know what's going on! Sometimes I've been in the kind of mood where I can't stay put somewhere for more than three days. Now it's the same, but with the one big difference being that I'm tied down, can't get anywhere and feel a huge sense of discomfort.

It's morning, I'm eating dried plums, looking through the *Sudmaliņas* journal, and I want to cry. I want Riga and I want *Sudmaliņas*, I want it to feel like the *Baltica-88* folklore festival. I don't really know, but I suppose you're having a good time right now. Things in my life have changed, but we'll talk about that when we see each other.

I am as ever—your Ieva

P.S. I'll call you all next week in the evening until I get a hold of you.

So I can't wait, I have to tell you—I'm going to the General Register Office today to register. July 9th. Good God! I'm eighteen years old.

So alright, I'll just lay it all out: I'm going to have a baby in the fall.

⸺

Hey, brother!

Thank you so much for your letter, which I only got once I was at the Zari house. That's why I'm writing back late.

I haven't written anything about myself all fall because the season seemed to stretch on for a lifetime for me. Getting used to a new life is the same as trying on new clothes. The fit is a bit tight in places, and loose in others. No joke, just up until a little while ago my eyes were still wide in surprise—is it really still fall?

As a result of all of it, I'm at the Zari house with Andrejs. We had a hell of a time with the repairs. We're not that far from Gran, but the wildlife is totally different. Black sand in the forest, grass to your armpits. When there's a storm the sea doesn't blow in through the windows, but instead crashes far beyond the wet fields. Gran cried when I left. Roberts has just been crying non-stop. He's survived the war and Siberia, and still can't wrap his head around the fact that Latvians once again have their own, independent state. He either cries, or sits with his buddies at the store and discusses Virza's *Straumēni*. Roberts gave me a cow for my dowry—Salna. She's a blue seaside cow, one of Zīlīte's calves. We put a string around her neck and led her all the way here along the roads through the pine forest. We made it without any problems. Now I have my own cow among Andrejs's brown cows, I can wrap my arms around Salna's neck and cry when I miss my old life.

I have to do my own cooking, draw my own water from the well and carry it, light my own stove with damp firewood.

The old collective farm stable is just beyond the orchard. There are still a lot of horses in it. The pastures stretch on until our vegetable patch. Sometimes voices can be heard coming from the old manor, but other than that we're completely alone.

At first I really missed home. I'd think of Gran and my friends, then go into the woods to cry. But then Monta was born and I didn't have much time for crying. My daughter is beautiful and healthy, born on the first day of frost. I looked at her, and only when I saw her little face did I understand what a child was. First and foremost—a huge responsibility. A person who will be by my side my entire life. That's for certain. As is the fact that one day she'll see me die. But I'm not thinking about that just yet. Old age is the last thing on my mind.

It's all work, work, work, and then it's already time for bed. So we can be up by 5 A.M. the next morning.

Alright, it's already 22:22, pretty late, time for me to go to bed. I'm exhausted.

Write to me, I really need it. Please!

Ieva

—

Brother!

Each letter I get from you is a reason to celebrate. My reply probably won't be the same for you.

I'm shattered into a hundred tiny pieces, glass shards. The bottom of the pot, black from soot, sometimes seems sweet and white to me, while a glass of milk sometimes pours red as blood. This letter is going to be that same kind of mosaic.

I suppose you're experiencing some breakage right now, too. I'll give you one piece of advice, though—don't drop out of school! Like the sun needs the moon, like a plant needs its roots, like a leg needs a foot, like a star needs its shine, so does every thing and every being need a foundation. Education will give you the foundation you need to stand tall. Once you finish, you can be a romantic, an anarchist, an artist, a mathematician—whatever your destiny may be. But for now, build your foundation and don't, don't drop out!

I'll admit that my hair stands on end when it suddenly hits me that right now I live in a harsh, base, and simple world in which Andrejs and I constantly ask ourselves questions, but don't bother trying to answer them or even hear them. And there's no joy in the mirror, in the birds, in nature, they're all a bunch of lies. The word "joy" itself is a lie.

People like us fall in love with unrealistic people who have a strange glow about them. Because I came to the conclusion—the only reason I like my husband is because he's my star with his own shine, some kind of special (maybe dark) internal shine. A person isn't yours, no, it's their glow or their shine—that's what's yours. The soul, not the body! You wrote—how can you like him, you don't even know what he's like! Yes and that's the thing, I don't know him—maybe that's why there won't be any disappointment?

Even if there are others, even if I'm with them, he'll still be my ideal. And to be with him together in life—it's the most I could ask for. See, I have nothing to give to the world if I have nothing to give to love.

And in the end I've kind of "lucked out," my grasp on life isn't as complicated and refined as yours. I can only be amazed by how you express yourself, the picture you sent of yourself, and feel sorry for myself. I can tell you that you are one of the rare wonders I know of. You absolutely have to finish what you started, absolutely.

There's a forester's house not far from Zari, where this odd woman named Stase lives. You can probably tell from the letter that I've been to visit her a few times. She scares me, but I'm drawn to her keen mind and her opinions. Each time I promise myself that I'll never talk to Stase again, but I quickly forget, and it's deathly boring around here. My husband isn't big on languages, we talk about planting, cows, mechanics, but sometimes whole days pass where we don't speak a word to each other.

Stase has a son, Aksels, who's our age.

He's a bright guy and—sort of peaceful. The last time I sat with Stase until midnight and Aksels walked me home. It's funny, at the gate he watched after me until I went into the house—and then I felt guilty because of Andrejs, who'd stayed home with our daughter. It's the first time I've felt like that. Strange. And SO WHAT!!!—as Jonsy, my Icelandic friend, would say. What was that look for when I told him I'd been to visit Stase and Aksels? Can't I have friends?

I asked Gran once if she'd ever had friends. She answered—what do you mean, friends, I had family and didn't have time for friends. Maybe what she meant was that guilty feeling, when each new person you talk to essentially uses up words meant for your husband? But can there ever be fewer words?

If something here doesn't make sense to you, then let me just say that I don't even really get it. It's simple: I've gotten to know our neighbors, that's all. That's what I'll tell myself and that's how it is!

In closing I'll write something that I keep rereading with my husband in mind.

God bless you!
Ieva

—

That I want thee, only thee—let my heart repeat without end. All desires that distract me, day and night, are false and empty to the core.

As the night keeps hidden in its gloom the petition for light, even thus in the depth of my unconsciousness rings the cry—I want thee, only thee.

As the storm still seeks its end in peace when it strikes against peace with all its might, even thus my rebellion strikes against thy love and still its cry is—I want thee, only thee.

R. Tagore

Holy shit, brother, I'm <u>18</u> years old! But is that a reason for us to cry?

I can't bring myself to say goodbye to you yet.

Speaking of Aksels.

Aksels has a lot of books in that forester's house. And he's read all of them.

Andrejs has read maybe one or two in his entire life—and it was probably an instruction manual for laying a brick stove. At first I used to read to him a lot—don't laugh, it was before we'd go to bed—and he'd always fall asleep after the first paragraph.

Aksels gave me a strange story to read. I'll write it down for you and then burn it afterwards, because I want to think only of Andrejs and don't want to keep strangers' letters in the house. I'll probably burn it! Yes, probably! No doubt! And if this sentimental piece had some kind of value! I don't know where he got it, if he copied it out of some book or came up with it on his own. But read it for yourself:

The star said it had already figured as much. And then it cried on my shoulder, probably melted bits of frost left over on its lashes from that other time. It said that it had been to see a poor poet living in an

attic room. The poet often prayed to the star in the pale moonlight—
he was ragged, voracious, and impassioned. And the star had gone to
him. In the literal sense. In the way that only stars can go to people.
But the poet? The star now sobbed more bitterly. The poet had stood
bewildered—so grey, grey, grey.

"How," he had asked, "can you truly be so cold?"

"How," he had asked, "are you not a planet, but a little star?"

"And tell me, star, what am I to do with you?"

The star said it had already figured as much. It went and lay
down on the Milky Way and, focusing all its concentration internally,
exploded. Hundreds of poets saw this and said to themselves: "Oh! A
falling star!" And a hundred poems with a hundred different descrip-
tions of stars were born.

I went to see that poet, to the high windowsill up in his attic
room, and looked down. And there he lay, having already frozen as he
fell. The star had wooed the poet. It didn't bask in the light of adoration, but instead came and looked directly into his eyes.

People will be unintentionally destroyed by the wandering stars in
their lives.

I'm waiting for mine . . .

—

Hi, my dear!

Do I even need to say that your letter gave me another fantastic
emotional high? This morning Andrejs tells me—you got a letter, get
excited! I went to the house immediately, put on some music—and
what a relief it was to read your letter . . .

The way in which the prophecies come true on the ideas circulat-
ing in the skies above us at any given moment is so strange. We're

on the same wave, brother. I read your letter and feel like all of it is happening to me. Even though I dare to say we live in absolutely different worlds. At least in an external, physical sense.

You've grown up taking care of your spiritual life. I've mostly let mine drift, which I sometimes regret.

Who knows how we're supposed to live? There isn't a specific formula, and now and then we feel so lonely and unprotected. Especially when we have to make tough decisions.

The weather today is nice, foggy, and warm, sprouts are shooting up out of the earth and birds are chirping in every branch. I can keep the window open and hear how newborn foals whinny loudly in the pasture and search for their mothers.

I also have a man who loves me, a baby that we both love, and we have a house—and peace and safety. They're wonderful feelings, really. And how he knows how to keep me on a leash with this peace! You could say he's almost unbreakable in his confidence—run around the world, be wild, do smart or stupid things, but no matter what, you'll come back to me when you need something real! It's like that's what he thinks, and maybe that's right. Time will tell.

You and only you are responsible for causing problems for yourself.

Always, your Ieva

⟋

Hello!

It's so superb
to be free of doubt, to not try to hide
flaws behind lace and hopelessness behind laughter
and to one night wager destiny
against everything like a trump card.

There—that's Amanda Aizpuriete. A fantastic poet, bright personality, and what's more, she raised four kids.

I said it, wrote it, and am now embarrassed. Is that something that can be said in a single, short sentence?

Next to me is a blue vase with blue cornflowers and yellow marigolds. There was an amazing sunset when I got your letter Saturday evening, but up here, in Heaven, they're all like that (by Heaven I mean my veranda). The sun was red, the clouds were violet and billowing, and the swallows were singing.

So where can I even begin?

Or rather: should I even?

I'm starting to think that people either take care of all the important things in one go, or else don't take care of them at all.

Ieva

> Don't ask me what words
> mean. They're
> only words.
> . . . What are words? Essentially a redundant
> cry from the burning house
> in which I have to stay.
> —A. A.

Brother!

So—that's it.

. . .

I have to confess to some lies. I try so hard to stay happy! In each letter to you, and in each sentence. I tried to read some books, get lost in quotes—nothing worked. I'm actually doing horribly. I don't know what to hold on to anymore. Andrejs thinks that I'm creating an imaginary world around me, not living in reality. Maybe the books are to blame? I've read books since I was little like I was obsessed, and the words have probably taken their toll on my brain.

What's happening to us?

I mean—to all of us. It looks like the country has lost its mind. The day before yesterday they liquidated a joint-stock company's cattleshed, you should've seen it! There are no words to describe it! Everyone rushed out like mad to find the best cow. They drove up in their compact cars and their trucks and fought loudly over the cattle. I saw respectable women, family matrons, tearing at each other's hair and spitting in each other's faces. Some men came in with a butcher already in tow to have their cows stunned with a hammer, mounted onto a hook, and skinned right there in the corridor. And there were kids around! I remember the cows' eyes, placed all in a row like a necklace stretched out on the dusty concrete. I was wading through blood, brother, and that's no metaphor.

Gran gave up her share for us to have, but I wanted to get out of there. Good thing Andrejs is so calm. "Look for a cow, not at what everyone else is doing!" he said. We noticed a younger cow by the door, greyish with a dark ridge along its back. We wrote its number down in the logbook and said we'd be back in a bit to get it. The poor thing was bucking at the end of its chain in fear from the scent of all the blood. I wanted to put a rope around its horns and get it away from the insanity as soon as possible. Well, but it would be a long way to walk and the baby was asleep in the car. We left that place behind as fast as we could. In the yard out front, a gypsy was tying a calf—ALIVE!—to the sidecar of his motorcycle and then took off down the road, the calf's head dragging along the ground.

What's happening to us?

And unfortunately, this morning Aksels asked Andrejs to come out to the horse stables. Aksels works with horses as the stable hand, and there was a horse that needed to be brought to the meat processing plant, but the stable tractor was broken.

I put Monta in the stroller and walked out to the stables. It was amazingly sunny after several days of rain.

And it was that horse!

I've already said that the stable pasture ends by our vegetable garden. Once, about a month ago, I was working in the furrows with a pitchfork when it suddenly seemed like a storm had picked up in the pastures. They were trying to break in a black horse. Later Aksels said that this horse had bad blood—the blood of a baron's horse. Horses like that are so mean that it's even rare for stronger men to be able to handle them. In order to get a saddle on this black horse for the first time, they'd called in an experienced man from a few districts over. But his expertise didn't help. The horse had pulled free and was galloping around the pasture like thunder incarnate, kicking up sand with its powerful, shaggy legs. The earth shook. The horse snorted, whinnied, and thrashed, tore at the leather bridle with its teeth. It was like the devil himself had broken out of hell, and the people just looked on helplessly.

In the end the horse slipped and crashed into one of the low iron bars enclosing the pasture.

Right into its own end.

Because, as Aksels told me, when it heaved itself back onto its feet, it broke its lower back. And that was it. They tried to nurse him back to health, but in vain. The vet said the best doctor for any animal is nature. And then I saw the black horse a few times hanging around the apple orchard. He'd been let out to be with the other horses—he was a slow-moving cripple under the blossoming trees. A victim of his pride.

Until he finally lay down under an apple tree and didn't get back up.

It was a group effort to get him back on his feet and lead him into the stables. Once there he dropped down in his stall, and everyone knew that this time he'd stay down.

What can you do? If a horse dies, it gets taken to the animal cemetery and tossed into a pit surrounded by green grass, thick blue-green fir trees, and black ravens in the branches—so shiny and robust as turkeys they can barely fly. And the giant snowdrops growing over the animals' graves!

If a horse is brought to a meat processing plant, the farm gets money, and that's no small matter when the employees haven't been paid for several months. But you have to take the horse there while it's still alive.

And I'm sure you understand, brother, that this horse couldn't just be picked up and carried to the butcher's truck. They thought and thought, then finally called Andrejs to bring his tractor, and I went with him. And that's where it all started.

The horse was lying on its left side in the same spot it had been a week before. The men strapped it into canvas belts and chains like a large rock, and Andrejs used his tractor to pull it into the corridor through the opposite window. Then he dragged it outside along the corridor. The horse stayed proud the entire time—kept its head high. It only whimpered now and then. Bits of skin and flesh from its bed-sores scraped off onto the cement.

Once outside, it was dragged through the mud to the butcher's truck and lifted by a scoop into the back. Then the horse disappeared down the lane—quiet, half-raw, and with its head still held high.

At the time Aksels had asked them to sedate the horse. They said no. Andrejs laughed at Aksels, then called him a little shit who was just getting in the way. It was mean. After that I called Andrejs a bad name, almost scratched his eyes out, and then left with Aksels. And with Monta in the stroller. Along the road and away. That night

I didn't even go home to milk the cows. Andrejs drove out to the forester's house completely drunk, threatening to shoot Aksels. Stase screamed at me to get back to my own house, and take my baby with me if I didn't want any trouble.

In a word, it was a complete mess. And this entire long introduction is because I want to ask you for your opinion as someone who's on the *outside*. What do you think, should I take Monta and run away to Riga to stay with Mom? I don't see this ending well.

Best—your sister

Brother, dear brother!

First I have to say a huge thank-you for the money you sent. It was an uncanny move on your part—to pick the day that I have nothing, absolutely nothing at home, and then to send me money. Things have been terrible. That's why I haven't written in so long. Andrejs lent our car to a friend, and on Friday night he crashed and flipped it onto its roof into a ditch. Now, to get it fixed, we need a lot of money. We don't have a car. We can't go anywhere. If someone were to get sick, there's no way for us to get to a doctor. Thank God Gran is staying with me right now, helping me look after Monta. But her pension isn't that big. My horrible husband isn't worried about the fact that we don't have anything to eat—everything has to go toward fixing the car.

And then the postal carrier shows up and says: "You've been sent money!"

I knew right away, I got such goose bumps, what a feeling! An entire fortune! No one really knows about the money and they're not going to find out, either. I'm going to use it to get food for Monta. I'm going to ride to the village in a bit on my bike. Little Monta already has it so tough. In Riga I saw a kid her age wolfing down bananas and yogurt, but my daughter only sees turnips and beans . . .

Life here is awful. I feel what's happening to me—I'm growing old and dumb. And I want to hang myself, too. Especially if the potatoes haven't been furrowed, if there isn't any firewood, if the electric stove is half-burned out. I'm going to lose my mind.

But maybe not, because Aksels is here. And the whole time I have this hope in my heart: Riga. Aksels and I might go to Riga in the fall, if Mom and Dad will let us stay with them. And we should be able to find jobs, right?

But at least we have our health, so I can't complain. Aksels still works at the stables forking hay. I go with him to help. We've already brought in around 13 tons. It's hard work, manual labor. They pay 1.50 lats a day. We still haven't seen a santim of it.

Gratefully—your sister

P.S.   And I soon grow tired of all the markets,
        But they still stay in my memory.
        Forward, my dream horses,
        Forward, my haggard friends!

        Let the headwind count our ribs,
        Afterward it can bite us where it wants.
        The rain rips us from eternity
        And already washes away our footprints.
        —M. Melgalvs

Hello!

I'm writing you quickly and in tears, because the stable owner Austrums was shot dead last night. He showed up at Zari last fall—he'd stopped in to meet his neighbors, say hello, and ask about partnership opportunities. Austrums wanted to build the first golf course in Latvia here. He already owns a hundred hectares, but our field by the corner of the forest with the big pine tree could be of use to him. And we were willing to give it to him—there's more sand than grass there anyway, and it's worthless for the livestock. Austrums was very sociable—on the short side, attentive eyes, as easy-going as a strand of seaweed in a current. He invited us to golf lessons, showed us how to swing a club and how to stand. The stable employees were also there—we laughed and made friends with them.

He drove out from Riga every weekend. Built a sauna by the pond—almost everyone from our country's new government would drive out to drink there Saturday nights. Aksels would grumble about it sometimes—at night the drunk men would go to see the horses and let them into the pasture, then wake up Aksels to help get them back and out of the farmers' crops! There were problems with the bunch from Riga, but on the other hand—things were active, lively, hopeful! The stables were renovated, the pastures sown with grass, the mass amounts of endless mud gone. There was a sense of hope in the air.

And now—shot dead! Then he was torched in the woods just outside Riga, in his car. Did robbers do it? Or the government? Everyone is stumbling around with sad expressions. No one can believe something like that happened. The first person shot since the Awakening. I can still see him clearly—as alive as a person can be. Those friends of his who spent every weekend at the lake and sat next to him drinking in the sauna, they're all on the news now shrugging their shoulders and claiming to have never met him in their lives.

There're rumors around here that the baron cursed his land before he died, so that no one living on it would ever feel happy. But those are just stupid stories—

I'm worried—Ieva

⟋

Pāvil, hey!

You scold me for not writing.

If only you knew.

Oh I don't even care.

I'll just give you the facts. Nice and simple. Please don't be surprised.

You already know about Aksels. Stase was his mother. Was, because the forester's house burned down. They say she fell asleep smoking. Drunk, maybe. Everyone here has taken up drinking. I don't even know when it started. But now we drive to Madara every Saturday.

Oh I don't even care.

What else is there to do here? At least the bar is fun, there are people. Champagne. Boys from the neighboring village drive out here, start fights with the local boys. There's some kind of strength inside us, it's crazy, I don't know, I've got a lot of power inside me. There's nowhere to put it. So we drink. Of course I'm embarrassed. One night I stepped out of the bar to get some fresh air, and I fell onto all fours. I got up and then fell backwards. And then again—on all fours. And then—backwards. Someone helped me up, I staggered to the bathroom to wash my hands, looked at myself in the mirror and thought: Ieva, you?

Gran also gives me disapproving looks, says I'm abandoning my child.

I've even started smoking.

Oh I don't even care.

It's fun to dance at the bar, to let loose. To drive around from one party to the next. It's even fun the morning after, I like it. I feel awful, but experience some kind of inner peace.

Stase said it's suicide. Told us to leave for the city as soon as possible, that we'll rot alive out here. The countryside is death. That's the only reason she moved out here, to find death. I thought she was a great woman, just that she'd have these bouts of anger where she'd hit anything that came within arm's reach.

She was such a smart woman, but kind of—ravaged by life. Ah, whatever, what am I saying, she was herself. Like Jonsy. Stase was Stase. Without any pretenses. Everything she did was spontaneous and her own, she could be terrifying one second and the kindest person in the world the next. But no matter what she was, she was herself. Even the burning was such a Stase type of death. Even as she burned, she lived. The whole fire was awful. When Aksels got back home in the morning, he opened the window. And everything inside just exploded instantly. That's what happens, if things have already started to smolder, oxygen creates an explosion. Stase was standing and just went up in a column of fire. I don't think Aksels will ever get over it. He didn't even go to the funeral, just stayed back in the bushes and glowered at everything like a wolf. His heart is breaking, you know, but Andrejs just laughs. It's awful.

The times when Aksels wasn't able to, Stase would go in his place and chase the horses out of the crops and back to the stables when the enclosures were broken. She'd catch the fastest horse and ride it bareback, with just the halter. She'd gallop ahead of them all like some kind of vision, a sorceress! Everyone's going to remember her like that—with her hair flowing behind her as she rides the fastest horse.

Aksels is living with me at the Zari house now. Everything is so screwed up for me with these men. Aksels and I—how do I put it—well we just couldn't live without each other anymore, but we didn't say anything to anyone, didn't even admit it to ourselves. But Andrejs sensed something, would look at us hatefully, grew even more aggressive towards me, in the end I even cried at how hard-hearted one person could be!

Of course Gran also scolded me, but lovingly. She had seen and knew everything. Now she's gone back to the seaside. Oh I don't even care. I'm sick of being the bad guy. It's better if nobody sees it.

Back then, the three of us would drive around to the bars as a group. Sometimes we'd take other friends with us. And that one time on the way to the bar, a rabbit jumped out of the wheat field right in front of the car. I begged Andrejs to brake for it, but he went after it like a maniac until he ran it down. He even pulled over to throw the carcass into the trunk, so I'd stew it for breakfast. But the rabbit hadn't been run over, just knocked back into the wheat field—its screams ripped through the quiet of the night. Andrejs was drunk, he couldn't find it. I got out of the car and started walking home, but he blocked my way and forced me back into the car.

And then—at the bar! Whether it was revenge or a breakdown, I don't know. More likely it was some third thing.

That beautiful song "Black Velvet" was playing, you know the one. And I went to dance with Aksels. A slow dance. The first time ever with him. I didn't care anymore. He didn't either. We only saw each other in this crazy, fucked-up world. It really was more of a breakdown.

And toward the end he kissed me. For the first time.

But I pulled away, recovered, and then saw—guess what? Andrejs's eyes. He was standing by the wall and watching us carefully.

I panicked! Because everything happened so spontaneously, you know, I still didn't realize anything, just got scared—for Aksels, for me, for Andrejs. What's going to happen to us now! And I ran home through the morning fog like a scared little puppy. Barefoot, with my shoes in my hands. Andrejs followed behind me in the car and tried to run me down the entire way. I'd just keep jumping into the ditch and then back out again. It was awful!

Back home Andrejs grabbed me by the back of my collar and shook me. And then he suddenly sat down at the table and started sobbing—please, that I wouldn't, for the love of God, leave him! That he'd already figured things out about me and that little shit.

I asked him—how could you figure things out if it only just started tonight? Maybe, I said, I hadn't even known it myself! I said, I now know clearly that it won't end with Aksels because I love him!

And I love you, he said in a voice I could barely hear.

You don't know how to love, I answered cruelly. Because at that moment I remembered that half-dead rabbit in the wheat field.

Then he retreated into himself, started selling the livestock and even sold the tractor so he could pay off the bank loan before term. He sold everything, didn't even leave me the kitchen table. He didn't talk to me anymore, was acting out of his mind, smoothing Monta's hair and crying. I was afraid he'd take her away from me.

And well, it was on that same insane morning that Aksels—who'd been left by himself at the bar—slowly made his way home to the forester's house. The door was locked from the inside, he pounded on it, pounded, then opened the window—he knew which one could be unlatched from the outside. And the entire house went up with Stase in it, with all of Aksels's belongings. Up in flames.

After the funeral he came to live with us. Yes, there was a time when all five of us were staying at the Zari house. How we made it work, I still can't explain. No, wait, I can—we didn't speak. At all. Nobody spoke to anyone else. For a long time it was as if the Zari house was a kingdom placed under a spell. Everything is possible when you don't speak. The only thing is that you can't deal with that kind of silence for too long. Then Andrejs went off to work as a car mechanic in Riga, and Gran went back to the seaside.

Aksels and I are going to leave for Riga soon. If we stay here we're just going to die of hunger. For now we plan on asking Mom and Dad if we can stay at their place. Your room is going to be empty for at least another year. If they say no, we'll figure something else out.

And that's all, little brother.

This time—without any quotes.

Keep your fingers crossed for us—Ieva

DESTINY

IEVA walks through the village and cuts down dandelions with a knotted stick.

She doesn't want to go home.

The head of the village, Sarmis, is a gaunt old man with bright eyes who can't keep his hands to himself whether it's in the store or village hall. A slap on the thigh, a tickle to the ribcage, a caress of the shoulder. And when he comes to order smoked salmon from Gran, he always says in a surprised manner—how beautiful Ieva's grown up to be, a woman, a real woman!

Gran just laughs and sends Ieva to the cellar for mushrooms—Ieva is happy to go, because this strange word "woman" and Sarmis's bleary stare sends blood pounding to her temples.

But a strange devil moves her to quickly get the mushrooms and hurry back, her hair whipping behind her. Back to sit near Sarmis and to laugh, pretending not to notice him staring. Let him look, Ieva tells herself, nothing bad will happen from just looking. It's a little scary, but Gran and Roberts are right here. But it's interesting—what does Sarmis see when he looks at Ieva? She'd like to find out sometime, but it's not possible to climb into someone else's skin.

Sarmis is a lesser evil compared to the forester Buliņš. They run into each other along the road and Buliņš speaks ardently. And his words stick to Ieva's heart like linden leaves—soft and gentle. His speech is sensible, his thoughts clear. Upward, beautiful, magnificent. School, studies, the future. But then Ieva happens to look at Buliņš when he doesn't expect it. The blue eyes staring at her have the same hungry look as Sarmis!

Buliņš doesn't let up. One day he comes to see Roberts with a bag filled with canned meats. He just happened to be passing by and decided to stop in to give them a taste! Gran thanks him, Roberts praises him—ground stag with bacon, a real forester's feast! Gran sends Ieva to bring the empty jars back to Buliņš at the forester's house, but Ieva refuses. "Just take them," Gran scolds her, "is that so hard? He had no trouble preparing the meats or bringing them over here, a single man living by himself in a forester's hut, but so hardworking!"

"I've got nothing to do with his troubles!" is Ieva's unexpectedly curt reply.

As if that's not enough, Buliņš sends them a load of dried pine logs. Enough to cover the yard of their small fishing hut. But it's such lovely firewood that Gran can only gesture and lift the logs to her nose and breathe in their scent. Yellow, light as a feather, strong as medicinal balsam, with the crisp scent of sap! Roberts, however, points out that burning pine logs clogs up the chimney.

"Don't look a gift horse in the mouth!" Gran scolds and shakes the two logs in her hands at him. "They could be wet! But they're dry, chopped! It would be a sin to complain."

Neither of them bothers to wonder why the forester has suddenly become so generous.

Soon enough Buliņš comes to the house in person, on a night when Gran and Roberts aren't home. No matter, he'll just sit in the kitchen until they get back and have a cup of tea. Ieva shrugs, makes him a big mug of tea and goes into the other room. Let him wait!

But Buliņš follows her silently. His hand searches for the light switch on the wall and—click!—the room sinks into darkness. Ieva gets up from the couch and heads toward the door to turn the light back on, she's stubborn and wants to scold the forester—what is he thinking!—but she runs like a fish right into his arms. He grabs hold of her by the elbows, says nothing, just brings his face to her and tries to kiss her. His eyes glisten in the light reflecting from the snow. Ieva feels like a hypnotized rabbit, because there's no reason to scream, or tell him off, or to hit him—the guy is being gentle and quiet. Ieva can only murmur—no, no! She lowers her chin, presses it into her chest, then pulls away and runs.

If she was less embarrassed, she'd tell Gran. But Gran is an angel who can't hear those kinds of things, and Ieva even feels that she herself would become impure from telling those kinds of stories. And in the end she neither likes, nor hates Buliņš.

Ieva wanders down the long stretch of road between the sea and the lake, whacking dandelions with a stick—she scatters their white, fluffy heads, and thinks, thinks. Wracks her brain.

"Hey, Ieva, what're you looking for?" asks Edvīns, the village driver as he rolls past.

"Yesterday," Ieva replies and turns her back to him.

"Maybe we can look together?"

"You're all talk!"

"What can I do, honey, I've gotta work! You coming to the bar tonight?"

"Yeah, when pigs fly!"

Edvīns's friend Armīns leans out of the other window.

"Then come swimming with us at lunch! I'd like to sit you down on my lap!"

"You can hold on to your piece yourself!"

To fall into the clutches of those loudmouths—like a honey pot to a bear! The entire county would know about it by the next morning. Ieva is too proud to let someone go around town bragging—I got Ieva Eglīte!

There is one boy who Ieva likes more than the others, but that's why she has to stay away from him. Because it's almost like it's meant to be, so strangely familiar that it terrifies her.

They met in winter at a dance at the community center. The entrance was swarming with people. Breaths steamed in the cold air, everyone was entertaining everyone else with exaggerated jokes. The main hall of the center was like a hot and sparse clearing. Couples sat at tables lining the walls, a disco ball hung spinning from the ceiling, and a local ensemble played on stage.

Nobody danced. Well, of course not; it was only ten, and the guys hadn't downed enough liquid courage. Around midnight they'd start to shake and thrash in the center of the dance floor like they were possessed.

Ieva stood around for a while, grew bored. She headed toward the exit. There was a fan by the wall, humming and blowing out the colorful streamers tied to it. And of course, it also blew up Ieva's lightweight skirt. She stepped back, smoothing the cloth back down.

She looked up. And right into Andrejs's eyes.

It was kind of like meeting the stare of someone you love intensely, but haven't seen in a long time. Like the eyes of a brother.

And that's why Ieva avoids Andrejs. Sex with a brother! She doesn't think incest is a good thing.

This strange feeling in the noise and chaos of the party only lasted a second. The long, distorted shadows of the spotlights, the sound of the fan, twirling skirts, music, other people—it all faded away to make room for a pair of very familiar eyes. She didn't see his face, his build, or his clothes. She saw nothing but his eyes. And everything life had in store for her was in those eyes.

Then the stranger stepped aside to let Ieva pass. She lowered her gaze and obediently walked out.

Now she was no longer bored, or cold. She had to wait for that official one o'clock point when everyone else would be wasted, but the unfamiliar boy would be looking for her. Ieva doesn't know how she's absolutely certain that he has to come look for her. She only didn't know *him*. She didn't know anything—where was he from that she'd never seen him before? If he's drunk when he finds her, she'll run away. She's got at least that much sense left.

He found her in a little over ten minutes. Took Ieva by the elbow with his large, warm hand and led her to the center of the dance floor.

No one was dancing, but that didn't seem to matter anymore. What was important was that Ieva was dancing with the stranger. She could think of a few times when a hopeful beginning had turned into a complete catastrophe.

This wasn't one of those times. They moved a little in one direction, and then the other, before they both suddenly spread their wings and took off across the creaking linoleum floor.

After a good half-hour the two of them ran outside—to throw snow at each other and cool down.

After that they spent half the night standing in the quiet hallway near the spare rooms like two horses standing neck-to-neck. He had his hands wrapped around her waist and was digging his strong chin into the hair next to her ear. At first Ieva was worried that she was sweating through her white sweater, or that her face was too flushed, but he just breathed into her hair and said nothing, and Ieva slowly relaxed, unwound, blossomed.

"You smell like cookies," he said, his voice thick. Ieva nodded. Before the dance she'd secretly taken a packet of vanilla powder from Gran's hutch and sprinkled the fine, snow-white powder into the material of her sweater.

And then they were kissing, their lips hot and eager.

"Let me go!" she suddenly rushed down the hallway, feeling agitated. She didn't smell like vanilla anymore, but like something even warmer and gentler than vanilla.

In the bathroom she turned on the cold water, rubbed her cheeks and looked into the mirror.

What now, Ieva?

She could still feel his breath in her tousled hair.

Best to go back and dance.

His name is Andrejs. He's from the inland, not from the seaside families.

He's almost ten years older than she is. Lives at the Zari house, which belonged to his grandfather and which he got back after the Awakening. Before Ulmanis, the property still belonged to Baltic Germans. When Mother Germany called her children back home before World War II, the Baltic German quickly sold the property back to Andrejs's grandfather, and then boarded a ship with the rest of his household to never again return to this marshy corner of the world. Back in the collective farm times, the Zari house was home to a cotton workshop.

After the dance, Andrejs walked Ieva home. It was an endless night, both wonderful and terrible, as if she'd been injected with something, a paralyzing substance—velvety black, volatile.

He told her he'd been in the army, fought in Afghanistan, but that he never wanted to talk about it. She shouldn't think the worst—but there had been a situation where four men had lost their lives on account of him.

His friends.

Men he had known very well.

It's not even possible for people in this country to comprehend that place, he said. He'd had a good instructor at officer training in Viljandi who started a lecture on Afghanistan with the following comparison: If there were a spring not too far from your house, and your house had no running water, what would you do?

Carry it with a bucket, someone had answered.

Eventually put in a water main, was another reply.

So, the instructor had emphasized, you're going to a country where people have carried and carried water from springs to their homes for thousands of years because that's what their fathers and grandfathers did. As far as the water main goes, you can forget about progress. It's not a country of progress, it's a country of traditions. That's something you're going to have to experience for yourselves.

And Andrejs had experienced it. He watched how a local grandfather passed a hemp pipe to his son, and then to his grandson. Accustomed to drugs from a young age as if it were bread. No drinking, though; alcohol turns a person into an immoral creature.

But—enough about that.

That's that, he'll tell her once and then no more! Sorry, but he'll say it right now—he wasn't going to talk about it.

Ieva shrugs—if not, then fine. Only there was no reason to get so worked up about it.

Andrejs used to live with his parents on the outskirts of Riga and worked as a car mechanic. Then they got back his grandfather's property and he didn't have to think twice—since the Awakening, everyone was rushing back to the countryside to renew, rebuild, and reconstruct. As the only son, this was also the path Andrejs had to take.

They'd kiss under the big ash in the Zari yard—it seemed that this ritual was important to Andrejs, to kiss Ieva right under the ash tree. The house itself was in bad shape. The cotton workshop had left behind its dark, sooty imprints on the walls. Like a person who wakes up from a restless night with a face full of pillow marks. The half crumbling staircase in the middle of the house, the tattered wallpaper fluttering in a draft. But Andrejs was hopeful—he had a tractor, the Zari house, and fifty hectares of Kurzeme land.

On a beautiful June evening Andrejs pulls Ieva down next to him in the apple orchard. They kiss as usual, but after a while a strange tension spreads from Andrejs to Ieva. She looks into the clear, clear eyes of her boyfriend.

Andrejs asks:

"What's with you?"

Ieva looks away.

"I want it to happen now."

Ieva sees the leaves against the sky. They're blue.

Then she closes her eyes. After a bit she feels Andrejs's excited breathing above her.

"It'll be alright," he murmurs.

Two currents struggle within Ieva. One is holding back, the other rejoicing—finally, it's going to happen! Since the time the fire first awakened in her, it's been suffering and waiting for release.

A massive force tries to break into her, it hurts, she moves away. Andrejs persistently follows her body, as if to say that it's only in fairy tales that breaking happens without pain. Ieva's eyes are full of tears, something in her bends like a footbridge over a river, and then gives, breaks.

Then the invisible river throws them ashore—the ground under her hips is hard and real like always. Andrejs lies on top of her, motionless as a rock. Then he kisses her, rolls off, and Ieva's eyes again see the vibrant blue. A lonely bird circles high, high in the air. Ieva thinks—what is it like for birds? To grow up, love, and fly. So naturally. Does that also hurt?

"Let's get married, Iev'," she hears Andrejs's voice. "No one will find us here. A marsh on one side, woods on the other, let's live here."

"I'm only seventeen," she says.

"I'll wait."

It hurts.

Two currents struggle within Ieva, two lightning strikes, two destinies. Until now, her life has always gone according to her plan. Now she feels like a caged animal. She can't go on living the way she did before, but she doesn't know how to live any other way and has her doubts.

Exactly when did the first crack form in the wall of this house?

And the discrepancies in the assumed moral obligation of a person's life?

At times fate gets underfoot like a stray dog, and sometimes it has rabies. It's great if the cards that fate deals you seem good. But what happens to the simple freedom of your childhood?

They'd already moved into the Zari house, already spent their days and nights together, but at the same time she told Andrejs: Don't wait for me, I'm not promising anything, I don't even want to see you anymore! Some sort of insanity came over her. She wanted it to be like before, before she met Andrejs, to live as free as a bird in a tree. She said those harsh words, and her own heart almost broke.

It wasn't possible to live simply anymore.

Andrejs said nothing in return, but got drunk by himself. Came to see Ieva looking wrecked. The tractor jostled along the road like a horse. Andrejs followed her through the rooms, crying, tearing, swearing oaths. Threatened to drive right then over the ice and into the sea! Ieva had never seen him like that. In the end she took pity on him, lay him down, took his heavy head into her lap, and watched as he fell asleep.

The first time she had looked into Andrejs's big, green eyes, with their flecks of brown and curious melancholy, she had sensed how cruel fate was, about how she would fight to pull away from it, cower in fear from it. But how she would oddly enough always be subjected to it.

Now, with Andrejs's head in her lap, she senses that twice as much. How can she escape it? Look at how comfortable he is right now, fast asleep! Does she love him? Supposedly yes. But at the same time she wants to run away.

Where is her freedom?

Even if she cried for help—she doesn't think anyone would hear her.

She tried to talk about it with Gran:

"What do you think about Andrejs?"

"What's there to think, sweetheart, he's a handsome boy, and hardworking at that."

"But something about him scares me, Gran. People say he's moody."

"Well, other people can think about him what they want, but for you he could be gold!"

THE SEVENTIES

THE EXTINGUISHING

HOW beautiful the clouds are!

Along with the wind and the sun, they're the best painters in the world. The sky is a canvas. Sometimes the clouds are joined by the full moon and the reflection of the earth in droplets of fog.

Masters of the chiaroscuro.

And then there comes a day when, as the clouds are painting, a person happens to tilt his head back to look up at the sky. Rays of light slide across his face. A never-ending cycle of extinguishing and flickering. You don't know where to take your next step because the earth blazes up in front of you, but in your eyes—it opens up wide. When it dies out it gets as dark as a peat bog pothole. You end up jumping from one spot to another so often that the earth trembles. When the clouds are painting light and dark.

The same thing happens in a person's life—a sunny corner can suddenly become overcast.

The only remaining letter after Ieva's brother Pāvils was born (from Lūcija's sister to Lūcija).

Lūcīt!

I'm once again rushing out to visit you. Yesterday I ran around like a mad dog, but wasn't able to find everything you asked for. I bought two bras, I could only find them in one store and only in a size 5. The sales lady said I should buy two sizes up. If they're too big you can cut off and re-sew the buttons. I couldn't find the straps you wanted, not even cotton or gauze. I'll run over to the pharmacies on Ļeņina Street, maybe I'll find something in that neighborhood, but I doubt it. There hasn't been any cotton or gauze in the city for two months. We'll have to think of something else.

I can't get myself to calm down—I keep thinking and crying about the negligence of those doctors. It's interesting that they all say the same exact thing, that the trauma will fix itself, but you say that your son is completely crippled. Maybe it'll really be like that, a month or so will go by and he'll be a normal boy. Definitely name him Pāvils. It's an old, good name. But you haven't even asked what his father thinks. Okay, I'll stop here, I won't wait for you to write back. If you can, call me, I'm putting in 2 kopeks.

With love to both of my heroes
(give the containers back right away, and wash the grapes)

This letter is addressed to Lūcija in the 7th ward. The word "ward" has been stubbornly crossed out, and the word "room" is penciled next to it in different handwriting. As if to say—there's no one sick in here! And yet, and yet . . .

It's been only a little over a year since Ieva was born, but that sunny corner is now overcast. Ieva's mother has already yelled at her husband. Ieva's father has managed to upset her. Any woman sitting at home with a child has an imagination more vivid than any writer—it doesn't take much to get upset. They barely talk to each other anymore. Only when absolutely necessary: when it's about food, the time, or sick relatives.

After a long and tormenting period of thinking it over and finally deciding to have a second child, Lūcija puts her trust in destiny and doctors, and her in mother's words that everything with a second child is twice as easy, and silently, deep down secretly hopes that after the baby is born her sky will clear up again. Like it had with Ieva.

But it doesn't. It grows even darker. Pāvils is in no hurry to be born. The doctors don't properly monitor her. Then the baby is far overdue and the poisoning starts. The labor itself is difficult, and Pāvils survives, but his movements for the rest of his life are palsied, even though his mind is exceptionally sharp.

And there's something else—a kind of malicious termite inhabits Lūcija's brain after his birth. There are a few days in the first month where her head aches so intensely she throws up and she isn't even able to take care of Pāvils herself. She lies motionless in a dark room. A typical, unexplainable migraine—so says the doctor. The forever-busy, mercurial Pauls is not happy about this. Even though he loves his daughter and son, he's not ready to quit his job for them. And what's more, Pāvils needs special care.

They decide to send Ieva to the seaside village where Lūcija's parents live. At first the grandparents are concerned, but when their granddaughter arrives and laughs for the first time, they feel as if they've been given an unexpected present. Every night, Gran gives her granddaughter a bath in a large tin bowl set on a warm stove. As she scrubs Ieva's back, Ieva faces the stove, inspects the kitchen utensils—clangs the pots, plays with the foam skimmers, touches the enamel cups and saucepans hanging from hooks.

Brother and sister grow up apart from one another. Lūcija and Pauls never separate, even though their married life isn't harmonious and Lūcija only feels happy once in a while. No sunlight shines into

302

their Riga apartment because it's unforgiving to Lūcija's melancholy eyes. How does that first crack in the structure of a person's life form? Is it the moment when assumed moral obligation is replaced by reality?

When the clouds start to paint, the sun grows overcast.

IEVA'S BIRTH

FOR the moment there are only three things to prove Ieva's birth—I'll whisper to you what they are—and they can be found in the attic of a building in Riga, in a yellow-painted wooden chest with stylized Latvian folk engravings on the lid. Attic mold hasn't held back—the contents of the chest are almost entirely overgrown with this fuzzy evidence of time. Fifty or so letters written in different hands have turned into a greenish-black turf; the letters are unsorted, stacked in a pile and secured by a half-disintegrated piece of twine. A foamy grey covers the glossy greeting cards, rings of moisture paint over the ugly color; time brings everything together with a robust drawing. The ugliness betrays its owner, the Soviet era, the era of ugliness. Moisture has eaten away at the black-and-white photographs—amateur handi-work from those times, when every self-respecting Soviet citizen had a small darkroom in his Khrushchev-period brick apartment building. A darkroom with an enlarger, a processer, chemical baths, and an infrared light bulb. With a wave to his family, such a perfectionist would disappear behind the curtain Friday evening, latch the door and, in the reddish-black light, rest a veneer sheet covered with all his treasures across the bathtub. There he'd sit on the closed lid of the toilet and watch intently as the developing chemicals conjured lost time onto the paper. The magnifier could be used to select individual faces from the crowd, and the developer used to regulate the level of bleakness in the facial features. Some photo paper was hard, which made the scene turn out a coffee brown. Other paper turned out gloomy, bluish and slightly pliant. The air in the bathroom would be positively charged, chemically fragrant. And the family would be annoyed because the only way they could get into the combined bath and toilet room to take care of their natural needs was to beg and beg. The photography enthusiast would make up for his offense by letting the children dry the wet photographs, lay them on the cutting board, and let them trim the edges with a straight-edged razor or a special blade. Additionally, whoever was trimming the picture got to choose how wide the white border would be. But God help anyone who forgot and flipped on the bathroom light!

Now the photographs have been cut up by time and humidity—here and there are the white teeth of broad smiles, the black scarves of funerals. The most popular subjects in photographs from that time are various foods and bottles set on banquet tables surrounded by happy guests, or funerals with a somber and grey forest in the background.

What has outlived this moldy turf is a time of receipts, a time of sending postcards, a time without e-mail.

And three little pieces of evidence to Ieva's birth.

The first piece of evidence—or rather, the first announcement of Ieva's birth—are small tags, the ones that were attached to gold jewelry in the Soviet Union. Tiny, calligraphy lettering on the cards explains that the gold items were rings made in the Riga Jewelry Factory: item 0611, 583-proof, weight 5.66 grams, price 11 rubles and 50 kopeks per gram, total item price 65 rubles and 00 kopeks. The second ring has a weight of 6.12 grams, total item price 70 rubles and 38 kopeks. Ieva's mother and father, like two tagged birds, slid these rings onto each other's fingers, following the worldwide tradition to thus express their trust in a single being among all other beings.

The second bit of evidence is an orange piece of laminated material bound with gauze thread; on it in black ink and in Russian are written Ieva's mother's name and surname, her father's name, that they have a newborn baby girl, weight 3 kg and 50 g, her birth date and time, and her mother's patient number—71. Red ink lettering indicates five seconds, apparently the amount of time that passed before Ieva's first cry.

This kind of tag was tied around a newborn's ankle, while the mother would have a smaller tag tied around her wrist with just her number. Every three and a half hours or so, a steel gurney would be pushed down the long hallway toward the wards carrying tightly wrapped, crying or quiet babies that the ward maid would bring to the mothers. And thus continued the Soviet era individual's greatest adventure, starting with pregnancy, birth, and the realization that, contrary to what the Soviet grandfathers of biology thought, children weren't actually clean slates to be scribbled on with the commandments of the Communist party. At least Ieva's mother Lūcija realized this on the first day of Ieva's life, she could easily tell Ieva's voice apart from the other babies on the gurney; and every newborn's face is its own, unique, almost like its character, already complete and mature at the moment of birth.

The third piece of evidence of Ieva's birth is a lock of her hair, wrapped in paper and dated around the time she was a year old—a silken and brightly shining substance. Who knows why this lock had been cut off. Maybe to mark her first haircut?

These incredibly personal passages can probably be best explained by the letters between Ieva's parents. In its paranoia of germs, Soviet science ignored her father. Left him standing on the other side of the hospital threshold, flowers in hand. A real man was supposed to be muscled, hairy, and smelling slightly of body odor, the kind of person who would crack open a bottle of cognac at the construction site and pass it around to his coworkers in honor of his new offspring, not the type to tramp through the flowerbeds surrounding the hospital.

Ieva's father Pauls doesn't quite fit this idealistic category of man. He was an engineer in one of the Latvian Soviet Socialist Republic's countless design institutes—a paper pusher in a button-down shirt— who'd met and married his wife right there in the institute, and who was now doing everything he could to get into the hospital to see her, if only for a second. When he couldn't get in no matter what, he wrote letters. The entire expanse of the Soviet Union, from the Baltic Sea to Sakhalin, was one big letter-writing workshop that constantly wrote and spread myths because citizens at that time didn't see each other often enough to talk face-to-face, and were always isolated from one another in consideration of the safety of the State. So in this country, people with imaginations and people of action, who were usually divided in society 50-50, were forced to become 100% imaginative. And what does an imaginative person do when the Cerberus-like ward maids keep him away from his wife and newborn child for an entire week? He either drinks, or he writes letters.

First letter
(from Ieva's father Pauls to Ieva's mother Lūcija),
written in black ballpoint pen on a torn-out sheet of lined notebook paper, most likely at home on the evening of Ieva's birth.

"Dear, dear, dear, Lūcija!"
The happy father admits his bewilderment, joy, and excitement, but this is nothing compared to what she experienced. He knows he has a daughter and that she weighs 3 kg and is 52 cm long. Then come questions:

"How's your health? Was it bad? And how is our first-born doing? Who does she look like—you or me? What color are her eyes? What does her nose look like? What color is her hair? Is she a loud crier? Is she healthy? Do you need anything—juice or fresh fruit, or something special?"

Immediately following these questions he starts in on choosing names—"our little girl is already tall, we should name her Skaidrīte, so she could be name-twins with Skaidrīte Smildziņa" (here he means the TTT team basketball player Skaidrīte Smildziņa). As far as names, he asks for time to think and for them to decide tomorrow if possible.

Then he writes a bit about the outside world. About how he slept poorly the night before, how he was only able to doze off toward morning. Woke up at half eight. Was late for work and called the hospital once he got into town to find out if there was any news. There wasn't, and they told him to call after lunch.

He decided to call after two. He was eating when his mother called him and, after giving him an update, congratulated him. A coworker had been standing next to him at the time and had seen him turn red, then pale; then the coworker congratulated him, asked if it was a boy or girl, then went to spread the word.

The new father then called the hospital himself. They told him that "everything is very, very normal and your wife is lying in bed smiling" (it's possible this is a standard line). "But I already thought as much," he writes. "After that I didn't want to work anymore. And tears kept welling up in my eyes for no reason."

After this the letter includes a description of several congratulations and greetings from coworkers and family members. One person said that they should definitely drink something to the occasion. Another said his wife had experienced a beautiful dream.

By 15:00 Pauls couldn't stand it anymore and went to beg his boss to let him leave early. His boss asked after the health of his newborn and his wife, asked, if his employee had hoped for a boy or girl. Pauls had grown flustered and answered that he'd hoped for both.

He has no new news, it's already 16:15, and he has yet to cover the distance between himself and the hospital.

(And it's true, he had to cover that distance to leave a care package and the letter with the receptionist, and to then slink along the side of the hospital garden in the hopes of catching sight of his wife through the window for a few moments.)

Second letter
(from Ieva's father Pauls to Ieva's mother Lūcija),
written in black ballpoint pen on lined notebook paper; the letter indicates that he wasn't able to see his wife yesterday.)

In the second letter he again writes that he was chased off hospital property at six, so could she please immediately answer the following questions and only then read on.

1. How are you doing in this hospital?
2. How's your health?
3. Could you write something more about the baby?
4. Are her legs bowed or do they look normal?
5. Do you need anything?
6. What's new?
7. Is it true new mothers don't get to see their babies for three days, and only then do you get to feed them yourselves?
8. What do you think of the name Helga?

Third letter
(from Ieva's mother Lūcija to Ieva's father Pauls),
in which she lovingly addresses her husband and thanks him for the care package, which she won't be able to finish off, as "there's a lifetime of things in it.")

"So we have a daughter," she writes, and adds that she was born very small. Other women gave birth to babies weighing 4 kg or more. She's the image of her father. Lūcija, in turn, held out courageously—there was one small gash, but it was sewn up. Tonight she'll be allowed to start walking again. Health-wise nothing interesting, just a slight temperature.

She writes lying down because she's not allowed to get up, but hopes that he'll be able to read her handwriting. She'll probably be able to go home in seven days. Their daughter is very beautiful.

"Don't worry, love, it's all over now." That's how she ends the letter.

The reader must not forget that this correspondence wasn't brought about by esthetic whim, an attempt at style, or an artistic craze, but life itself, livelihood. The desire to connect and utilize one's human advantage—words. And with this little stack of letters Ieva Eglīte's name was pulled from the stream of time.

True, is should be pointed out that the stream of time is always very close by. It's already reaching with its furry paw of mold for new ground, and this name and surname will also soon be washed away by time.

It should also be said that Ieva Eglīte herself has never known about the existence of her birth certificate, and maybe that's for the best because, having read these letters, she would never believe that she had been the size of a large cat at the time the pen touched the paper.

But she was.

It becomes clear to anyone who has been present for the birth or death of another person that life is no laughing matter. It can and must be treated as a good, successful joke, but in essence it's not a joke.

If you've been touched by a ray of light, if it's pulled you from the darkness—that's no joke.

Sitting on a pretty hill, I often daydream, and this is what I think: there is neither essence in money, nor in the number of women, nor in old folklore, nor in a new wave, but we end up in strange places by feeling our way there, and the only things that belong to us are joy and fear. Fear that we are worse than we could be, and joy that everything is in good hands. And in each dream I can't resist but run to who knows where. But, when I wake up—I hope you'll be with me.

B. Grebenshchikov

Inga Ābele (born 1972) is a Latvian novelist, poet, and playwright. Her novel *High Tide* received the 2008 Latvian Literature Award for prose, and the 2009 Baltic Assembly Award in Literature. Her works have been translated into several languages, including Swedish, English, French, and Russian, and have appeared in such anthologies as *New European Poets*, *Best European Fiction 2010*, and *Short Stories without Borders: Young Writers for a New Europe*. Her most recent book, *Ants and Bumblebees*, is a collection of short stories.

Kaija Straumanis is a graduate of the MA program in Literary Translation at the University of Rochester, and is the editorial director of Open Letter Books. She translates from both German and Latvian.